DEATH
DOWN THE AISLE

BOOKS BY VERITY BRIGHT

DEATH
DOWN THE AISLE

VERITY BRIGHT

bookouture

Published by Bookouture in 2022

An imprint of Storyfire Ltd.
Carmelite House
50 Victoria Embankment
London EC4Y 0DZ

www.bookouture.com

ISBN: 978-1-80314-714-7
eBook ISBN: 978-1-80314-698-0

No man is rich enough to buy back his past.

~ Oscar Wilde

1

Lady Eleanor Swift shifted uncomfortably in her seat. It wasn't the stifling heat of the unseasonably warm September sun that made her restless. It was that all eyes in the packed room were on her. And she was acutely aware of it.

Why they were, however, eluded her. From the third row of hard wooden chairs in the side chamber of the Town Hall, she looked around at the other members of the Chipstone and Little Buckford's Women's Institute, trying to fathom why she was suddenly the centre of attention. Formed in 1917, it had taken the Women's Institute four years of fighting to be allowed to meet in the Town Hall at all. And even now, a year later, the council looked on the organisation with almost the same fear and distrust they reserved for newcomers to the town. Of which, Eleanor was one.

Brushing a stray red curl from where it had bounced onto her eyelashes, she looked down at her open notebook again. An agenda item was scrawled in her usual hasty hand. *Surely that couldn't be why, Ellie? Goat husbandry?* However, she knew the government was keen to get people to grow their own food and keep livestock after the shortages of the war. Perhaps, therefore, she'd missed them asking if they could use the grounds of her country estate, Henley Hall, to graze a communal goat herd?

Keen though she was to play her part in the local community, she hesitated. She loved the idea, but wondered if her traditionally minded butler would consider herds of goats wandering around quite as befitting a country estate as deer? And she wasn't sure how Joseph, her gardener, would take to his prize shrubs being ravaged. Goats were such splendid creatures, but they could be rather destructive.

The trouble was, Eleanor had only inherited Henley Hall a few years ago, on the passing of her last remaining relative, her uncle Lord Byron Henley. She'd spent most of her life abroad, having been brought up by unconventional parents until the age of eight, then travelling solo across the globe after being freed from her hated British Boarding School. She'd only returned to England on news of her uncle's death. Her unexpected inheritance of his estate, however, had not included a much-needed manual on how to be the lady of the manor. This left her needing to rely on Uncle Byron's rigidly proper butler for advice.

At the head of the gathering, the nest of heavily pinned greying hair swung left and right as the chairwoman surveyed the group. 'We'll move on once we've, er, confirmed all our members are in agreement. La—'

'Not afore I get back, I'll thank you.' Five chairs along from Eleanor, a pinched-faced woman with a figure to match, wrapped in a worn brown cardigan, scooped up two large enamel teapots from the bench behind her.

The chairwoman sighed. 'Mrs Harris, we are not here just to drink tea, dear.'

'Don't go pretending you don't need a cuppa as much as the rest of us, Madam Chair. Fighting talk needs a wet whistle to be heard, as well you know.'

A murmur ran around the room. The chairwoman frowned.

'Yes, but we aren't here to pick a fight!'

'That's as maybe,' Mrs Harris said, 'but we also didn't haul our worn feet all the way up here so as we could play at who can speak the most pretty.' She slid her gaze pointedly at Eleanor. 'It ain't like it used to be. And not for the better.'

Aware that the rest of the eyes in the room were fixed on her again, Eleanor stood up. She'd smooth things over with her staff somehow.

'My apologies, ladies,' she said brightly. 'Still being the new girl at this, I fear I may have missed your request. I think it's a wonderful idea to graze goats at Henley Hall. I'll ask—'

'Oh goodness, no, Lady Swift,' the chairwoman said. 'We voted that motion down. Goats, indeed!'

There was a general nodding of consent among the members.

'Smelly little blighters they be,' a voice called out from the back.

'And vicious. Bite you sooner than look at you,' another answered.

The chairwoman rolled her eyes at the vice-chair. 'Quite.' She turned back to Eleanor. 'We were just waiting to, er, check that you were also happy with the decision?'

A snort came from the pinched-faced woman. The chairwoman shot her a warning glare. Eleanor held up her hands. 'Well, yes, of course, I'm happy to go along with the general consensus.'

The chairwoman nodded. 'Good. Then I suggest we move quickly on, ladies, to your suggestions for the cause we shall champion this month. And, Mrs Harris, we'll toast our decision with tea at the end, thank you. So, starting on my left, each present your idea. Succinctly, please.'

Eleanor sat down, relieved she wouldn't have to wrestle a herd of goats into the Rolls while Clifford looked on in horror. She soon shifted uncomfortably in her seat again, however, while waiting for her turn to suggest a cause to support. It wasn't that she didn't have any suggestions; it was just that she felt strongly that other, longer-serving members had a far better idea of what their community needed than she did. After all, she'd only been in Little Buckford a couple of years, which counted for nothing in this part of the world.

The next suggestion was so quiet that she missed whatever had been proposed. Many of the members nodded and shared approving looks.

'So sorry, I couldn't hear,' Eleanor called out. 'What was that?'

The chairwoman raised her voice. 'She said we should petition to have women back in the local police and I wholeheartedly agree. Women served in the police force during the dark days of the war with pride!' A general cry of 'Hear! Hear!' went up. The chairwoman nodded and continued. 'And we did as good a job as the men, I might say. It's a crying shame we were all removed when peace was declared. We women see and understand different things, things even the best men in uniform can't. Sometimes, we just *know*.'

'Oh, yes. Hear! Hear!' Eleanor shouted. She quickly clamped her hand over her mouth. 'Oops! Sorry, I got carried away there.'

The chairwoman smiled. 'No one objects to your enthusiasm, Lady Swift.'

Another snort erupted to Eleanor's right. All eyes swivelled to the cause.

Mrs Harris stood up. 'None like her! Them's the rules. When is the Madam Chair going to do summat about it?'

Eleanor was lost again. She looked questioningly at the chairwoman, whose cheeks burned at her gaze.

'Hush, Mrs Harris, please. 'Tisn't the time for that now. Any more suggestions, ladies?'

'Yes!' Mrs Harris said sharply. 'That we do as we're

supposed, not what suits. If that carry-on's going to happen here, I'll be going elsewhere!'

From the few discreet glances around the table, Eleanor deduced that this threat might not be too unwelcome for some members.

She stood up again. 'Could I ask, what exactly is *"them rules"*?'

'I don't like to explain, Lady Swift,' the chairwoman said awkwardly. 'Not in front—'

'Then I will,' Mrs Harris called out.

'No, Mrs Harris,' the chairwoman said firmly. She sighed and turned back to Eleanor. 'Begging your pardon, but you see the rules state that our local Women's Institute group should have no, umm...' She winced. 'Oh lawks, how to say it without sounding rude?'

'Upper classes,' the kindly faced woman beside Eleanor said gently. 'Titled ladies, like yourself, Lady Swift, can make things difficult for the likes of us to speak up, being more educated and such. And they can... dominate the proceedings.' She threw her a warm smile. 'Only, you're not a bit stuffy or overbearing like most of them.'

'Thank you.' Eleanor gathered her things. 'However, you are all too dedicated, and our wonderful community far too needing of your efforts, for me to scupper that. It's been an honour, if a sadly short one.' She rose and then hesitated. 'The only thing I don't understand then, is why you allowed me to join in the first place?'

'Because,' a voice called from the back, 'you stood as Chipstone's first woman MP.'

'And are still offering to pay anyone's doctor bills if they haven't enough shillings themselves,' another shouted.

'And you provided extra allotments to the village for nowt!' a third chipped in.

'Well said!' The chairwoman turned to Eleanor. 'The

Women's Institute is for women who do, not those who talk about doing.' She shot Mrs Harris a sharp glance. 'And you proved you were one of us, titled or not. So, we waived the rules and' – she shot Mrs Harris another look – 'are happy to continue doing so.'

Eleanor smiled. 'If you're sure. I mean. I'd love to stay. I just want to help.'

'We know, dear,' the woman beside her said. 'Never been a doubt about that to most of us.'

'Then,' the chairwoman said with evident relief, 'it's time to vote on our next cause.'

It was agreed by the vast majority that petitioning to allow women back into the police force was most worthy of support.

'Us women would be a great help with our extra sense for knowing when summat don't smell right,' one voice called out. 'We'd all feel better with women in the police as well, wouldn't we, girls?'

Most of the room nodded.

The woman behind Eleanor spoke again. 'And if a woman in uniform had knocked on my door in the middle of the night with the terrible news that my John... wasn't coming home no more.' She swallowed hard. 'Would have been easier to hear, alright.'

'Absolutely,' the chairwoman said. 'Now we need to think about how we're going to achieve our aim. Thoughts, ladies? The floor is open.'

After a few rejected suggestions, an idea was hit upon that received unanimous support. 'That's agreed then. A procession through the town.' The chairwoman noted it down. 'Now, there's no time like the present so we should do it next week.'

Eleanor's mind was whirling.

'And we should end in a rally outside the local police station and hand in a petition. That would definitely draw the crowds.'

A frisson of anxiety tapped at her thoughts. *What would*

Hugh think of the idea, Ellie? Her almost-beau was Hugh Seldon, a detective chief inspector who worked out of Oxford and London. They hadn't seen much of each other lately as she'd been out of the country, and on her return he'd been as busy as ever. Her attention was brought back to the room by Mrs Harris raising her voice.

'I don't see why none of you will say it out loud. Especially as...' – she smiled thinly at Eleanor – 'we've been reminded as how we're all equal here.'

'Quite right,' Eleanor said sincerely.

Mrs Harris scowled at her. 'Then if there isn't an axe to hang over our heads about being superior hidden in that there handbag, it would prove it for sure, wouldn't it?'

'Mrs Harris,' Eleanor said as gently as she could, 'I'm no one special. If any members require proof of that, so be it.'

Mrs Harris smiled triumphantly. 'Good. Madam Chair, I'd minute that as a "yes"!'

The chairwoman looked less certain. 'Lady Swift, you're sure?'

Despite a prickle of panic running up Eleanor's spine and her having no idea what she was being asked to do, she found herself nodding.

'That's settled then!' the chair said. 'Lady Swift will organise the procession and then the rally and petition.'

A rousing round of applause drowned out Eleanor's gasp.

'Next Saturday morning it is, then,' the chair said. 'Ladies, we will be making an enormous difference.'

'As always. And for always,' the room chorused.

'Next Saturday!' Eleanor gulped, trying to catch the chair-woman's attention as the women collected their coats and bags and filed out. 'But I have to attend a—' Catching sight of the clock, she jumped up in horror. 'Oh gracious, I'm already late!'

Outside, she hitched up her sage tweed skirt and ran down the Town Hall steps. At the bottom, she waved frantically to her butler waiting beside her late uncle's beloved Rolls Royce, holding her even more beloved bulldog next to him.

'Clifford, get Gladstone in and start the car, or I'm going to be fearfully late for the fitting of my bridesmaid's dress.'

'Indeed, my lady,' he said drily, stepping around to open her door. 'But, rest assured, your reputation for tardiness will remain intact. Since' – he held up his pocket watch – 'there is no "going to be" about it.'

She slid into the passenger seat. 'Never mind that. I've just got myself into the most hopeless barrel of hot water in there.'

He eyed her sideways. 'Chin up, my lady. At least if you survive the roasting at your next appointment, you'll be leaping from the frying pan into something marginally less painful than the fire.' His lips quirked as he started the engine. 'Perhaps.'

2

Eleanor sprinted up the steps of One Cromwell Street and into the reception area. Set in a cul-de-sac of two imposing Victorian townhouses, the exterior was as solid and respectable as the interior was chic and flamboyant, decorated as it was with a monogram-tiled reception area and ivory staircase. A woman stepped out from one of the white-painted doors, the swing of her ankle-length soft-grey skirt making not even a hint of a rustle.

'Welcome to Melrose Wedding Couturiers. Can I help you, madam?'

'Gracious, I hope so. The Davencourt party, please. I'm here for a fitting and,' Eleanor said with a grimace, 'I'm rather late.'

'Actually, that's quite the understatement, wouldn't you say!?'

Halfway down the stairs, a woman in a high-necked oyster silk jacket eyed her coolly. She was of advanced years but neither frail nor feeble.

'Ah, you must be Lady Davencourt,' Eleanor said rather too brightly. 'Peregrine's mother.' She stepped to the bottom stair and smiled. 'I'm Lady Swift, but do call me Eleanor. I'm one of the bridesmaids.'

'Yes, I know. The others had the good grace to arrive on time. And do call me *Lady* Davencourt.' Her thin smile failed to reach her cold hazel eyes.

Somehow, Eleanor managed to bite back the retort on her lips. 'Well, if you'll forgive me, I had better hurry along for my fitting.' She hastily followed the assistant down the corridor, glancing backwards with a shudder. *Let's hope we don't bump into her too often, Ellie!*

'Eleanor! Is that you?' a disembodied voice called from behind an ivory curtain in a room swathed in pearl-white silk and satin. Her friend's head of waist-length spirited blonde waves appeared. 'Oh, thank goodness.' She bounced over and threw her arms around Eleanor's shoulders. A good five inches shorter, she was the epitome of the comely English beauty. 'You're late, but here now, which is all that matters. And' – she laughed good-naturedly as she ran her eyes down Eleanor's unbuttoned sage tweed jacket and matching skirt – 'you are clearly going to be the least fussy of all my bridesmaids about your dress.'

Eleanor gasped. 'Says the girl who has taken months to choose her wedding gown! And rightly so.' A flicker of confusion showed on her face. 'Besides, what is there for me to be fussy about? It's your most special day ever, which means your choice about everything rules. I'm just thrilled you asked me to be part of it.'

'Thank you, love.' Constance bobbed up on her toes to lean her head on Eleanor's shoulder. 'You couldn't somehow get everyone else to see it the way you do, could you?'

Could she be referring to Peregrine's mother, Lady Daven-court, by any chance, Ellie?

Whether or not she was, Eleanor decided it was better to be tactful. 'Oh dear. Bit of mutiny among the troops, is there?'

Her friend groaned and tugged Eleanor down onto a velvet, deep-buttoned chaise longue. 'More a case of too many self-appointed wedding experts!'

'That can't be easy, I imagine.'

Constance nodded. A worried look came into her eyes. 'I promised I wouldn't say a word, but...'

'But what?' Eleanor tried to read her friend's expression.

'I just hope all this doesn't, you know, bring back... upsetting memories for you.'

A flashback to her disastrous marriage pierced Eleanor's thoughts, making her heart falter momentarily. Eight years earlier, she'd met a dashing army captain in South Africa who'd turned out not to be an army captain at all, but a rogue. He deserted her only a few weeks after they married. And at the outbreak of the war, he'd been sent to the firing squad for selling arms to the other side. Wrongly, it transpired. The fact she had mentioned any of this to Constance was a testament to how quickly they'd grown close.

Her friend wound a lock of hair around her fingers. 'Honestly, I deliberated for ages before I asked you to be a bridesmaid. You can still back out, you know. The wedding is not until Saturday. I can ask—'

'Don't be daft, I wouldn't miss this for all the world. And, anyway, I've reconciled the whole episode of my marriage... mostly. Unlike you and Peregrine, who are a match made in heaven, for sure. As for me, sometimes one just meets the right person at precisely the wrong point in their lives. Or the other way around.' She shrugged. 'That's my speciality, don't you know?'

Constance hugged Eleanor's arm. 'I don't believe that because, actually, I'd say your speciality is being the perfect friend.'

The sound of Lady Davencourt's sharp voice on the other

side of the door issuing demands to all and sundry interrupted them.

Eleanor winced. 'Still perfect? After I managed to light a match to your mother-in-law-to-be's ire on my very first meeting?'

Constance laughed. 'Trust me, one need only breathe to do that with Peregrine's mother. Or offer a suggestion. Or be blonde. Or' – she patted the top of her head – 'be Miss Constance Grainger.'

Eleanor scanned her friend's face. 'Don't panic. You're marrying Peregrine, not his mother.'

'I know. And he's such a dear, always telling me not to mind her relentless comments. But as the weeks have gone on, he's started insisting I stand up to her more.' She grimaced. 'I know he's right. If I don't, she'll only grow more and more impossible.'

Worried by Constance's disheartened tone, Eleanor wracked her thoughts for something positive to say. Then her eyes fell on the rows of white gloves in the glass display case. They reminded her of her butler's gloves and the myriad occasions when he had imparted his comforting wisdom to her. She wrinkled her nose. 'It can't be easy for her, if we think about it. She must feel as if she's losing her only son. Which is probably doubly hard after his father passed away only recently.'

'Mmm. She could choose to look at it as gaining a daughter-in-law instead?'

'Y-e-s. And in time she will, I'm sure. But right now,' – Eleanor thought back to Lady Davencourt's dark-hazel eyes and the hint of something they carried – 'perhaps you being so beautiful and full of life might be an unwanted reminder that maybe she was like you on her wedding day. And now, well...'

Constance clapped her hands. 'Oh, Eleanor, that's so much a better way for me to try to think of her. Thank you.'

Eleanor smiled. 'Thank Clifford. There's a chance his

amazing ability to see both sides of every coin, as it were, is rubbing off on me. At least a little.'

'Clifford, who? You mean your... your butler?' Constance laughed as she grabbed Eleanor's hand and dragged her towards another curtained changing booth. 'You know, you really are the most unorthodox lady I have ever met.' Her eyes shone. 'Oh, how I wish I could see the look on Peregrine's mother's face if I told her even a snippet of your adventures or your outlook on life.'

Eleanor blanched. 'I wouldn't do that. Instead, how about I slide into whatever gorgeous creation you've chosen for me and we appear like two grown-up ladies who do this sort of thing every day?'

Over the next ten minutes a flurry of assistants helped Constance into her dress and then adjusted the silk train of her exquisitely embroidered gown, while others fiddled with the headdress of rosebuds crowning her loosely looped tresses. Meanwhile, Eleanor slipped on her dress. Constance looked her over.

'I just knew you'd love the cut and colour of yours.'

'Umm... oh absolutely.' Eleanor crossed her fingers and swallowed her horror at the yards of salmon pink she was wrapped in. With a contrasting band of mint green directly under her rather modest bust-line, and mint-green frilled lace-edged sleeves, she felt, well, *ridiculous, Ellie*. The addition of a matching fur muff for her hands, also in mint green, made grabbing the long skirt each time she caught her toe in the hem doubly tricky.

'Ladies, please!' a clipped voice called.

Eleanor turned to see an angular woman walking towards them dressed in a tailored navy suit dress and vivid apricot silk scarf.

'Think about the bride's entrance into the church. It must be spellbinding! This is the prime opportunity to practise.'

Constance turned to Eleanor. 'Madame Melrose, our French couturier and gown designer. And this is Lady Swift, madame. My third bridesmaid.'

'So I gather, Miss Constance. Good morning, my lady.' The woman's eyes strayed up to Eleanor's fiery red curls, then down over the bridesmaid's dress with a flinch of her groomed brows.

Never one to fuss about fashion, even Eleanor couldn't miss the designer's dismay. Clearly, Constance had omitted to mention she was a vibrant redhead when discussing colours with Madame Melrose.

Eleanor turned and hugged her friend. 'I'll just scurry inside and let you make your grand entrance. You truly are the most beautiful bride I have ever seen.' Leaving Constance, she slipped through the door that Madame Melrose opened for her.

The large, hexagonal room she entered was hung with silver-edged floor-to-ceiling mirrors on every one of the six walls. Only two of the white velvet boudoir chairs at the far end were occupied, the centre seat having been commandeered by Lady Davencourt. The other by a lady that Eleanor was horrified she barely recognised. Constance's mother had been ill for some time, that she knew, but she was unprepared for just how frail the poor woman had become. She was painfully thin, her skin as brittle and yellow as old parchment paper.

Over to one side, two women were adjusting the frills on the skirts of the three young flower girls. The striking resemblance of all five left no doubt they were Constance's two older sisters and her equally blonde, blue-eyed nieces. Eleanor jerked to a stop as a marble rolled across the floor. As she bent to pick it up, a small outstretched hand appeared in her view.

'Ah, this must belong to you?' She smiled at the little blond boy, who she guessed to be about five years old. Although, where his smart, blue, velvet knickerbocker suit ended at his knees, there were none of the usual scrapes and bruises she would have expected at that age. He merely blinked back at her and thrust his hand further forward.

'Bertie, darling.' One sister glided over. 'What did we say about people thinking you are rude if you don't reply?'

This drew only another slow blink.

'So sorry, Eleanor,' his mother said. 'It's just a thing of his. Not speaking, I mean. The best we ever get is a monosyllabic grunt. And that's rare enough.' She brushed his cheek with her hand. 'We've taken him to all the best doctors and there's nothing actually wrong. He's really a very bright and perceptive child.'

'That's alright, Beatrice.' Eleanor bobbed down to the boy's eye level. She rolled the marble around her palm, noting his eyes watched her, not the movement. 'Some days I haven't many words either.' She ran the marble down her fingers into the child's hand and whispered, 'I bet you have lots of words you just fancy keeping inside, don't you?'

The young boy blinked and pocketed the marble before walking away.

Eleanor looked up to see Constance's mother gesturing to her. She hurried over. Even standing next to the woman, she had to bend forward to catch her stilted, breathless words.

'My dear Eleanor.' She patted the chair next to her. 'Do sit down. Isn't this too wonderful?'

Eleanor sat, trying – and failing – to arrange the yards of fabric she was wearing into some kind of order. 'It really is, Lady Grainger.' It was all she could manage, overcome by the tremor and weak grasp of Constance's mother who now held her wrist. She rallied her composure. 'Constance looks every inch the fairy-tale princess, Lady Grainger. But you know that already.'

The frail woman shook her head slowly. 'No, dear. I wasn't quite up to attending the last two fittings.' Her papery cheeks hollowed as she smiled wistfully. 'It's every mother's dream to see her girls married before...' She took a shallow breath. 'Before—'

'Before they reach thirty,' Eleanor said quickly. 'Which would have made me a terribly disappointing daughter since I have reached the disgraceful age of thirty-one without having a husband to answer to.'

Lady Grainger tinkled an uneven laugh as she patted Eleanor's arm with all the force of an exhausted butterfly. 'No right-minded parent could ever be disappointed in the remarkable young woman you are.'

'Thank you.'

'And I shall be enchanted to see you at the service on Saturday.'

Eleanor tried to keep the panic off her face. *The same day as the Women's Institute procession and rally you agreed to organise and run!*

'And now,' Constance's mother pointed a tremulous finger as the door opened, 'it's handkerchief time. Oh, my!' As Constance stepped over the threshold, her mother failed to stem a trickle of tears. 'Just look at my beautiful daughter.'

'Oh dear, no, no, no.' Lady Davencourt stood, her arms folded. 'Madame Melrose, what were you thinking of? Two inches too much width in the sleeves and three too little on the hem!' She marched in front of Constance and looked her up and down. 'And insufficient embroidery on the bodice.'

'Lady Davencourt,' Madame Melrose said with great aplomb, 'I was following the bride's instructions. I sent specific measurements to Paris where they made the dress exactly to them.'

'I think she will leave Peregrine speechless,' Eleanor said.

The icy look this earned her made her shrink back in her seat.

Lady Davencourt clicked an impatient finger at Madame Melrose. 'The gown will have to go back. And to Paris.'

Madame Melrose stepped forward. 'I am sure our seamstresses here can carry out any alterations, Lady Davencourt.'

'Possibly. But I am not having my son's bride parade through the church in a wedding dress butchered in a rural backwater like Chipstone. The alterations will be made in Paris and that's final!'

The room held its breath. Even the flower girls stopped spinning in circles.

Catching Eleanor's encouraging look, Constance managed a smile. 'I really like it just as it is. The—'

'Tsk! That is as maybe, but one must think of the photographs as well. Why, imagine looking back through in a few years and realising what a poor figure you cut on my son's wedding day!'

Eleanor winced as Constance's mother opened her mouth. How could the poor lady argue when she could barely be heard? Before she found out, the assistant who had greeted Eleanor at the reception hurried in bearing a telegram.

'I do so apologise for interrupting, my ladies, but there is an urgent message for Miss Grainger.'

She held the folded paper out to Constance, who opened it, looking bewildered. Her face clouded over on reading it.

'It appears our discussion over my gown will have to wait.' She looped her arm through her mother's. 'It's from Father. He's demanding I return home urgently!'

3

Back home at Henley Hall, Eleanor went straight outside to throw a tennis ball across the lawn for her exuberantly lumbering bulldog. It was a beautiful afternoon, with clear skies and plenty of warmth left in the sun.

'Dash it!' she grumbled aloud as the ball disappeared into the thick of the surrounding shrubbery borders. 'Why do I always end up in such awkward predicaments?'

'An unwavering disregard for decorum, perhaps, my lady?' Clifford's measured tone heralded his otherwise silent approach. He placed the tray table he carried beside the cane garden chair next to her.

'Very funny. But why a plate of Stilton crackers and a sherry, Clifford?' She stared up at him. 'And a bucket of tennis balls?'

He picked up her jacket from where it had fallen onto the grass with a quiet tut and produced a miniature clothes brush from his inside pocket.

'With sincere apologies, I have just been informed that your luncheon is not ready. Mrs Trotman did not expect you to return from the wedding fitting until after two this afternoon. And as she is preparing one of your favourite dishes, I trusted you would rather wait?' Whipping her beloved late uncle's pocket watch from her jacket, he held it out between white-gloved thumb and forefinger. She nodded.

'That's almost another hour, Clifford! Mind you, that's not a problem for me since I have no other engagements today. So, yes, I'll wait, thank you.' Her stomach let out an unladylike gurgle. 'But if I throw all these extra tennis balls you have brought me in this heat, poor old Gladstone will be on his last legs.'

They both looked to where the bulldog was already panting heavily, his tongue lolling like a slice of boiled ham, his back legs sticking stiffly out sideways. The pyramid of earth wobbling on his nose gave away the fact that the ball he had retrieved was now forever interred in one of the nearby beds. Clifford waggled a disapproving finger at him.

'Indeed, my lady. However, perhaps not all the contents of the bucket are intended for Master Gladstone.'

'Ah!' She rummaged under the balls and smiled as her hands closed around a book. She drew it out. 'A new penny dreadful! But you're forever suggesting that these books are the work of the devil. Don't tell me you've changed your mind?'

His inscrutable expression flinched in horror. 'Most assuredly not, my lady. However, it is something to occupy your thoughts, rather than whatever troubling matter you encountered this morning. And the tennis balls will preserve the latest of Joseph's dedicated efforts in the flower borders from Master Gladstone.'

'Actually, I was about to seek him out and apologise.' She hesitated. 'Umm, Clifford—'

He nodded. 'Naturally, after luncheon, I shall be free to discuss whatever you may wish.' He shuddered and pointed at the novel. 'On the proviso that it is not *that*. Does that answer your unspoken question?'

She laughed. 'Absolutely. Now, be off with you and leave me to my disgraceful romantic highwayman antics we shall both pretend I didn't succumb to.'

An hour later, with her muddled thoughts enlivened by adventurous tales of derring-do, Eleanor tucked into her luncheon with gusto and waved a loaded fork at her butler.

'You know, Clifford, this would have been worth going hungry a whole week to wait for!'

He sniffed. 'It appears your appetite considers it has been.'

She shrugged as he offered her a salver of roasted field mushrooms. 'I can't help it if I have a hearty appetite. After all, this lamb is too tender and delicious for words, and Mrs Trotman having baked it in her sublime pastry is an absolute masterstroke.'

'I believe the defining characteristic, my lady, might be her generous basting of dark rum. And then the careful rolling in wholegrain mustard and caramelised leeks before the pastry is applied.'

'Well, I just hope she realises how much I appreciate her hard work. In fact, all the staff's hard work, including you, of course, Clifford.'

He bowed. 'Thank you, my lady. Myself and your band of aproned musketeers are indeed aware.'

She frowned at his description and pondered the minted potato on her fork. 'Musketeers? You've given me a spiffing idea, you know!'

He eyed her suspiciously. 'Why do I feel an urge to request a retraction of what I just said?'

Lunch finished, Clifford accompanied her to the kitchen.

'Ladies, her ladyship would like a word with us all.'

Over at the sink, Eleanor's youngest maid, Polly, tried to bob a curtsey as she spun around, resulting in an arc of washing up water soaking Mrs Trotman, the cook. Stoically ignoring her drenching, Mrs Trotman hastily wiped her hands on her flour-covered apron.

'Please forgive the mess, m'lady. We weren't expecting a visit.' She grabbed the arm of Eleanor's other maid, pulling her into line. 'Lizzie, quick as lightning, my girl.'

'Oh, my stars!' Mrs Butters muttered. Eleanor's house-keeper swept up the bowls and baking trays from the large wooden table. From his quilted bed by the range, Gladstone let out a woof and tumbled out to get in everyone's way.

Eleanor held her hands up. 'No, it's my fault. I didn't mean to catch you all unawares. Especially after such a wonderful luncheon. I just have a question, so if Clifford could bear to permit that you all pause for a few minutes?'

All the women turned to him. He gave a brief nod and pulled out a chair for Eleanor, then stepped over to the oak dresser. Eleanor motioned for everyone to join her at the table. Polly's eyes widened as she stood rooted to the spot, shaking her head.

'Come on, Polly. Park your skirts here, girl.' Mrs Butters patted the chair beside her.

'But... but sitting in front of the mistress is against the rules.'

Eleanor smiled fondly at the young girl. 'True, Polly, but you've done it before.' She cupped her hand and pretended to whisper. 'Anyway, the mistress sitting in the kitchen is also against the rules, so let's get this done quickly before Mr Clifford notices?' All eyes swivelled to her butler, followed by a quiet round of giggles at the sight of him with his back half turned, his fingers in his ears. 'Now, everyone,' she continued, 'it's a bit of a cheeky request, but I've got myself into a hole.

And the thing is, I'm rather hoping you might all be kind enough to help me dig myself out.'

Mrs Trotman beamed. 'The likes of us? Helping the mistress with summat important? I should say so!'

'So exciting! Nothing like this ever happened when I worked at Ranburgh,' Lizzie, the second maid, said. They'd brought her back with them from Scotland last Christmas and her thick Scottish burr still delighted Eleanor.

Eleanor shook her head. 'But none of you know what it is I'm asking yet.'

Mrs Butters gave her a motherly smile. 'And neither do we need to, m'lady. But 'tis always a pleasure to help out.'

All four heads nodded. Clifford bowed from the shoulders.

'Thank you. Well, it's like this. The Women's Institute have asked me to organise a rally...'

Even before the kettle had let out its piercing whistle a minute later, her staff were nodding animatedly. Except the youngest, whose lips trembled as she fiddled with her apron hem.

'Is something the matter, Polly?' Eleanor coaxed.

'Beg pardon, your ladyship, but... but we'll all be fearfully worried about you.'

Clifford reappeared from the pantry, tapping his fingers on the tin of crystallised ginger he carried. He paused in the doorway.

'Polly,' Eleanor said gently, '*I'm* not going to join the police force.'

'You're not, m'lady?' her young maid said breathlessly,

'No. Gracious, no. But there will be women who do. I mean, the government was happy to have them in the police force during the war, but the minute it was over it seemed their services were no longer wanted. Well, this rally is to persuade the Chipstone police to put pressure on the powers that be so that those who wish to have the chance to join again. So, ideas, ladies? Clifford?'

Mrs Trotman tapped Polly's arm. 'Pencils from the groceries ordering shelf and some paper from the messages pad, quick smart, girl.' She stood up and pulled Lizzie to her feet. Sliding the girl's hands onto her perfect pear hips, she set off walking around the kitchen. 'Here we are in Chipstone, trying to get folks' attention. How do we do that?'

Mrs Butters laughed. 'You could hypnotise them like the man did to that woman in that travelling show we saw last year.'

Mrs Trotman snorted. '*Helpful* suggestions needed, thank you, Butters!'

Polly dropped the pencils and paper she had returned with onto the table and joined the end of the line as she was bidden, failing to stifle her giggles.

'So,' Mrs Trotman looked thoughtful, 'we're part of... floats, my lady! Not just people walking with a sign nailed to a stick. How about we get the likes of old grumpy Cartwright to haul out his tractor and tow a row of his flat hay wagons around? They'll carry a fair few of them Women's Institute members.'

'Brilliant!' Eleanor wrinkled her nose. 'But I seem to remember he's not my biggest fan. Or a fan of women's rights!'

Mrs Butters chuckled. 'Oh, he's nothing but bluff and bluster, m'lady. I'll handle him.' She started jotting down the idea.

'And you could sweet talk Wilkes into driving his milk float on the day, Butters,' Mrs Trotman said. 'Ask him when he's making up to you on the back step tomorrow.'

Mrs Butters gasped. 'Says the mare who's got Giggs the fishman calling so many days you have to give her ladyship herring, sprats and eels at least three times a week! So, he's your job to tackle about his horse and cart.'

So that's why there's so much fish on the menu, Ellie!

'Ahem!' Clifford stared around the table. 'Her ladyship is present.'

The ladies blushed.

Lizzie paused in her tour of the kitchen, causing Polly to bump into her. 'Beg pardon, m'lady, but if as you were thinking of having banners, Polly has a t'riffic way with drawing. And I know writing. The nuns taught me.'

Eleanor nodded. 'That would be wonderful.' She figured the other staff would help tidy up the young girl's enthusiastic efforts, and Clifford would correct Lizzie's spelling if needed.

Mrs Butters wrote the last of this down. She added the words "clever slogans" and "Mr Clifford?" then turned the papers for him to see.

Eleanor looked up at him eagerly, but he merely gazed back with his usual inscrutable expression, which made something dawn. 'You've been very quiet, Clifford?'

He realigned his cup to line more precisely with the pattern of his saucer. 'Perhaps now might suit you to have that discussion you asked for, my lady? If you will forgive the suggestion?'

Waiting for her butler in the small room referred to affectionately as 'the snug', Eleanor was mystified as to what might be troubling him. Then, as he joined her, she clicked her fingers and slumped back onto the chaise longue beside the sprawled Gladstone, hand over her eyes.

'I'm sorry, Clifford. I never meant to undermine your authority in the kitchen just now. You must be silently seething, me asking the ladies to help without running the idea past you first. After all, it's your responsibility to see Henley Hall runs like clockwork, and a fabulous job you do.'

He shook his head as he slid out his leather pocketbook and flipped it open to a double page with the black silk ribbon attached to the spine. 'I have already reconciled the staff's duties with their extra-curricular activities, as it were.'

She stared in wonder at the neatly drawn-out grid filled in his ever-meticulous hand detailing an amended schedule for each of the ladies. He re-pocketed the notebook.

'And for clarity, my lady, I am your butler.'

'Meaning?'

'I do not seethe. Silently or otherwise.'

'Noted. But then what is it that has rattled you about all this? You've always been behind every chance to champion women's rights, so that can't be the cause?'

He adjusted his perfectly aligned cufflinks. 'Indeed, my lady. However, notwithstanding, it is my firm belief that no member of the female gender should be called upon to enter dangerous professions. Or situations. Outside of national emergencies, at least, and even then, it is beyond regrettable.'

She smiled. 'Ever the chivalrous knight. But, don't worry, we can agree to differ. You don't have to help if you don't want to.'

He held her gaze momentarily, then permitted himself the luxury of a small sigh. 'Would that I am never the man who inflicts his will on another.'

'Which means?'

'I retract my objections and offer you my assistance in this matter, my lady.'

She scanned his face. 'Well, only if you're absolutely sure?'

He nodded. 'I would feel churlish in the face of your magnanimity.'

She smiled. 'Thank you, Clifford. But,' – her nose wrinkled – 'do you think this rally might scupper my chances once and for all with Hugh?'

'Have you envisaged the rally being of the extreme variety?'

'With us women chaining ourselves to the railings, you mean, and throwing stones through the windows of the police station? Far from it. I don't think Chipstone's very conservative residents will respond kindly to that sort of a rally.'

The jangle of the telephone bell sounded in the hall.

A moment later, Clifford returned. 'Miss Grainger for you,

my lady. And in some considerable perturbation,' he added in a whisper.

She followed him out into the marbled entrance hall, where he held the handset out to her.

'Constance! Whatever is it?'

Her friend's distraught voice came over the line. 'Oh, Eleanor, it's simply too awful! Please come now. Please, please!'

4

'Oh, Eleanor, thank you so much for coming.' Constance's arms enveloped her from behind. Before Eleanor could spin around to check her friend's face for tears, Constance lowered her voice. 'We need to sneak upstairs.' Her curtain of shiny blonde waves swung as she scurried on ahead.

Mystified by what the problem could be, or why they couldn't talk about it in one of the four reception rooms, Eleanor shushed Gladstone and followed. They tiptoed around the base of the staircase and down a long side passage. Three-quarters of the way along, at the bottom of the servants' stairs, Constance grabbed Eleanor's wrist and led her silently up to the top floor. Gladstone's nails, however, clattered on every bare board, his excited breathing resembling an express steam train by the time they reached the top.

Throwing open the fourth door along, Constance charged in, barely waiting for Eleanor and the exhausted bulldog to duck inside before she closed it behind them. She leaned back against it, brushing the long lock of hair that had fallen over her face out of the way.

'Oh gracious, you *have* been crying.' Eleanor took in the red-rimmed and puffy lids staring back at her. Reaching out, she pulled her friend into a hug. 'Whatever it is, I'm sorry.'

'Well, I'm not.' Constance pulled away. 'I'm furious!'

Eleanor frowned in confusion. 'Ah! Well, I think then we need to start at the beginning.' She took a quick look around the simply appointed sitting room. 'Are you sure we're not intruding, though, in whoever's quarters we've just barged into?'

'Hardly. Nanny's no longer with us.' Constance stepped over and rolled one ball of wool back and forth dejectedly with her finger. 'We still all miss her. She was such a rock when things went awry. Even Father grew very fond of her. Not that he seems capable of understanding anything of import now. The beast!' She slumped down onto the settee. 'Oh, it's the most awful and hideous mess.' She pulled Eleanor down into the seat beside her. 'I really don't know what to do.'

'Pour it all out to start with?' Eleanor shuffled sideways to let Gladstone lean against her legs.

'Alright. Well, it's Peregrine. He... he's being sued for breach of promise.'

'But...' Eleanor fumbled for a gentle way to ask but came up empty. 'Isn't that only applicable when one has... umm, broken off an engagement to be married?'

Constance took a deep breath. 'Yes.'

Eleanor stared into her friend's eyes. 'But that's impossible! He can't be reneging on marrying you. He loves you. I know he does!'

'I know he does, too. And no, he isn't.' Constance held a hand over her eyes. 'The lawsuit has been issued by his... his former fiancée.'

Eleanor gasped. 'Former—'

'Fiancée. Yes, you heard correctly.' Constance shook her head as her hand strayed to the silver locket around her neck. 'The silly boy only went and got himself engaged to a... a chorus girl. Some time ago, it seems.'

Eleanor was still trying to grasp the situation fully. 'Then you... you knew nothing about his former engagement until this lawsuit came through?'

She nodded.

'Goodness, you don't seem quite as, I'm not sure what the word is, incensed or horrified maybe, as every other soon-to-be bride would surely be?'

Constance shrugged. 'I feel rather foolish, if that's what you mean. And obviously rather... shaken. But Peregrine is very individual. That's most of what makes him so special. He's also devastated it has come to my knowledge in this way.' She jerked around to face Eleanor. 'Despite his dragon of a mother being determined that I only want to marry him for his money, I couldn't care less. I love him desperately. Which I'm entirely convinced is how he feels about me, especially as he is marrying way below his station.' Her shoulders shook, but no teardrops fell. 'It's pathetic. I've run out of tears already.'

Gladstone let out a soft whine and nuzzled his wet nose in her hand.

Eleanor shook her head. 'No, it isn't. This is an enormous shock for you.'

'Oh, Eleanor.' Constance ran her fingers along the bulldog's wrinkled jowls. 'Peregrine is the only man I've met with the courage to follow his own convictions. He does what he believes, not what he's expected to. Which is doubly hard for a man in his position. You'll understand that because you're of just the same mind.' She squeezed Eleanor's hand. 'That's why we've fallen into being such good friends so easily.'

Eleanor smiled sheepishly. 'I'm not likely to be much help over matters of the heart though.'

'Nonsense. Can you bear to hear the whole sorry tale?'

'Of course. As Clifford says to me almost daily, poor chap, "I am, my lady, all ears".'

Constance gave a wan smile before hugging her knees to her

chest. She rested her chin on the top. 'Peregrine was very honest with me. Finally, at least. That is, until Father waded in and threw him out, so I probably don't quite know everything. Anyway, what I do know is that he met this person, whoever she is, years ago and after a short while they became engaged. Secretly.' She sighed. 'It all sounded rather romantic.'

'Ah, so his mother didn't know until now either?'

'No.' Constance grimaced. 'I can only imagine the vehement dressing downs he'll be getting right now. And likely will for the rest of his life, too. Sons of earls are definitely not permitted to do such things.'

Eleanor trod warily. 'Following one's convictions is one thing. But to... to let a girl down with such a crash is quite another, wouldn't you say?'

'Absolutely. But he didn't, you see. The engagement was ended by mutual agreement. They both confessed to each other after a while that it had been an infatuation, not love. Being the gentleman he is, he offered her a reasonable sum in apology because he was worried she'd lost ground in finding the husband who would support her. I think that was very noble, don't you?'

'Umm, I think to act on one's principles is always noble.' Eleanor phrased her next remark carefully. 'But if they had a mutual agreement, I don't understand why he is now being summoned over a breach of promise?'

'Well, obviously, this woman hasn't done so well in life. And when she heard that Peregrine's father had passed away, she knew the man she was happy to let go back then is now wealthy in his own right.'

'But his father passed away months ago.'

'Yes, but what better time to pressure Peregrine into agreeing to a huge financial settlement than just before his, very much in the public knowledge, wedding?'

'Ah! Let me guess. This woman's lawyer came not just with

the lawsuit but also with an escape clause to simply pay up sufficiently so she disappears again?'

'And all threat of public mention will be dropped too.' Constance's jaw tightened. 'But it's no escape! The sum is so vast, Peregrine would have to split up the family estate to meet the cost.'

'Oh golly!' Eleanor said quietly. 'Lady Davencourt must be—'

'*Apoplectic?* All she can see is that he went against expectations and, if it all comes out, that he's disgraced the family name and may be responsible for breaking up the family estate.'

Again, Eleanor trod carefully. 'Which is probably how your father is viewing it all?'

Constance groaned. 'Yes. I know he's just trying to protect my reputation, but by forbidding me to marry Peregrine, he's choosing *for* me. And he's choosing wrong! What's the point of a respected reputation if you're miserable and unfulfilled for the rest of your life? In fact, what's the point of life at all if your heart is never made whole?'

Unable to answer without her emotions spilling over, Eleanor tried a different tack. 'Might your father come around, though?'

'Absolutely not. I'm twenty-five and I have never heard him raise his voice. He's always maintained that a gentleman can argue through reason or he's no gentleman. But he positively flew at Peregrine, saying he would never permit him to marry me if the breach of promise is proven against him.' She shook her head as if remembering the scene. 'I was quite scared for a moment!' She sniffed back more tears. 'But he also said if Peregrine pays the settlement this woman is demanding, he'll still refuse to let us marry because he'll take it as an admission of guilt. And then he practically threw Peregrine out. It was so awful!'

'Oh dear, that sounds like he's pretty adamant.'

'But it's even worse than you think.' Constance clamped her hands to her face.

Failing to see how it could be, Eleanor waited for her friend to continue.

'It's Mother,' Constance finally managed in little more than a whisper. 'The shock – and her subsequent argument with Father – caused her to have another episode. We had to call the physician. And now...'

Eleanor squeezed her hand. 'Take it easy, darling.'

Constance shook her head. 'And now she won't get her dying wish.'

Eleanor gasped. 'Constance! You don't mean?'

'Yes, Mother is a lot sicker than any one of us will admit to. Father included.' A fresh stream of tears fell. 'The doctors have said she may not live to see the year end. And all she's ever wanted is... is...'

'Is to see the last of her dearly loved girls married, I know,' Eleanor said softly. 'She told me at the dress fitting. Constance, I'm so sorry.'

Her friend's face suffused with anger. 'Well, I'm not! As I said, I'm furious! Furious that my poor Peregrine is being black-mailed by this terrible creature. Whatever she might have been when he thought he loved her, she's a monster now. And I'm furious with Father, too. He's broken Mother's heart. That's why I've been hiding up here. If Mother sees how distraught I am, I fear...' She tailed off, her eyes closed.

Eleanor's efforts not to lose her composure finally failed. The two women held hands, foreheads together, silence saying everything that words could not.

After several minutes, Constance's tears diminished. She sat back and managed an exhausted smile at Gladstone, who had somehow wriggled his entire top half into her lap. 'My legs have gone completely numb due to your wonderful cuddle.

Thank you.' She looked up at Eleanor. 'Oh, to be a dog and not have all this heartache!'

Eleanor tried to find her friend a morsel of comfort. 'Maybe Peregrine will hit on a solution in time?'

Abruptly, Constance pulled her hand out of Eleanor's and folded her arms. 'But we don't have time! That's why I need your help. Oh, *please,* say you will?'

Eleanor's brow furrowed. 'I'll do anything I can for you, you know that. But I honestly don't see how I can help.'

'I do. You can do what you've proved you're brilliant at. You can investigate for me. You can prove Peregrine isn't guilty of a breach of promise.'

Eleanor was flummoxed. Her desire to help her friend was burning in her chest, but the request was an impossible one, surely? She'd inadvertently helped solve several murders over the last few years, but nothing like this. She opened her mouth, but Constance leaned across and pressed her hand over it.

'I can't go to the police because no crime has been committed, so you're my only hope.'

Eleanor spoke as gently as she could. 'But how do you think I might prove Peregrine's innocence?'

'I haven't the beginning of an idea. But despite everything, I must marry Peregrine on Saturday for three unshakeable reasons.'

'Which are?'

'Because I love him with all my heart and if I entertained the idea of postponing the wedding even a day, it would show a lack of faith in him. And because I want him, and only him, to be... the father of my children.' She broke off with a sob.

'Still a few more tears left then,' Eleanor said gently, scrabbling first in hers, then in her friend's pocket for a handkerchief. 'And the last reason?'

'I am going to fulfil Mother's wish before... before she dies.'

She grabbed Eleanor's hand again. 'Eleanor, please, even if I had half an ounce of knowing how it might be done, Father won't hear of my even attempting any such thing. In his present state of mind, he'd likely lock me in the house. You're my only hope.'

Eleanor looked into her friend's eyes. 'And I don't want to dash that in any way, but...'

'You're still doubting Peregrine?'

'I can only be entirely and sincerely honest and say I'm not sure.'

Constance patted her hand. 'I understand. But that's easily rectified. Will you at least meet him and hear his side of the story?' Another cascade of tears fell. 'I'll respect your answer either way.'

Eleanor swallowed hard. 'Of course I'll meet Peregrine.' Silently, she groaned. *If you believe him, Ellie, you're stuck with a seemingly impossible task. And if you don't, you're stuck with watching your best friend's happiness destroyed.*

5

Even Clifford appeared uncharacteristically out of sorts as he eased the Rolls along the winding lanes to the Eagle Hotel in Chipstone where Constance had arranged for Eleanor to meet Peregrine. She caught him eyeing her sideways a third time with pursed lips.

She sighed. 'Oh, whatever it is, please get it out and over with.'

'I was merely going to offer the suggestion, my lady, that Master Gladstone be relegated to the footwell, rather than hanging his head out of your window. His portly frame is creating quite the unsightly crease in your skirt.'

'Well, since he's already made it, there's no point in my spoiling his fun of letting the wind whistle through his jowls. But thank you for pointing it out.'

He arched a brow. 'If that is how you wish to arrive at the notable Eagle Hotel to meet whomever you have an appointment with, far be it from me to press the matter.'

'No pun intended, of course.'

'None.'

They rode on in silence for another few miles. Eleanor's

mind was too full to delight in any of the hints of the autumn colours beginning to appear among the majestic beech woods. Even the thick banks of hawthorn lining the narrow lanes and swarming with sparrows and blackbirds passed without her usual delighted comments filling the car.

Clifford cleared his throat. 'My abject apologies, my lady.'

'For what? Speaking your mind for once? Not a problem. It's a very rare treat to meet the man lurking beneath your impeccable butlering togs. But I'm sorry too.'

'For speaking your mind? As always?' He winked. 'In truth, my disgraceful display of ill humour was, in fact, borne of concern. Despite our spending yesterday afternoon together addressing the long-overdue household accounts and the evening playing chess, you did not divulge what was troubling you. Which is beyond unusual. I feared your close involvement in your friend's wedding had awoken too many, ahem... upsetting memories for you.' He hesitated. 'However, please do not think I am prying, my lady.'

'I wouldn't. Thank you for being concerned.'

She accepted a mint humbug from the striped paper bag he held out and popped it in her mouth. 'I wish I had blurted it all out to you earlier since we're hurtling towards me grilling Peregrine and I feel hopelessly unprepared.'

Clifford arched a brow. 'Lord Peregrine Davencourt?' He winced. 'Good luck with your grilling then, my lady. Whatever it is for.'

'Why? He doesn't have a reputation for having a temper that I've heard.'

'Indeed. Quite the opposite. The young Lord Davencourt is widely known for being of a particularly even and genial disposition.' He met her gaze. 'And for his headstrong approach to all matters. As headstrong as a certain lady sitting beside me.'

'Well, we will get along famously, then. Which should make

asking about his former fiancée suing for breach of promise easier.'

Clifford stiffened.

She winced. 'I know. It sounds terrible, doesn't it? Especially as Peregrine's family – and Constance – didn't even realise he'd been engaged before.'

'If you are asking my opinion, my lady?' At her nod, he continued in a taut tone. 'It would sound terrible however one was to articulate it. The sons of earls do not engage in secret engagements. Well, not the morally upright ones.'

'Oh, just secret liaisons with a mistress – which are deemed acceptable, of course, as a man has needs – if they are discreet enough?'

'Never, ahem, having been the son of an earl myself, my lady, I couldn't say.'

'Artfully deflected.' She smiled, but it quickly faded. 'But you're right. However, we don't know Peregrine's side of the story yet.'

'Whatever it may be, a gentleman's word is his bond. And none more binding than the promise of marriage.'

Not for the first time, she was plagued with curiosity about Clifford's previous matters of the heart. He was too handsome and distinguished-looking not to have attracted a bevy of female beauties in his day. And she'd frequently seen he still did, to his horror, when she was present. He was also far too thoughtful and intelligent not to have found a special girl at one point. But, like so much else about his private life, that whole topic was a mystery and would likely remain so. She reluctantly settled for hoping he had some wonderful memories to enjoy in his quiet moments.

'Clifford, we really should be astride your white charger, rather than in the Rolls, given the chivalrous passion with which you said that. It was my first reaction too. However, Peregrine told Constance the engagement was broken off by mutual agreement.'

He merely sniffed in reply.

'Go on.' She gestured he had the floor. 'All insights welcomed.'

'It is hardly an insight, my lady. But if the engagement was dissolved in such a convivial manner, why is the lady now going to the time, upset and expense to bring a summons for breach of promise?'

'Constance thinks it is purely to obtain a vast sum in late recompense, since Peregrine has now inherited the family estate and money.'

'Or perhaps because ungentlemanly pressure was exerted when the engagement was first broken off and the lady has had time to reflect and realise she was wronged?'

Eleanor groaned. 'I didn't think of that. Nor did Constance. She's besotted with Peregrine and can't believe he'd ever behave like a cad.'

'Love is blind always, and cannot see.'

'William Shakespeare?'

'Geoffrey Chaucer, from 'The Merchant's Tale'. Although the eminent bard also proposed the same motif. Interestingly, in the similarly named *The Merchant of Venice*.'

She frowned. 'What does that say about merchants, then?'

'Nothing specifically of note, my lady.' He changed gear for the steep hill ahead of them. 'At least not in regard to matters concerning Lord Davencourt's regrettable actions of which hopefully we have now spoken sufficiently of.'

She wrinkled her nose. 'Uuum, not quite, Clifford, I need your help.'

'With the Women's Institute procession and rally, we are now in accord.'

'I meant with this whole breach of promise thing. And I

think you anticipated I'd ask for your help the minute I let slip who I was meeting and why.'

'My lady.' He paused. 'Unusually, I am fast running out of respectful ways to hold an alternative view to yours.'

'I know. And like I said yesterday, I wouldn't ever expect you to go against your beliefs. But this is Constance's happiness at stake. And you've been nagging me since I inherited Henley Hall to make some friends of my age and se— gender.'

'Just some friends at all,' he said gently. 'And not only in the hope that it would keep you from getting mixed up in any more of the' – he shook his head – 'distressingly unpleasant matters that, peculiarly, have occupied the greater part of the last few years.'

'You mean murders? But maybe you've also nagged a little so that I'd stop pacing Henley Hall, wittering on to you about all my insecurities in letting Hugh get closer?'

'I really couldn't say, my lady. But, yes.' His ever-inscrutable expression softened. 'Forgive my speaking out of turn again, but relationships of any depth have not been something you have ever permitted yourself to have, in my experience. Not since your parents regrettably disappeared. And your husband.'

'I'm trying with Hugh.'

'Indubitably. Just as the gentleman is, too.'

She sighed deeply and buried her face in Gladstone's fur. 'I know. But we're both so dashedly guarded and fearful about all that awkward falling in love palaver. We're a terrible match, aren't we?'

'Most assuredly.'

She groaned.

'And, I suspect, my lady, a perfect one too. Not that it is any of my business.'

'Thank you. But back to Constance. She is reconciled to Peregrine's previous mistake and still desperate to marry him on Saturday. So, who am I not to try to help if I can?'

Clifford's tone was incredulous. 'Miss Grainger still intends to marry Lord Davencourt?'

'She is beyond unwavering in her determination.' She glanced at him and noted he appeared to be deep in indecision. She crossed her fingers under Gladstone's generous belly.

Finally, he spoke. 'My lady, does aiding Miss Grainger in whatever she asked you to do mean a great deal to you?'

'Genuinely it does.' She'd said it so vehemently, she was surprised herself. 'Constance is the first real friend I've had in longer than I can remember. I look forward to our times together as eagerly as I look forward to Christmas.'

'And what precisely has the lady asked you to do?'

'Prove Peregrine is innocent of breach of promise. Her father won't let her marry him otherwise. And the amount of money Peregrine would have to pay if he did settle is so great it would force him to sell off much of the family estate.'

'As I feared,' he muttered. The beech woods and sheep-strewn fields of the Buckinghamshire countryside had given way to the outskirts of Chipstone, the nearest market town to Henley Hall. He swerved to avoid several children rolling a hoop down the middle of the road. 'And are you resigned to what you might discover?'

'You mean that he is a guilty rotter who treated the other woman disgracefully? Yes. Because it's better Constance knows the truth, whatever that is.'

'Then my answer is yes. But I must warn you, with some heavy reservations.' He brushed the fingers of his driving gloves against each other as if trying to remove something dirty. 'I feel we are the deplorable characters of a penny dreadful novel, engaged in the shoddy activities of grubby private detectives. Private detectives set on besmirching the character of a woman we are not even acquainted with.'

She winced. 'I know what you mean, Clifford, but what can I do?'

'As a loyal friend of Miss Grainger, my lady, exactly what you are doing. The challenge, however, is great. In the case of a breach of promise, the onus is entirely on the gentleman to prove his innocence. He needs to show that the lady agreed to break off the engagement with either letters or reliable witnesses. Indeed, there was a famous case a few years back involving the 6th Marquess of Northampton. He was forced to sell off much of the family estate in settlement in the end. Mmm.' He stroked his chin. 'I wondered when you told me Lord Davencourt's former fiancée had asked for such a large sum in recompense if she was indeed inspired by this particular case.'

'Golly! If so, that sounds ominous for Peregrine.'

'In all probability, yes, my lady. Now, before you meet with Lord Davencourt, might it assist you to know the three grounds upon which a gentleman may be considered *not* to be in breach of promise? Despite, that is, him having broken off the engagement?'

'I should say so, as I'll probably have to find evidence of at least one of them if I'm going to help Peregrine. Hang on.' She struggled to shift Gladstone first to one side and then the other to reach her pockets. 'Dash it, I should have brought my—'

'Ahem.' Clifford produced her notebook.

'That. Thank you, my suited wizard. Right. Oh, Gladstone, you will have to slide into the footwell.' With the grumbling bulldog removed from her lap, she looked up at Clifford expectantly.

He nodded. 'The defendant – that is Lord Davencourt, in this instance – must be able to prove that his previous fiancée lied about her past. And in such a way that he would have had cause not to propose marriage – and thus become engaged – had he known.'

'Number one, got it.' She scribbled furiously. 'Number two?'

'That the lady lied about her financial situation in such a way that he would have had cause not to propose marriage.'

'And...' Her pen flew across the page. 'Lastly?'

'That the lady was covertly of poor character in such a way that he would have had cause not to propose marriage.'

She looked up. 'But that's rather subjective, isn't it?'

'In general, the term refers to her being of criminal bent or, ahem, of a certain unmentionable profession.'

'A prostitute, you mean?'

He sighed. 'The very unmentionable profession which you have just mentioned, my lady, yes.'

'Sorry. But how wonderful that you are such an incredible mine of information.' She waved her notebook. 'Knowing this will definitely help me steer the conversation appropriately.'

Clifford brought the Rolls to a stop at the base of the broad steps leading up to the entrance of the Eagle Hotel. 'You'll forgive my not sharing your confidence on that particular score, my lady.'

The tall Georgian facade gave the Eagle Hotel an imposing air. To one side of the steps an archway led to a cobbled courtyard, once used for switching the horses for the last leg of the journey to London. The sixteenth-century black-timbered stables and precariously leaning outbuildings still remained but were now used to house guests' cars.

With Gladstone left to snooze happily on the passenger seat of the Rolls, they mounted the steps.

'Lady Swift, welcome to the Eagle,' the doorman said. 'It has been a while since we've had the pleasure of seeing you.' His Buckinghamshire accent rounded his vowels with a soft country air. 'And Mr Clifford, right through—'

His words were lost to an ear-piercing scream that made Eleanor's heart stop.

6

Eleanor sprinted past the stunned doorman, across the lobby and down a passage in the direction the scream had come from. Ahead, she could see an open door. Next to her, Clifford increased his stride. As she reached the door, he thrust out his arm.

'My lady, please. We do not know what scene—'

But she ducked underneath and ran into the room, her eyes scanning the area. The first thing she saw was a woman in a housekeeper's uniform standing at the far side. By the look of shock on her face, Eleanor deduced she was the one who had screamed. Out of the corner of her eye she also noticed at the opposite side of the room – yes, it was! – Beatrice with Bertie. What were they doing here? And what was the young boy's mother shielding his eyes from?

Before Eleanor could answer any of these questions, the housekeeper fainted. But neither she nor Clifford moved to help. Because in the middle of the room lay another woman whose expression stopped them both dead. Clifford strode forward and kneeled down. Eleanor was aware of people crowding in behind her, but everything was happening so quickly, she had no real time to take it in.

First Lady Davencourt, of all people, appeared, closely followed by Sir Grainger. Before Eleanor could react to these new arrivals, two staff entered from the door near where the housekeeper had fainted. They hurried over and helped the housekeeper, who seemed now to be semi-conscious, into a chair. With a jolt, Eleanor recognised her as Mrs Harris from the Women's Institute.

Before she'd had time to respond to this new development, or to return her attention to the poor woman lying in the middle of the room, a strenuous voice rang out.

'Stand aside, please, if you would be so kind.' A stout chap in a plum waistcoat made a path through the onlookers. The hotel manager, Horace Flint, drew up short on seeing Clifford kneeling over the woman on the floor. His mouth fell open as he saw two of his staff over another, one waving what looked like smelling salts under her nose. 'Would someone please tell me what is going on here? I heard a scream—'

'That was the woman who fainted – Mrs Harris.' Eleanor pointed to her left. 'And this woman—'

At that moment Clifford turned around, the expression in his eyes telling her everything.

She swallowed hard. 'Is dead.'

The manager ran a handkerchief over his brow. 'But how? I mean—'

'It doesn't matter how. You must call the police.'

His jowls wobbled. 'But maybe she just fell? This is the Eagle Hotel. I don't see the need—'

'She didn't fall, Mr Flint.' Clifford stood up and strode over. 'Now kindly call the police immediately, as Lady Swift requested, and have your staff clear this room. Everyone needs to remain on the premises, however.'

Mr Flint seemed to be about to argue, but then glanced at

the body on the floor once more and gulped. 'Right, will do. What about Lor—'

'Leave him to me, Mr Flint,' Eleanor said. 'He seems to be in shock.'

Flint nodded and scurried over to two staff gawping by the door. Clifford nodded at Eleanor and helped usher everyone from the room. All except one. Someone Eleanor had noticed just after she'd entered. He was still kneeling, staring down at the body. She tapped him on the back. He turned like a man under a hypnotist's command. With his dark-hazel eyes, Roman nose and unmistakable thick lock of fair hair, which curled wilfully back over his head, there was no mistaking Lord Peregrine Davencourt.

'Hello, Eleanor,' he said blankly.

She looked past him to the figure on the floor. Then she scrutinised the area in which the poor woman lay. Aside from the three long burgundy velvet settees spread with bolster cushions, there were two pairs of contrasting cream-print armchairs. A series of light-oak bookcases, built into the ancient building's architectural alcoves, abounded with well-thumbed leather-covered books as well as several low-fronted wicker baskets of newspapers and farming journals. Despite the wide windows, the light was dimmed by the panes of bottle-bottom glass. The room also faced out onto the rear of the hotel's cobbled yard, the building's grand expanse casting a broad shadow. Clifford checked the silk-stringed pull cord of the nearest floor lamp before whipping out a handkerchief and using it to add some much-needed illumination to the scene.

Her scrutiny of the room was far from morbid curiosity, rather the need to record any pertinent details before Sergeant Brice, head of the local police, arrived. Although his sense of duty rested in the right place, she also knew his powers of observation and his stomach for death were both firmly hidden beneath the tightly laced bindings of his stout boots. He was more at home recording stolen bicycles and other common misdemeanours of a sleepy country town than a murder. *For that's what it is, Ellie!*

The dead woman at Eleanor's feet looked to be only a few years younger than she was. The patch of her face not covered by her auburn waves showed a youthful complexion, the folds of the pretty cotton floral dress a slim figure. The backs of the woman's modest shoes had slipped from her heels, revealing a hole in her stockings on the heel of one foot. And the yellow scarf wound tightly around her neck... was too tight. Eleanor swallowed hard. An open handbag lay beside her, a few of the contents scattered on the floor.

'She's gone,' Peregrine said in an absent tone, still staring glassily at Eleanor. 'Daisy's gone.'

So, he knows her!

By now the room was empty save for Clifford, Eleanor, Peregrine and the woman's body.

Eleanor waved at Clifford and mouthed. 'Shock?'

He looked back at Peregrine and nodded. Stepping forward, he slid a hand under the man's arm and hoisted him to his feet. 'This way, my lord.' He pressed the dazed figure into a leather wingback chair, rescuing his arms from dangling over the chair's sides by settling them in his lap.

It was only then that Eleanor noted Peregrine was clutching small sheets of what looked like letter paper.

A familiar voice out in the corridor penetrated her thoughts. 'Alright, folks, show's over. Move along.' The heavyset rear view of Sergeant Brice backed into the room as he repeated his somewhat breathless command. 'I'll thank you all to do as I've said and await my official instructions. Lowe, look sharp about it, my lad.'

The young constable accompanying him shrugged. 'But where shall I take them, Sarge?'

'I should think the main lounge,' Eleanor called over. 'The others are already there.'

Brice spun around. 'Lady Swift.' He whipped off his policeman's helmet and scratched his head, making his thick moustache quiver. 'You? Really? Again, m'lady?'

'Yes, Sergeant Brice,' she said resignedly. 'Again, sadly.'

He peeped over her shoulder, blanching at the sight of the woman's body. 'Beg pardon for saying, but 'tisn't it a bit rummy how bodies seem to turn up so often when you're around?'

'Sergeant!' Clifford stepped to his side. 'Perhaps the only appropriate question might be how this poor lady came to die, wouldn't you say?'

'Right, you are, Mr Clifford. No offence, I'm sure.' He reached an arm over his stout chest to unbutton his breast pocket. 'I'll just take down all the... all the details.' Casting a hesitant glance at the body again, he made a short half page of hasty notes. After stepping closer, he paled and coughed into his bear paw of a fist. 'Suppose you've both had some thoughts already, m'lady? Mr Clifford? Probably comes natural after all you've seen of late.'

'Only amateur musings, Sergeant,' Eleanor said, 'but I think you'll find the poor woman's been strangled. With her own scarf.'

Brice looked down at the woman again. 'Cor, stone the crows, m'lady. You've a point, alright.'

'We'll let you get on here and wait in the lounge with the others for your instructions.'

'And leave me on me tod with a dead lady!' he muttered into his notebook, wide-eyed. He seemed to tune into the fact that Peregrine was also in the room and was staring straight through him. He jerked his head over at the wingback chair. 'Someone you know, Lady Swift?'

'Yes, Sergeant. That is Lord Peregrine Davencourt. He's rather shocked, I believe.'

'Oh, lummy!' Brice's jowls wobbled. 'Lord, you say.' He snapped his notebook closed. 'Well, this is a job for shinier brass than the buttons on my uniform jacket, Lady Swift. I'll place a call up the ranks. Yes, that'll be the thing to do.' Tapping his forehead with his pen, he frowned. 'Lock the scene up first, mind.'

'Excellent suggestion, Sergeant,' Clifford said. 'This way now, my lord.' He eased Peregrine to his feet again and arched a brow at Brice. 'With your permission, Sergeant? I believe we might need to swing through the bar en route. Brandy needed.'

Brice peered sideways at Eleanor. 'Her ladyship ain't usually the fainting sort, I'd always thought, Mr Clifford?'

Eleanor's sharp ears caught her butler's heartfelt reply. 'How I would that you were wrong, Sergeant! But I was referring to Lord Davencourt.'

Taking one last look at the tragic figure of the young woman lying on the floor, Eleanor followed them out of the room.

As she joined everyone else in the enormous U-shaped lounge that spanned the left half of the inn, she felt the tension in the air. In front of her the staff were huddled in a group, with the patrons of the Eagle scattered throughout the rest of the room. Looking closer, she realised that the staff were actually congregated around Mrs Harris, the woman who had fainted. Now propped up in a chair, she was staring at her hands, shaking her head repeatedly. Despite being at odds with her in the Women's Institute meeting, Eleanor hoped she'd recover quickly from her shock. Mrs Harris lived in Little Buckford, the village where Henley Hall was situated, but Eleanor assumed, given the scarcity of work in the area, she'd sought employment in Chipstone, the nearest town.

Sergeant Brice entered and nodded at Constable Lowe, who had stationed himself by one of the massive wooden vertical beams that formed an arch at the head of the room. Brice looked around and took a deep breath.

'Right, folks, I'm sure as you've no wish to be here any longer than—'

'At all!' Lady Davencourt's voice cut through the air like a poisoned arrow dipped in ice. 'What is the meaning of all this?'

Brice tried to puff his chest, threatening to pop off the already beleaguered buttons of his jacket. 'If I might be allowed to explain, madam.'

'Madam!'

Eleanor nudged Brice's arm. 'That's Lady Davencourt,' she whispered.

'Oh lummy! Sorry, m'lady, but I'm only repeating orders from above, so don't be shooting the messenger. No one is to leave. Nor be talking to each other, since all of you are considered witnesses. So, patience please, folks.' With surprising agility for such a rotund man, he shot out of the lounge as the room exploded in a cacophony of raised voices. 'Keep them quiet, Lowe,' he called over his hurriedly retreating footsteps.

'Witnesses!' a raft of separate voices chorused in horror.

'I didn't see owt!'

'I cannot see why we're being cooped up like criminals!' a frustrated male voice muttered. Eleanor recognised it as belonging to Sir Grainger. She frowned.

It seems odd he is here as well as Lady Davencourt, Ellie? And Constance's sister, Beatrice?

The Eagle was in the centre of the town and also, being an old coaching inn, was still used to break the journey to London or back from the North. But it seemed odd so many of Constance's family – and family-to-be – should be there. She shared a look with Clifford, who gave an imperceptible shrug in reply.

Lady Davencourt glowered at Constable Lowe. 'Whatever this ridiculous nonsense is about, it's no business of the Davencourts. The moment my son reappears, we shall leave instantly.'

He looked panic-struck. 'Well, m'lady, as you heard, my instructions were to keep you here until—'

'Your instructions mean nothing to me. I—'

'Lady Davencourt.' Eleanor came to the young constable's aid. 'Your son has had quite a shock. My butler attended to Peregrine before he went in with Sergeant Brice. And the fact of the matter is we need to stay here until the police arrive from Oxford.'

'Preposterous! There is no reason—'

'Lady Davencourt, that poor woman in there obviously did not die by accident. Or by her own hand.' She held her stare.

'Preposterous!' Lady Davencourt hissed again, striding huffily to the back of the room where she commandeered a chair and looked pointedly out the window.

Sir Grainger, who had come over to the constable with Beatrice, opened his mouth, but closed it with an exasperated snort. He strode to the opposite side of the room to Lady Davencourt and perched on a chair.

It seems there's no love lost between Constance's father and Peregrine's mother, Ellie.

Beatrice gave Eleanor a quiet nod and bent to scoop up her son's hand. 'Bertie, please. We need to go with Grandpapa.' But the young pageboy Eleanor had met at the dress-fitting stiffened his legs so he couldn't be moved. He turned and looked at her, his face expressionless.

Thinking that her ever-inscrutable butler had nothing on the boy's impossible-to-read expression, Eleanor offered him a wave. 'Hello, Bertie.' This drew a series of slow blinks before he slid his hands in his pockets and walked on after Sir Grainger.

For the next hour, Sergeant Brice reappeared at regular intervals trying to placate the growing anger and frustration in the room. Finally, he announced that the 'top brass from Oxford' had arrived and would take the first statements. It was almost an hour after that, however, when he approached Eleanor.

'Your turn to be interviewed now, m'lady.' Brice let out a long, low whistle. 'Good luck, mind. Ne'er seen him in such a foul mood!'

7

It was cramped inside the manager's office. A desk with a chair either side occupied one end, the green leather-tooled top obviously having been cleared by sweeping the swathes of papers and files onto the side table. At the other end were a couple of filing cabinets against one wall. And that was it. Until, that is, she spotted a blue woollen overcoat hanging on the back of the door and her heart skipped. It was usually worn over a distressingly flattering charcoal-grey suit fitted to a long athletic frame. One that belonged to a head of chestnut curls she'd missed seeing for too many weeks.

'What do you mean you arranged for them all to take tea, Brice!?' a deep voice on the other side of the frosted pane barked. 'This is an investigation, not a picnic! Oh, never mind. I'll need an extra fifteen minutes for this next interview, anyway.'

Behind her, she heard the door open.

'Ah, Lady Swift.'

'Ah, Inspector Seldon.' Once the door had clicked shut, she dropped her casual air. 'Hello, Hugh! I thought you'd be chained to your London desk for at least another week?'

Seldon's deep-brown eyes lit up, but his expression quickly fell grave. He ran a hand through his hair and took a hesitant step towards her, looking every bit as awkward as she felt. Their opportunities to meet were so few and far between that they managed more progress in rubbing each other up the wrong way than in getting to know one another better.

In the end, he just nodded. 'Hello, Eleanor. I should be, given the mountain of serious cases I've left behind.'

'Then why were you dragged here from London?'

'I wasn't "dragged here", actually. There was a problem in Oxford, so I'd already come down this way for the day.'

She took in his leaner-than-ever cheeks and the shadow of dark circles under his eyes, wishing he didn't always work so hard. Once she was seated, he folded his endlessly long legs awkwardly under the chair behind the desk and then back out again.

'I wasn't expecting to see you here, but...'

'But what?'

He shrugged. 'Wherever there's a dead body...'

She rolled her eyes. 'I don't do it on purpose, you know. They just seem to... appear when I'm around. I don't like it any more than you do.'

He grimaced. 'How about you give me your statement?'

She nodded and recounted all she could remember. Now that she was reflecting on those first few minutes when she'd arrived at the dreadful scene, something was bothering her, but what she couldn't fathom. It was as if her unconscious brain had registered certain information, but only filtered part of it out to her. Then again, everything had happened in such a hurry. It was such a vague feeling, she shook it out of her head and stuck to the facts.

When Seldon's pen had finally stopped travelling across his notebook, he looked up.

'Now, I've already spoken with Lord Davencourt, who you

obviously know. So, are you well acquainted?' This was delivered with a look that suggested he hoped her answer would be no.

'We're friends, actually.' At his groan, she shrugged. 'More so with his fiancée, Constance Grainger, who I've become quite close to.'

'In other circumstances I would be delighted as' – he held her gaze – 'you rarely mention any friends you've made.'

'I didn't know you noticed.'

He cleared his throat. 'Moving on. Isn't "fiancée" a bit of a moot point for Miss Grainger now? Not meaning to be insensitive, but Lord Davencourt already had one in the wings, as this breach of promise business seems to indicate.' He frowned. 'Actually, it's a pretty poor show all round, I'd say.'

She bristled. 'You sound rather like Clifford. He wouldn't countenance any justification for Lord Davencourt's actions.'

Seldon stared at her as if she'd just declared the world was flat. 'That's because there can be none for dabbling with a woman's heart. *Ever.*' Rubbing his neck, he looked down at the desk. 'Not to my mind.'

Feeling a glow at his chivalrous attitude, she fought the urge to reach out and take his hand. 'Hang on, how did you know about the breach of promise? It's supposed to be—'

'A secret? Well, it was until Lord Davencourt told me about it.'

She frowned. 'Why would he...' She stared up at him. 'Daisy! He called the dead woman by her name.' Her confused look turned to one of horror. 'You don't mean—'

He nodded. 'I do. The deceased is a Miss Daisy Balforth, Lord Davencourt's previous fiancée. And plaintiff in the recent lawsuit issued for breach of promise.'

Eleanor's brain refused to comprehend the information. 'But... but what was she doing at the Eagle?'

'Meeting with Lord Davencourt, it seems.'

'Oh, no!' she groaned. 'What will Constance think? She was absolutely resolved to marry him on Saturday. But now...' She looked up. 'Does she know?'

He shook his head. 'Not that I'm aware. So she also isn't aware that Lord Davencourt was the one found hunched over the body and that he will remain in custody while he answers some pertinent questions.' He held up a halting hand at her gasp. 'Please, Eleanor.' He looked her over in concern. 'What I really want to concentrate on is Clifford letting you see yet another body. What was he thinking, blast it?'

She shrugged. 'He tried. Trust me, he really tried.'

He looked uncomfortable. 'Actually, Eleanor, would you mind if I brought Clifford in now? I... I need to ask you both something.'

'Of course not,' she lied with a quiet sigh at yet one more lost moment alone with the man who made her heart falter and her temper bristle in equal measure.

He yanked the door open. 'Ah! You're already here, Clifford. Would you come in, please? Oh, and Gladstone too, it seems.'

Clifford stepped in, throwing Eleanor an imperceptible nod of apology. As he entered, Gladstone launched his top half into the inspector's lap, treating him to a licky kiss.

'Agh! Seriously, old friend.' Seldon grimaced as he ruffled the dog's ears. 'This, like every other instance, is not the time.'

After Clifford had pulled off the dog and settled him by his feet, Seldon stared at them both.

'Right.' He hesitated, then seemed resigned. 'At the risk of repeating a conversation we've had too many times, my department is impossibly short-staffed. And under-budgeted at the moment.' He threw his hands in the air. 'And I'm already caught up in a raft of other serious cases.' He frowned. 'Blast it! Could this be any more difficult to discuss with you, Eleanor?'

'I'm listening, Hugh.' She peeped sideways at Clifford. 'Really, I am.'

'Good. Because this is far from what I want to say.' He swallowed hard. 'Therefore... I need your help. Again.'

Had she not been sitting down, she would have fallen over. Clifford, however, had stiffened, his brows flinching.

'With this case?' she breathed.

'Yes.' Seldon held her butler's firm look. 'And before you say anything, Clifford, it won't be dangerous in any regard. Besides, I want a word with you about letting Eleanor see the deceased. A word I will save for later. Although I don't envy you the task of ever trying to restrain her from any idea that pops into her head, no matter how inappropriate.'

Clifford bowed. 'Forthcoming admonishment duly noted, Chief Inspector. Perhaps, however, I might respectfully ask the reason for requesting her ladyship's aid in this regrettable incident?'

'Yes, you may. Although, Eleanor, you need to consider carefully before you reply, please. Firstly, this case involves a certain strata of society—'

'Toffs, you mean?' she said to ease his discomfort.

Clifford pinched the bridge of his nose in despair.

Seldon fought a smile. 'I meant the aristocracy, Lady Swift. Secondly, a member of that aristocracy has already threatened to complain to her good friend, who happens to be one of the highest-ranking police officers in England.'

'Lady Davencourt?'

'The same. So, I need... a female to accompany me when I interview her – and some others – to try to cover my back.'

She hid a smile. 'And you haven't got any female officers, of course.'

'No, we haven't, as you well know. Though, there are a few of them in the London force.'

'Which is quite ironic as I'm organi—' She caught Clifford's warning cough. *Not really the time to tell him about your involvement in the Women's Institute petition and rally, Ellie.* 'Ah, never mind. Why do you need a woman, though, Hugh? A man would do just as well.'

'No, he wouldn't. Because, Eleanor, this whole matter revolves around a wedding.'

Seldon and Clifford shared a look of sympathetic understanding.

'So?'

Seldon waved at her butler. 'Your turn to translate for me now, please!'

'My lady, I believe the chief inspector may already have experienced the rather heightened emotions which tend to proliferate.'

'Among who?'

'Among members of the female gender over such important occasions, my lady.'

She turned to Seldon. 'Seriously? Is that it?'

He nodded. 'To my shame, yes. Hysteria and titled ladies, when interviewing, does not bring about a conclusive set of answers, in my experience.'

'But,' – she looked between the two men – 'that's not like either of you. You're normally far more open-minded.'

'Eleanor, it isn't a personal attack on your gender. Or... or class. It's that I'm a policeman. And a senior one, for my sins. And, trust me, that does not put anyone at their ease, especially when weddings and murder are on the agenda.' He managed a wan smile. 'Not that you've noticed, of course.'

'I really couldn't say, Chief Inspector,' she said, imitating Clifford's signature phrase. 'But, yes.'

Even her butler's lips quirked at that.

'So, what do you say, Eleanor?'

Avoiding Clifford's gaze, she nodded. 'I can't really refuse, can I? I mean, I may have promised to help out Constance and

Peregrine, but at the same time this poor girl Daisy needs justice – her killer caught.'

Seldon clapped his hands. 'Splendid. Now, I've arranged to interview Lady Davencourt properly tomorrow. We'll meet up then. And afterwards go on to...' He examined his notebook. 'Mrs Beatrice Wilton.' He looked at her awkwardly. 'I'm very grateful, Eleanor, especially as the bride and groom are your friends. It's going to be blastedly difficult for you to be objective. But I am entirely confident you can do it.'

As if pulled on an invisible string, Clifford glided to the door with Gladstone and slid out.

Once alone, she leaned on the desk. 'Are you, Hugh?'

He nodded. 'Unreservedly.'

Something dawned on her. 'But you didn't explain why you decided to investigate this if you had only dashed down to Oxford to sort out whatever problem was there. Couldn't you have sent someone else?'

He stared at her hands. His lips parted, but no words came at first. 'Y-e-s, in truth, I possibly could have. But that would have meant missing the chance to see a certain lady. So, somehow, I found myself haring over here.'

'Me?' At his nod, she frowned. 'But you didn't know I was here at the Eagle.'

'Obviously.' He blushed. 'Which made the hope all the more ridiculous.'

Outside, on the top step, Clifford was untangling Gladstone's lead from the doorman's legs, the bulldog having got the wrong impression that the doorman had treats in his pockets. Once extracted, he followed her down the steps.

She took a deep breath. 'Fancy getting my telling off over and done with before we get back home?'

He pursed his lips. 'Naturally, I am disappointed over your

agreement to become involved in yet another distressing matter.'

'But dash it, you would have said the same in my position.'

'Undoubtedly, the very same. But without all the social faux pas, my lady.'

'You total terror!'

'Oh, Lady Swift! Thank goodness,' an anxious voice called from along the pavement. In a neat navy coat with a high collar, a vaguely familiar female figure bobbed a curtsey. 'I'm Miss Grainger's maid, my lady.'

'Ah, of course.'

'Please excuse my calling out, but I have an urgent message. Miss Grainger asks if you would be so kind as to meet her. Now.' Her voice shook as she added, 'Only it'll have to be in secret.'

Eleanor groaned to herself. Somehow, Constance had obviously found out at least some details of what had happened at the Eagle.

'I'll come immediately.'

Clifford's sympathetic look spoke volumes.

He's right, Ellie. What on earth am I going to say?

8

At the top of the winding path, at the furthest corner of the modest Grainger estate, stood a lonely classically porticoed stone temple. Its colonnade of thirteen Doric columns rose from the balustrade flagstone balcony to the wide plinth below the domed roof. It was a fine example of the last century's appetite for building the ultimate garden extravagance, a folly.

'Hopefully, not an apt location, my lady,' Clifford said in a low tone as he stopped at the base of the weathered stone steps and passed her Gladstone's lead.

'Hopefully not, indeed. Wish me luck, anyway,' she whispered.

He shook his head. 'Would that luck might be a sufficient calve.'

Fearing her words of comfort would be inadequate, Eleanor tiptoed in through the nearest opening. But she was even more unprepared than she'd feared.

'Constance! Oh gracious, look at you.' She hurried over to where her friend he sat in an alcove hugging her knees, head pressed to the life-size statue of what Eleanor assumed was a

Greek goddess. She pulled her friend into a close hug. 'I wish I had a magic wand to make all this hideousness go away.'

Constance wiped her tear-stained face. 'Thank you, love. It was too good of you to come. Really.' She tugged Eleanor down to perch beside her. 'I must look absolutely awful.'

'That might depend on your definition of "absolutely".'

Constance managed an exhausted laugh. 'Well, if I don't stop crying soon, I'll be the puffiest-eyed bride to ever say, "I do".'

Eleanor flinched. 'You're still just as determined in that regard, then?'

Constance pulled away. 'Well, of course! You can't imagine for a moment that Peregrine would have committed' – her hand flew to her mouth – '*murder*. Even though that woman, that monster, was trying to ruin him and our happiness?'

Eleanor put her arm around her friend's shoulder. 'Stay calm. I'm not saying I think he killed Daisy.'

Constance traced the stone folds of the statue's gown. 'So that was her name, was it? Daisy. It's pretty. Like she probably was too, I imagine.'

'Constance,' Eleanor said soothingly, 'Peregrine adores you. We both know that.'

She nodded. 'And we both know he wouldn't hurt anyone. Especially someone he used to... love.' She shrugged. 'Or at least he thought he did at the time. Oh, what a mess! My poor Peregrine held in jail for something so awful, when these should be some of our happiest days ever. But I'm being horribly selfish. Even though she behaved unforgivably, that woman is dead. She didn't deserve that. I can't believe it.'

'Me neither.' Something struck Eleanor. 'But how did you find out about it all so quickly?'

'Beatrice telephoned me from the Eagle Hotel. She's such a dear. She played the outraged-daughter-of-a-sir card to the police sergeant. She bullied him into agreeing by demanding she be allowed to let someone know she would be home far later than expected. But she was genuinely close to hysterical when she finally told me that Peregrine had been hauled away. I can't believe the police are convinced it was him just because that Daisy creature had brought that terrible breach of promise against him.'

Fearing her friend might press her into divulging too many upsetting details – like the fact they'd found Peregrine hunched over the body – Eleanor opted for a sympathetic shake of her head. 'Who are we hiding from here, by the way?'

Constance looked around, her face lighting up for a moment. 'This is where Peregrine proposed to me. It was so perfect.' Her face darkened again. 'And we're hiding from Father. And Mother. She is so frail. The physician said she's only hanging on now to see me married. If she knew her dream son-in-law-to-be was being held for... for murder' – she pulled out a handkerchief – 'it would be the end of her, I'm sure.'

'I'm so sorry.' Eleanor wished she knew how to comfort her friend better.

Constance grabbed her wrist. 'Oh, Eleanor, please reassure me you believed Peregrine when he told you his side of how his relationship with that Daisy person ended?'

'Umm, we didn't manage much of a conversation, actually.'

Constance rose slowly, her back turned. 'I *am* going to marry Peregrine on Saturday, no matter what. For my mother. For Peregrine's and my future together. And' – she spun around – 'to prove I am worthy of being his wife.'

Eleanor hesitated. 'Do you mean so you can prove that point to Peregrine's mother?'

'No. But it will do that too. Well, actually, nothing will do that, I'm sure. She's so hung up on the fact that no girl will ever be good enough for her precious son.'

'Peregrine's a very lucky man. Truly.'

'Oh, thank you.' Constance ran back to Eleanor and

wrapped her in a hug that nearly squeezed all her breath away. 'So, you haven't given up on trying to help us?'

Eleanor's heart constricted. 'No. No, of course I haven't.' She hoped her friend hadn't noticed her hesitation.

'Thank heavens because Peregrine needs you more than ever now. It was awful enough I begged you to prove he didn't commit a breach of promise, but now I need you to clear him of suspicion of murder!'

It took all Eleanor's control not to wince. 'Constance.' She fought for the right words. 'I'm no expert in such things. And even though I completely understand your determination to marry Peregrine as you've planned...' She sighed. 'Oh, my friend, I need to say, *please* don't pin all your hopes for happiness on my being able to clear Peregrine's name. I... I just can't guarantee I can.'

'But you have to.' Constance's eyes filled. 'At least *try*. Please promise you will.' She ended as her tears spilled over.

'I promise I'll try. But—'

'And you'll talk to Peregrine?'

'I would but Peregrine's in, you know, in police custody.'

'But he'll be released on bail soon, for sure. He's a member of the House of Lords now his father's passed away.'

Eleanor's thoughts ran back over the conversation with Seldon and Clifford in the hotel manager's office. Seldon hadn't specified how long he planned to hold Peregrine for. Or indeed how long he could.

'Well, fingers crossed for that, then.'

Constance slid her arm through Eleanor's, wiping her eyes with her free hand. 'It's a fearful cheek to ask, but will you wait with me for him? So... so I'm not alone. And so you can finally talk to him about all this... this horridness?'

'Of course.'

Eleanor shuffled up closer to her friend to offer all the

comfort she could. And together they waited for Peregrine to arrive.

She had no idea how much later it was when Gladstone, letting off a flurry of barks, roused them. The sound of feet running up the steps and across the flagstoned balcony made them both hold their breath.

'Constance, my darling!' A wrung-out Peregrine dashed over and scooped his fiancée into his arms. 'I charged straight here from that awful jail knowing this is where you would be.' He buried his face in her hair and closed his eyes. 'I can never say sorry enough for all this. Never. But please know it will be my greatest regret forever.'

'Oh, Peregrine,' Constance said softly. 'Let's never live with regrets. Just love.'

They embraced again.

He seemed to notice Eleanor for the first time. 'Please forgive my shocking lack of manners, Eleanor. No excuse, but it's been something of a day.' He gave a wan smile. 'Thank you for being with Constance. I'm so grateful. You really are an outstanding friend.'

She smiled back. 'It's good to see you, Peregrine. Are you... alright now?'

'Of course. Thank you so much for your help at the Eagle.'

Constance tugged on his jacket. 'You must tell us exactly what happened, Peregrine.'

'I wish I knew,' he said wearily. 'But genuinely, I don't.' Gathering his wits, he pulled his fiancée to his side. 'But you've been through too much already to discuss any of it now, surely.'

'No, it has to be now because Eleanor said she'll help us.'

Peregrine frowned. 'Thanks, but how...' He slapped his forehead. 'I forgot, you've done some fiendish detecting stuff before. But... but I can't ask you to help me. I mean, it's—'

'It's what friends are for,' Eleanor said. 'But one thing I must make clear. I will try my utmost, but try is all I can do.'

Constance pulled her into their huddle. 'And no one is asking anything more.'

'Then all I ask is that you are completely honest, Peregrine. Not' – Eleanor held up a placating hand – 'because I doubt you would be, but sometimes we hold things back.'

He nodded ruefully. 'Or don't mention them at all because... because it seems unimportant. Or too hard, perhaps is nearer the mark. Well, I've been a fool in doing that before, so I swear to you, Constance – and you, Eleanor – that I will tell the whole truth.'

Eleanor nodded. 'And, just as importantly, omit nothing?'

He nodded back. 'I swear. So where do I start?'

'At the beginning. Tell us why you were at the Eagle Hotel today.'

'Because Daisy contacted me by letter and asked to meet me there. But it had to be in secret. I wasn't to tell anyone or she wouldn't show.' He took Constance's hand. 'Please understand, darling, her letter said it would be to our advantage.'

'It's alright, love. Go on.'

'Well, when I arrived, the hotel manager told me Daisy was already waiting in a room I'd arranged so we could talk privately. So, I went on down there, but when I opened the door...' he swallowed hard, 'she was lying on the floor. Just still, not... not moving at all.'

'So, then you?' Eleanor said.

'I guess I dashed in, although whatever I did was automatic. I can't recall doing it consciously. But I was then definitely on my knees, trying to rouse her.'

'Rouse her how?'

'Well...' He ran his hand over his forehead. 'The usual sort of thing. I called her name, shook her shoulders and held my hand up to feel for her breath.' He paled. 'But there wasn't any.'

'Why not feel for her pulse in her wrist?'

Constance bristled. 'He was just acting as anyone would on finding someone, weren't you?'

Peregrine shrugged. 'Absolutely. I'm not medically trained and I was in shock. I just did what came to me. Anyway, I heard a scream and turned around and some woman – a maid or something I think – had come in the opposite door. Then you arrived, Eleanor. And I remember the maid fainted.' He shook his head. 'And then more people crowded in and you know the rest.'

Eleanor pursed her lips. 'You've forgotten to mention one important detail. You promised to omit nothing, remember...' She tried to keep her voice neutral, coaxing. 'Have you... forgotten anything that happened in between you realising poor Daisy was no longer with us and the housekeeper appearing and screaming?'

He stared up at the domed ceiling for a moment, and then his eyes widened. 'My letters! They were lying there, amongst a few other things that had fallen from her handbag.' He frowned. 'It was like time had slowed. Like watching a moving picture that's got stuck and is flickering out each frame. I saw myself pick them up.' His hand reached out as if to grasp something, but then he held it up in dejected surrender. 'As I told that police inspector, I can't explain that part of what I did. I was in shock.'

Eleanor had stopped listening. '*Your* letters?'

He nodded. 'I recognised the handwriting. They were my letters to Daisy when we were...' He grasped Constance's hand. 'I'm so sorry, my darling.'

Constance's eyes flashed. 'Don't be. If she hadn't brought that breach of promise against you, none of this would have happened.' Her voice wobbled. 'Not that I wish her to have been murdered over it. Never.'

Eleanor shook her head. 'We don't know that Daisy's death had anything to do with this breach of promise affair.'

'That's not how the inspector viewed it,' Peregrine said grimly. 'But you do believe me, don't you, Eleanor? I mean that I didn't kill Daisy? I realise it must have looked awfully suspicious to you when you ran in. And it's tricky with us all being friends and everything. But surely...' He backed off. 'I'm behaving terribly again. My apologies.'

'It's alright, Peregrine,' Eleanor said. 'I do believe you.' And she meant it. The chairwoman at the women's institute had been right. As a woman, she just *knew. But you can't present that as evidence in court, Ellie!*

'Darling.' Peregrine pulled Constance into his arms. 'I can't believe you still want to marry me after all this.' He flinched. 'But what about your father? He said he would never agree to you marrying me with a breach of promise, let alone a murder charge against my name.'

Constance shook her head. 'No, he wouldn't. He has already declared that unless you are unreservedly acquitted of both, he will never countenance our marriage. Oh, Peregrine.' Constance breathed, burying her face in his chest. 'We've got a week. One week.' She looked up beseechingly at Eleanor.

'Then,' – Eleanor clapped her hands – 'I'd best get to it.'

'Any help you need, in any way, just let me know,' Peregrine said.

'Thank you. I will.'

As she walked down the steps, leaving them embracing, she groaned inwardly. *And just how are you going to clear Peregrine of both charges when the chief witness in both cases is dead? Apparently killed at the hand of the man you're trying to prove innocent!*

As she cleared the last of the stone steps, Clifford tutted at Eleanor's apology for the time she'd been. 'Entirely as I had anticipated, my lady.' He held up one of Voltaire's works. 'I brought along reading matter for the eventuality.'

Halfway back to the car, she was hailed by three excited voices. 'Lady Eleanor, wait for us!'

She turned to see Constance's young nieces skipping towards her, chains of daisies in their long blonde hair. They huddled around her, three sets of big blue eyes staring up at her. The middle one nudged the tallest forward.

'Please say we still can?'

'Can still what?' Eleanor said.

'Be flower girls!' they chorused.

'Something's happened,' the eldest said. 'But we don't know what. But we overheard Grandpapa shouting.'

'We love Uncle Peregrine. Is he not going to be our uncle, after all?' the middle one said.

'And no bridesmaids' dresses or flower crowns?' The youngest's eyes welled up.

Eleanor bent down. 'Do you know, girls, I think you need to skip back over to the lawn and start practising.'

'You mean?' The eldest jumped up and down on the spot.

'Yes.' Eleanor's gaze slid to Clifford's arched brow. 'Aunty Constance and Uncle Peregrine will be getting married on Saturday. I promise.'

9

The next morning held the promise of the best and the worst experiences imaginable thrown together. She would get to spend time with Hugh, but only while he interviewed witnesses to a murder. And starting with Lady Davencourt! Despite this – or because of it – she decided she'd make a special effort not to rub him up the wrong way. And maybe to even advance their 'two steps forward, one step back' relationship. Or was it 'one step forward, two steps back'?

Peeping sideways, Eleanor cursed silently as she realised Seldon had caught her watching his curls flutter in the breeze from his open car window.

'Too draughty for you?' he said teasingly.

She blushed and wondered if he was making an extra special effort as well.

In the passenger mirror, she saw Clifford's lips quirk, though he pretended to be absorbed keeping Gladstone's paws from scratching the leather of the back seat.

'Really, it's fine, thank you.'

'Ah, here.' Seldon slowed the car as he turned in through the imposing gates of Davencourt House. The winding drive ended in an enormous Baroque fountain, the house itself being a six-storeyed symphony of ornate English baroque columns and balustrade balconies. Stepping out, he waited awkwardly for Clifford to open Eleanor's door. Once she was out, he nodded to him.

'I don't imagine we'll be long.'

He turned and motioned her up the steps with an impassive wave of his hand. She concluded that, as a detective, inter-viewing suspects really was his daily diet. Because if he was experiencing even a hint of the nerves she was, he was doing a remarkable job of not showing it. But as they reached the top, he turned to her.

'It's awfully good you're here, Eleanor. Though, I confess, it feels very odd.'

She looked away so he couldn't see her cheeks flush. 'Tsk, tsk, Chief Inspector. I was once informed by a very eminent policeman – named Hugh Seldon, actually – that there is no room for "feelings" in investigations. Facts and solid evidence are all that count.'

'Well, apparently, he was wrong. Because this definitely feels odd. And something else,' he ended in a mutter.

The Davencourt's butler met them at the top of the steps.

'Her ladyship is in the Windsor suite. This way, please.'

Following behind, Eleanor looked about her, taking the opportunity to see where Peregrine had grown up. Acres of black-and-white marbled hallways led them past opulently appointed rooms dressed in velvet and silk, the oak-panelled walls sporting floor-to-ceiling portraits.

It makes Henley Hall seem quite unassuming, Ellie.

Finally, the butler stopped at the open door of what she assumed must be the Windsor suite.

'Detective Chief Inspector Seldon and Lady Swift,' he announced.

'Lady Swift?' There was no mistaking the icy tone.

'Good morning,' Eleanor greeted their frosty hostess brightly as she stepped into the room.

Perhaps the long expanse of Wedgwood-blue walls and ivory-silk settees had been chosen to befit the grandeur of the rest of the house. But like Lady Davencourt's demeanour, they merely added another layer of chill. Even the proliferation of gold frames and ornamental clocks glinting in the weak sunshine filtering through the floor-to-ceiling windows failed to add any warmth to the room.

'Thank you in advance for your time, Lady Davencourt,' Seldon said in the businesslike tone Eleanor always dreaded when he used it with her. 'I'll come straight to the point.'

'The only point of the matter, Inspector, is why you have one of my son's bridesmaids in tow? Explain yourself.'

Seldon seemed unfazed by the hostile reception. *He must be used to this, and worse, Ellie.*

'Lady Swift is here in the capacity of observer. An option which is entirely within police protocol if the situation warrants.'

Lady Davencourt's eyes blazed. 'The only situation is the one you created by hauling my son away so disgracefully. I sincerely hope you lose your misbegotten badge over it!'

'Thank you for your candour. However, if I might propose we waste no further time discussing my career. Unless, of course, you prefer this to take up more of your morning than necessary?'

'Oh, get on with it,' Lady Davencourt snapped. 'I suppose you had better sit. Both of you.'

Seldon waited for Eleanor to take a seat and then took one several chairs away.

Opening his notebook, he paused for what felt like forever before speaking. Eleanor tuned into the uncomfortable fact that Lady Davencourt was glaring at her. She stared back with, what she hoped, was her butler's inscrutable expression. She wasn't sure if she'd got it right, but it had the desired effect. Lady Davencourt looked away with a snort.

Seldon glanced up from his notebook, pen poised. 'Lady Davencourt, I know I asked you some initial questions yesterday, but can you tell me again what you were doing at the Eagle Hotel?'

'Yes, Inspector. I was being held against my will by one of your inept colleagues. In some sort of hideous lounge area with all manner of types unfit for a lady of my standing to be with.'

Seldon eased back an inch in his seat. 'I have all day, Lady Davencourt.' He held her gaze. 'Just in case it helps you to be aware of that.'

She glared at him and then threw up her hands. 'Preposterous! But if you must know, I was there purely by coincidence.'

'I see. So, you were there coincidentally to do what?'

'To talk to the manager about a room for one of the guests coming to this now aborted wedding.'

Not aborted yet, according to Constance, Ellie!

Lady Davencourt shrugged at Seldon's raised eyebrows. 'They needed to take the first train in the morning back to London. Obviously, they would normally stay here in Davencourt House along with the other guests, but the branch line in our local village has no direct trains to London.'

Seldon's brows remained raised. 'Isn't it a little unusual for a lady like yourself to become involved in booking rooms? Wouldn't a member of your staff normally arrange such a thing?'

She looked at him icily. 'I wanted to see the hotel manager personally because last time one of our guests booked a room, they were told when they turned up that it was already occupied.'

It was obvious to Eleanor that Seldon no more believed Lady Davencourt's story than she did. However, he nodded and made a note in his notebook. 'Thank you. And why were you in the room where the deceased was found?'

'Because I have ears, Inspector. I heard a scream. And I was far from alone. I do not appreciate your inference.'

'No inference made, Lady Davencourt. So, who did you hear scream?'

'Good heavens! Does one have to teach you how to suck eggs? It was that woman.'

'Which woman?'

'Why, the one in uniform, of course.' She gestured disparagingly at Eleanor. 'Lady Swift saw her faint, didn't you?'

'If you mean the member of the housekeeping staff who slid to the floor as I arrived, then, yes, I did.'

'Well, whom else could I have meant? Honestly!'

'Lady Davencourt,' Seldon said, 'did you actually see the lady in question,' – he referred to his notes – 'a Mrs Harris, scream? Did it occur to you that the scream may in fact have been the victim?'

Lady Davencourt clucked her tongue. 'Are you sure you are an inspector? Because I should have thought it was rather obvious, even to you, that someone who is being strangled cannot scream at such a volume?'

'Thank you, Lady Davencourt.' He kept his eyes down, his pen moving across the page with short, efficient strokes. 'Although, of course, no one has mentioned that Miss Balforth was strangled.'

She shrugged. 'Peregrine told me after you so impertinently interrogated him.'

'Mmm. Did you recognise the deceased?'

Lady Davencourt arranged the folds of her dress. 'No. She was not the sort of woman with whom I would ever be acquainted.'

Something in her tone transported Eleanor back to the room where Daisy had been murdered. Again, she had a feeling that she'd seen something, but not registered it consciously. She became aware that Lady Davencourt was staring at her again.

'Of course, some who have inexplicably been granted a title appear happy to consort with all manner of people. I, however, do not.'

Seldon coughed. 'Lady Davencourt, did you find out the identity of the deceased from your son?'

She folded her arms. 'Yes.'

No! Eleanor needed all her self-control not to shout the word out loud. She'd remembered! When Lady Davencourt had first come into the room, a look had flashed across her face. A look of... *triumph.*

Lady Davencourt's glacial tone broke into her thoughts.

'Have you any more pointless questions, Inspector?'

She became aware Seldon was looking at her quizzically. She shook her head almost imperceptibly. He cleared his throat again and returned his attention to Lady Davencourt.

'I beg your pardon, Lady Davencourt?'

'I said, do you have any more pointless questions? I don't have all day. I am the widow of an earl.'

'My sincere condolences. So, just before you heard the scream,' he continued calmly on through her outraged huff, 'you were where exactly?'

'In the lobby, I think.' She waved a vague hand.

'Hmm, strange then that you arrived where the deceased was found *after* Lady Swift. Even though she was entering the lobby when she heard the scream and never mentioned passing you on the way to the crime scene?' At Lady Davencourt's silence, he turned to Eleanor. 'Lady Swift, do feel free to correct me?'

'No, you're quite right.'

They both looked at Lady Davencourt.

She huffed loudly. 'Yes, alright. If you must pry, I went to powder my nose, although your lack of decency in asking such questions knows no bounds.'

He nodded. 'Hence Lady Swift's presence.'

'Really. And you thought that would diminish my discomfort over such outrageous discussions?'

'No, Lady Davencourt, *mine*. Now, I will thank you to answer my final question. If we can return to Miss Balforth?'

'With pleasure.' Lady Davencourt smiled cruelly. 'If you want a motive for her murder, then I will give you one. She was an odious tramp who took advantage of my son's good nature some time ago and then saw fit to try to defraud him of his father's fortune. Be sure to write down that I am extremely glad that she is dead.'

'Thank you.' He made a note and looked up. 'But that wasn't my question. It can't have been easy to learn that your son's previous betrothal had become common knowledge? Nor that it was a matter of a breach of promise?'

'How dare you! That is an accusation.'

'No, Lady Davencourt, it is a fact. A breach of promise was issued against your son. I made no comment as to my belief of his guilt, or otherwise, in that regard.'

Lady Davencourt rose. 'Inspector, I have run out of patience. My son made a grave error of judgement where that creature was concerned. Even gentlemen fall prey to indiscretion on rare occasions. But one thing I will stake my life on is that Peregrine did not kill her.'

Seldon glanced at Eleanor, clearly asking for her to step in.

'Because he is a gentleman?'

Lady Davencourt looked at her witheringly. 'No, Lady Swift. Because, despite being my son, Peregrine does not have the stomach, nor the steel, to do so. He is too weak-willed.' Lady Davencourt's top lip curled. 'Obviously, however, someone of the scandalous classes did.'

Seldon shook his head. 'Forgive the observation, Lady

Davencourt, but in my experience, murder is not the sole province of the lower classes.'

'Really? Are you proposing that a countess could also be considered capable? Should I be preparing legal representation? Is that it?'

Seldon put away his notebook. 'I am not proposing anything. I came to ascertain what you know about Miss Balforth's death. Nothing more.'

'Nothing is correct. Since I know nothing.'

Seldon stood up. 'Thank you. Our discussion is concluded.' He gestured for Eleanor to follow him. 'And, actually, you've been most helpful. More so than you might imagine.'

'Inspector!' Lady Davencourt said hurriedly, her voice less sure than before. 'My family's good name was at stake, for goodness' sake! Of course I hated that woman the very moment I learned of the breach of promise being issued. She put her name to the lawsuit against my son. And then threatened to tell the world if he didn't relinquish into her filthy hands an outrageous sum that would have forced Peregrine to sell off the family estate. And for what? So that she could live in the style of the wife of an earl. Her! That common trollop!'

Seldon raised his hand. 'Lady Davencourt, must I ask you to moderate your language while there is a *proper* lady in the room?'

Eleanor silently gasped. For a moment she thought Lady Davencourt was going to stride over and strike him. Instead, she looked daggers before pulling the bell cord next to the fireplace.

'My butler will be here in a moment to show – or rather throw – you out. But before he does, get one thing into your uneducated skull, Inspector. If you want to find that woman's murderer, I suggest you look for another innocent soul whose life she had already ruined, or was about to. Personally, though, I feel it would be a waste of public money.'

Seldon nodded. 'Thank you for your advice. Good day.'

The butler appeared at the door. Lady Davencourt smiled thinly.

'Inspector, I normally forget the name – and face – of any of the lower classes I have the misfortune to come into contact with. But yours, yours I will remember.'

'Aren't I the lucky one,' Seldon muttered as he and Eleanor followed the butler out of the room.

In the hallway, as they were being led to the front door, he peered sideways at Eleanor, a smile playing around his eyes. 'Actually, I think I may be.'

She recalled his remark about a proper lady being in the room and her heart skipped. *No, Ellie, I think I am.*

10

As she settled into Seldon's car, Eleanor was struggling to work out if the interview had gone well or not. But as he started the engine, she caught a quick sigh.

'Right,' he said as if jerking back to the present. 'That's for another time.'

'What is?'

'Hmm. Oh, Mrs Wilton. We can't see her today. Sorry, I should have told you earlier.'

'You mean Beatrice, Constance's older sister and mother of a rather unusual little five-year-old called Bertie?'

'Yes. When I was at the Eagle Hotel, Sergeant Brice tried to send her into me in near hysterics. I shall definitely need your help to interview her properly. Tomorrow, hopefully.' He ran a hand through his hair. 'If that isn't too much to ask, of course?'

'No, it's fine. But I didn't think I was much help at all in there with Lady Davencourt.'

'On the contrary, you were exactly what I needed. I'm eternally grateful. Now, I'll run you all back to Henley Hall and then crack on.'

Eleanor's shoulders slumped.

Here we go again. Another opportunity to spend even an hour together, lost to his wretched groaning pile of case files.

A few minutes after they set off, Seldon seemed surprisingly taciturn. He stared forward with only an occasional sideways glance at her. Even for a man who had more awkward moments than not where she was concerned, she was unsure what the matter was. Finally, she realised from the repeated tiny jerks of his shoulder he was having an argument with himself. Catching her eye in the passenger mirror, he blushed and cleared his throat.

'There is, I seem to remember, a small country inn, the Clumsy Pheasant, just around the corner. They have a telephone. I need to check in with HQ. Ah! There it is.'

The Clumsy Pheasant was a small, half-timbered Tudor building, with a white-and-pink daisy-patterned lawn which was being caressed by the rays of the late-summer sun. A small stream gurgled and burbled by, a stone bridge crossing it to the pub entrance. Eleanor sighed as Seldon strode inside, dreaming of spending a pleasant hour or so with her beau on one of the carved wooden benches out the front talking of this and that. *Anything but murder, Ellie.*

A moment later Seldon returned and they set off. He glanced at her.

'Apologies. I'm always the stuck phonograph record about having a mountain of work waiting, I know.'

Resigning herself to the inevitable, she shook her head. 'No need to apologise, Hugh. And talking of work, what did you mean about my having helped with Lady Davencourt's interview?'

He slowed for a hay wagon. 'Well, without you having been there, the "interview" would have been a three-minute-at-most tirade against my unthinkable audacity in even requesting an appointment before I was escorted out by the butler.' Seldon chuckled. 'Lady Davencourt said exactly what I expected. And a few things I didn't.' He winced. 'But if we're going to talk through the prime suspects, I shall have to include Lord Davencourt in our conversation as well, even though he is your friend. So, perhaps we'd better stop before there's another blasted row.'

In the back, Clifford patted Gladstone, discreetly staring out the window.

'That's not very fair,' she said as gently as she could. 'I wasn't going to rip your head off about Peregrine.'

'Just my ears, perhaps?' he said, with a relieved twitch of his lips.

'For starters, maybe.' She smiled. 'Come on, we've managed this a few times before without actually falling out.'

She waved for Clifford to join in the discussion.

'So, back to Lady Davencourt,' Seldon said as Clifford indicated he was all ears. 'I can't say I was convinced by anything she told us.'

'Except how much she hated Daisy?'

'No, not even that.'

Eleanor's jaw slackened. 'But if Daisy's breach of promise had been successful, Peregrine would have been forced to sell off half the family estate. The one her husband practically died trying to maintain financially by all accounts. Of course she would be vehemently set against the girl.'

'True. But that doesn't explain why she referred to it three times. And why she insulted her son in front of us by claiming he was of weak character.'

Clifford gave an imperceptible nod.

Eleanor gasped. 'You both believe she was trying to persuade us that she might have killed Daisy herself because... because she believes *he* murdered her?'

'Or she knows he did.' Seldon held up his hands in surrender and quickly placed them back on the wheel as they drifted onto the other side of the road. 'Eleanor, she is his mother. Who else would know him that well?'

'His fiancée,' she said firmly. 'No, listen. I know you're thinking that love is blind and all that, but he and Constance have a bond. A rare, magical and unshakeable bond. And that doesn't occur unless you've both poured out your hearts, your dreams, your fears and every one of your weaknesses and failings to each other.'

Seldon looked more awkard than ever. 'Well. Quite. But Lord Davencourt hadn't told Miss Grainger about his previous engagement...'

'I know,' she admitted quietly. 'Well, since we've jumped to Peregrine, let's get all your thoughts about him out of the way, please, Hugh.'

He looked doubtful. 'Are you sure you can be objective about him?'

'If you can,' she said rather more sharply than intended. 'Sorry. Yes.'

'Well, at the risk of sparking more conflict, be honest with me. If you didn't know Lord Davencourt, on learning that he had received a breach of promise lawsuit against him, would you see him as a less than honourable man?'

'Not without hearing his story, I wouldn't.'

Seldon's brows met. 'He asked a girl to marry him, Eleanor, and then failed to go through with it! As to his story that the engagement was broken off by mutual agreement, I neither believed, nor disbelieved him. I did get the uncomfortable feeling, however, that he'd convinced himself it was by mutual agreement whether it was or not. And the letters – found in his hand! – mentioned nothing about them breaking up by mutual accord. Indeed, the last one declared how much he looked forward to making her his wife.'

'I can see that he might have grabbed those in a daze. He was in terrible shock when Clifford and I got to him.'

'You mean when you found him hunched over the deceased?'

She shook her head. 'It's no use, Hugh, I'm a woman. And women are partly governed by instinct and always will be. And mine is insisting Peregrine didn't kill Daisy.' She looked up to see Seldon was listening intently. 'And it's asking why on earth would he kill her somewhere so public? We know Daisy contacted him to meet alone for some reason. If he'd intended to kill her, he would have insisted they met somewhere more private. Somewhere quiet and secluded.' She threw out her hands.

Seldon nodded. 'All commendable theorising. But what if she refused to meet him anywhere else? Or he didn't intend to harm her? Not to start with. He turned up to find she had kept the letters he probably thought were long lost. He grabbed them, and she started screaming or fighting back.' He looked pained. 'Maybe he panicked. Men don't know their own strength too often, especially with women. I see it every day.'

'And I wish you didn't, Hugh. Truly,' she said gently. 'But Peregrine doesn't have a fiery temperament. Honestly, it would be like trying to rouse Clifford into a rage!'

'That doesn't wash, Eleanor. We've both seen what your impeccable butler here is capable of in certain situations.'

'But not in anger.'

'Then I shall have far stronger words with him than I ever intended.'

'What?'

'Eleanor, the only shred of comfort I have when you have been up to your neck in something dangerous is that Clifford will do what's needed to keep you safe.'

'Hugh. Stop worrying. I'm not up to my neck in anything at the moment. But my instinct *is* quietly driving me mad because there was something odd at the murder scene.' She frowned. 'But no matter how hard I try; I can't put my finger on it.'

The countryside had given way to an increasing number of

villages, mostly of Cotswold stone, as they reached what looked like *the outskirts of Oxford, Ellie?*

Seldon slowed for the increasing traffic and shook his head. 'Eleanor, however you look at it, in any other case you've worked on, you wouldn't discount the facts. Especially when you add in that Lord Davencourt is strong enough to have strangled Daisy Balforth with ease.'

Having no answer, she looked out the window. *Oxford? Surely you don't need to go through all of Oxford to get back to Henley Hall?*

As if reading her thoughts, he cleared his throat. 'Just need to make a small detour. Won't take long.'

They lapsed into an awkward silence, broken by Clifford.

'I assume, Chief Inspector, after Lord Davencourt and his mother, Sir Grainger is your next suspect?'

'He is.'

'Might I enquire as to Sir Grainger's explanation for his presence at the Eagle Hotel?'

'He said he had gone there to find a business associate with the hope of having a spur-of-the-moment meeting.'

'And did this business associate confirm that they had their meeting?'

'No. He couldn't because he wasn't there.'

'I see.'

'Sir Grainger said he'd followed the man in after seeing him in the village, then searched the public areas of the hotel without success before realising he had mistaken the man for another. Then he heard a scream and you know the rest.'

Eleanor wrinkled her nose. 'Bit of a thin story.'

'Normally I'd agree. But the person he pointed out in the lounge to Sergeant Brice as the one he followed inside in error does look considerably like the business associate he named. I checked that myself by calling on the man on my way back to the office.'

'So, Sir Grainger had the opportunity, since his story itself tells us he was wandering all around the hotel on a supposed wild goose chase.'

Seldon nodded. 'He is also strong enough to have overpowered Miss Balforth without difficulty. But his motive isn't as strong as the others, even though Miss Balforth bringing the breach of promise was threatening his daughter's future and happiness.'

Clifford raised an eyebrow. 'Chief Inspector, Sir Grainger is a most successful gentleman of business. The loss of his daughter marrying into a considerable fortune – to say nothing of his family's elevated status were his daughter to marry an earl – might be a stronger motive than it seems on paper. That is, what option did he have? Other than to ensure Miss Balforth could neither threaten his family's forthcoming rise up the social ladder, nor reduce the Davencourt fortune his daughter was about to marry into?'

'Only murder,' Seldon said thoughtfully.

Eleanor grimaced. 'Is it terrible of me to say I hope it turns out to be Lady Davencourt? For Constance's sake. And her mother's.'

Seldon sighed. 'I am sorry, Eleanor, but on all available evidence, Lord Davencourt is still the most likely suspect.'

'Clifford?' she asked tentatively.

'Regrettably, my lady, since I am unable to find a legitimate reason to disagree with the chief inspector, I must concur. If you will forgive my overstepping, Lord Davencourt's previous actions have shown unreservedly that he is a gentleman of... chequered principles. On the other hand, it is also true that Lady Davencourt and Sir Grainger both had much to gain from Miss Balforth's demise. Perhaps, therefore, they came to the same conclusion at the same time and decided to join forces to remove this obstruction to both their families' futures?'

Seldon stroked his chin. 'It's an interesting idea.'

He'd grown increasingly on edge in the last two or three miles through the busy streets of shops and long rows of terraced housing. Now he turned into a quieter tree-lined avenue where the houses were semi-detached. He pulled up to one with red-brick paving leading to a blue front door, all the others in the street being black or white.

'Please excuse me one moment.' He leaped out of the car and up to the door. Unlocking it, he disappeared inside.

Eleanor turned to Clifford.

'This is all very cloak and dagger. What do you think he's doing?'

He mimed buttoning his lip.

'It's not much, I'm afraid, Eleanor,' Seldon said a minute later as he opened her door and offered a hand for her to step out. 'But this... this is my house.'

11

On the doorstep, Eleanor hesitated, her breath caught in her throat. He motioned her to continue inside, his deep voice tickling her ear. 'Sorry to spring this on you. I... I hope it's alright but' – his lips twitched into an awkward smile – 'I seem to remember you mentioning several times about not knowing where I lived.'

'I did.' She wished she didn't sound so breathless. 'But I shan't press you as to why now.'

He laughed awkwardly. 'Thank Lady Davencourt. But don't ever tell her I said so. So... umm, please come on in properly.'

With its patterned circular rug and narrow settle seat, the soft-blue hallway felt more like a room than merely somewhere to pass through and hang up coats. A white-painted staircase ran up on the right-hand side, a carpeted runner in matching blue leading the way. In the arched recess below, a door led to what she imagined was a boot cupboard, but surprisingly had a framed photograph of a smart young policeman hanging in the centre.

He caught her peeping at it. 'It's so I remember why I do what I do. On the really difficult days.' He nudged her forward. 'You can giggle at it later. Come on.'

The small but bright sitting room he showed her into had the feel of a room rarely used, despite the welcoming settee and two matching duck-egg patterned armchairs. In the fireplace, fire irons stood ready but no basket of logs or coal awaited. The mantelpiece, devoid of framed photographs, held just one ornament that was a sculpture of a family embracing. The bookcase was full but mostly, it appeared, with overflowing case files. He stepped over and closed the small writing bureau in the corner filled with neatly filed papers.

She shook her head and smiled at him. 'Hugh, are you ever at home with even a moment to relax?'

Before he could answer, Gladstone lumbered in and up to Seldon, tail wagging furiously. He patted him on the head.

'Hello, old thing. Welcome too, but it won't take you a second to explore, I'm afraid.'

Eleanor wished she knew what to say to ease his discomfort over the vast chasm between the size of their homes. Clifford stepped in behind her, carrying a crate.

'I took the liberty of accepting your delivery, Chief Inspector. Through there, I presume?'

'Good, they were quick. But look, give it here. You're a guest too, Clifford.'

'Thank you, sir, but I can manage.' He glided off towards the back of the house with his burden.

Seldon shook his head. 'And I thought *you* were impossible.'

'I am. Sometimes. And Clifford's trying to play the chaperone without intruding, Hugh.'

He groaned. 'I need to get something out of the way and then hopefully you just might still be speaking to me.'

She blanched. 'That sounds rather ominous.'

He stood up, running a hand around the back of his neck. 'No, but I expect you're going to be furious. And I don't want to row with you. Especially not here. But first, I know you want to ask me something?'

She bit her lip. 'True. But, however carefully I phrase it in my head, I'm sure it will come out all wrong.'

He smiled. 'That's guaranteed. Let me say it for you, then we can both breathe more easily. Number one, you want to ask how long I've lived here. But you fear that it will be long enough that it must have been when my wife was still alive, which it was. Number two, you're wondering why there are no photographs of her anywhere. That's because I rushed in to take them down before you came in.'

'Oh, Hugh, I wouldn't have said anything.'

'It wasn't so you didn't see them. It was so... oh, blast it!'

'So,' she said softly, 'she didn't see me?'

He spread his hands. 'Stupid, I know.'

'No, it isn't. Not a bit. It's beyond admirable that you worry there's any hint of you being disloyal.'

He sighed. 'You'd think after six years I'd be able to let a paid help inside or entertain a female... friend for tea, but I felt—'

'Guilty?'

He nodded.

'Hugh, I'm no different. Since my husband turned out not to be who I thought, and after travelling alone for so long, I'm pretty hopeless at anything even vaguely romantic.'

'Well, I've decided not to be hopeless any more,' he said determinedly.

They both let out a deep breath.

'You alright?' she said quietly.

He smiled. 'Better than I imagined I would be.'

'Clifford's gone very quiet, even for him,' she said, offering them both a reprieve from the conversation.

'Poor chap.' He cleared the room in three long strides.

She caught the indistinct sound of a hushed exchange.

'No, I insist.' Seldon returned with Clifford in tow. 'It's through there. But it looks rather more like my office, so one moment.' He disappeared again.

'Clifford,' she whispered. 'How did you know we were coming to Hugh's house? He said it was all spur of the moment.'

'I didn't know, my lady. "Knowing" and "hoping" on your behalf are entirely different beasts.'

They looked up to see Seldon hovering in the doorway. 'Umm... there's food.'

Eleanor stared at him in surprise. 'Wonderful! Food is my favourite lunch. Especially toast?'

Seldon tutted. 'Such accusations!'

In the dining room she gasped as she stared at the array of dishes standing in a neat line along the centre of the small table. 'Gracious, Hugh, what a spread!' Three places were set with a napkin as a mat and one set of cutlery. It made a welcome relief that she wouldn't have to juggle formality and all the emotions coursing through her at the same time.

She slid into the seat he held out and threw Clifford a grateful look as he took another without argument. 'It looks and smells delicious. What's on the menu, chef?'

Seldon looked abashed. 'I have no idea. Your toast comment was spot on, as bread was all I had in, as usual. Oh, and a hunk of suspect cheese. So, after checking in with HQ from the Clumsy Pheasant, I quickly telephoned the restaurant at the end of my road that does food to take out. But your wizard of a butler has somehow arranged what they've sent into a proper set of dishes I didn't know I had. Clifford?'

'Cupboards can be so deceitful, Chief Inspector.'

Seldon sighed. 'Well, I don't think I've opened most of those cupboards since...' He looked away. 'Anyway, however you managed it, thank you. Let's dig in.'

Eleanor noted Clifford didn't even try to serve her, clearly to ease Seldon's awkwardness. But she also noted how much his lips quirked with every spoonful she helped herself to.

'I thought we could eat and finish the conversation about the case, if that's alright?' Seldon said.

'As long as it doesn't stop me attacking this delicious roast beef, Hugh, go ahead.'

'It might,' he said ruefully. 'While I was speaking to my office from the Clumsy Pheasant, my boss came on the line, Eleanor. There's no easy way to say this.'

She closed her eyes momentarily. 'Sinking feeling coming on?'

'Yes,' he said softly. 'He won't allow anything more than the very minimum of police resources on this investigation. Just enough to tidy up for the records, basically.'

'Because?' she said hesitantly.

'Because it's a classic open-and-shut case. Please, Eleanor, hear me out. Hear *him* out, actually, because I'm merely relaying what he said. With all the evidence we have, it's close to a foregone conclusion. All my boss believes I would be doing is spending time proving what we know already. That Lord Davencourt is guilty.'

'But we don't know that!' She paused to calm down. 'Hugh, you can't really decide it was Peregrine who killed Daisy without more investigation. You don't know him like I do.'

'Eleanor, I'm not saying it's an automatic given that Lord Davencourt killed Miss Balforth. But as an earl, he is a member of the House of Lords. Even if I were to find enough to charge him, he would simply claim "Trial by Peers".' He rolled his eyes, 'And we know how that goes all too well.'

She shrugged. 'I don't, actually. Clifford, please translate for me?'

'My lady, "Trial by Peers" is a privilege that allows any

member of the House of Lords to be tried by his peers. That is, the other members of the House, rather than a traditional court of law.'

She frowned. 'Maybe I'm being cynical, but that sounds a bit like the old-school-tie routine?'

'I really couldn't say, my lady. Perhaps, most notably, because the House of Lords is in fact also the High Court of Parliament. Though it is rarely referred to as such, since the privilege is not often called upon as few lords are charged with murder!'

Seldon nodded. 'The last time anyone claimed "Trial by Peers" was decades ago. Surely even you don't know who, Clifford?'

'Lord William Byron, 5th Baron Byron, I believe, Chief Inspector.' He turned back to Eleanor. 'On being charged with murder, he claimed the right and the House of Lords found him guilty of manslaughter.'

'Oh,' she said in surprise, 'my apologies for the old-school-tie remark then, since he didn't get away with it entirely.'

'Ahem, there is a second right available to peers. That of "Privilege of Peership" which allows for all charges against a member of the House of Lords to be dismissed, including—'

'Manslaughter, I'm guessing?'

'Quite, my lady. Only treason or murder cannot be dismissed.'

'So, Byron walked free,' Seldon gruffed.

'Gracious.' She felt another shudder of awkwardness at having a title. Clearly Seldon felt equally so at his lack of one. 'You're very stoic about the injustice of it all, Hugh.'

'Not when I'm alone at night I'm not! One day I might even confess the ridiculous activity it's driven me to.' He stopped, staring at his plate, and then looked back up at her. 'But Lord Davencourt hasn't tried to claim any privileges. Yet. Which, I have to admit, has impressed me and unseated my initial assessment that he may be guilty. Slightly,' he added quickly at Eleanor's hopeful look. 'Either way, I cannot allow an innocent man to be wrongly found guilty. Nor can I allow a guilty one to go free.'

'So where does that leave the case, Hugh?'

'But for window dressing, closed, Eleanor.' He hesitated. 'However, only officially.'

'I don't follow you.' She glanced at her butler. 'But I see Clifford does, dash it! What am I missing?'

Seldon raised his hands. 'Eleanor, I have been caught up in these matters with you too many times before. I know that just because I'm being forced to slam a case-file drawer firmly closed, doesn't mean you'll do the same. Or that you'll take any notice if I forbid you to get involved. Even threatening you with arrest hasn't deterred you in the past.'

Clifford nodded. 'As it wouldn't now, Chief Inspector. I too have learned the hard way.'

The two men shared a sympathetic look.

Seldon's tone was serious. 'Eleanor, I am going out on a wild limb when I say that I will quietly and unofficially do what I can to help you investigate. But it might not be much.' He ran a troubled hand through his curls. 'But I want to ask you to promise me two things first.'

As if by magic, the door closed behind Clifford, leaving them alone.

She smiled. 'Try me. Because I really appreciate what you're offering, Hugh. But mightn't you get into fearful trouble?'

He leaned in. 'Eleanor, I *always* get into fearful trouble when you're involved. But first, I need to know you'll be alright whatever truth you uncover.'

'I will. But it might take a while if you're right and I'm wrong about Peregrine.'

'Fair enough. Then second... umm, when this investigation is over, despite any bruising arguments we might have had, say you will at least consider coming to my home again?'

12

'Oh, Clifford, why is time always against us in these dreadful affairs?'

Despite Gladstone delighting in the wind whistling through his jowls, she was finding the scenery between Henley Hall and Chipstone was passing frustratingly slowly.

'Perhaps because murderers tend to run away, my lady?' Her butler stared impassively through the windscreen. 'Invariably rather quickly, I have heard.'

She laughed despite herself. 'Well, since nothing seems to impede your lightning wit, couldn't you urge the Rolls on faster? Because I was actually referring to Constance and Peregrine's wedding being only a matter of days away.' She felt a wash of sadness. 'And her poor mother is unlikely to last much longer than that according to the doctors.'

'It is far from an easy time for the Grainger family, my lady.' His brows flinched. 'But neither for yourself.'

'I'll be alright. I've been caught up in these matters before.'

His silence spoke volumes.

At the Eagle Hotel, with Gladstone left snoring happily in the Rolls, Eleanor peered through to the bar and then into the lounge. 'Gracious, Clifford! It looks like our plan of trying to buttonhole the staff and regulars might be defeated before we start. Somehow, I didn't expect there to be so many patrons. Not so soon after poor Daisy was cruelly dispatched here. The chef's reputation must be even better than I thought.'

He eyed her like a small child of minimal intellect. 'My lady, I would suggest that Miss Balforth's murder is entirely the reason half the townsfolk are here spending a significant portion of their meagre week's wage.'

'Well, I would say that sounds rather macabre, to come in with the secret hope to pick up some gossip about the dreadful affair.'

'But since we are here to do precisely that...'

She nodded. 'True. So, please employ that superlative memory of yours to remember everything we find out. I might not be hiding the fact I'm investigating, but pulling out my notebook would be far too much like a formal police interview. Everyone would just clam up for sure.'

'Quite.' He raised a gloved finger to attract the attention of a waitress.

'Tea for two, please.'

'Right away, Mr Clifford,' the young girl replied.

'Thank you, but do not rush on our account. We have a matter to attend to first.'

Eleanor smiled at the waitress. 'You've got a particularly busy shift today. Mind, yesterday evening had quite a crowd too before the unfortunate incident. I assume you've managed to rest in between?'

The waitress shook her head. 'Not really, m'lady. The manager, Mr Flint, needed us all to stay on a fair while extra after... after that terrible thing happened.'

'Ah, naturally. I hope you didn't see anything too upsetting at the time?'

'No, m'lady. But I was luckier than Mrs Harris. And Mr

Flint. Maybe that's why today he's still so...' She stared anxiously at her shoes. 'Apologies for speaking out of turn.'

'Not at all. But perhaps you can tell me where Mr Flint is at the moment?'

'I'm here,' came the tart reply.

She turned to take in the sight of the generously proportioned Horace Flint eyeing her with less than the hospitable expression he had always shown her in the past. In truth, she'd been embarrassed on previous visits to the Eagle by how he'd fussed around her, harrying his staff to attend to a raft of whims she didn't have. He strode up, his stout chest threatening to burst his plum waistcoat's buttons.

'Matilda! Back to your duties,' he barked. Her footsteps hurried away. His glance slid towards Eleanor. 'Lady Swift, would you do me the honour of popping into my office for a moment?'

In his managerial domain, Eleanor slid into the seat across from the desk while Clifford adopted his customary hand-behind-his back stance, off to one side.

'Is something the matter, Mr Flint?'

He hesitated and then sat behind his desk. 'Save for the exceedingly good name of the Eagle evidently being under scrutiny, Lady Swift, no.'

'But you must know I wouldn't be here to try to besmirch your fine establishment's standing?'

He hastily held up his hands. 'No, no, of that, I'm sure. But' – he ran his hand over his thinning crown – 'you won't mind my saying, as you do have something of a reputation locally for helping the police with, er... certain matters.'

You can't really deny that, Ellie. She pondered how to reply. 'Y-e-s, but I am not helping the police with this particular case. I do, however, have a personal interest in it. And surely you are as keen as I am to find who murdered one of your patrons?'

He looked away. 'Of course. But if you're here to ask questions about the lady that died, please confine them to me only. I'm sure you understand it's in everyone's best interests.' He stroked his flaccid chin. 'And you not being an actual police officer, it'll only rattle folk harder than a coin in a tin to think there's something further amiss than they already do. No offence intended.'

'And none taken, Mr Flint. For the purpose of my visit to your office, then, I shall do as you request and direct my questions to your good self only.'

The ambiguity of her agreement seemed to flummox him. He reached for the small pile of papers on the corner of his desk and made a show of squaring their edges. 'Of course, though I'm a very busy man. There's another delivery due soon, so I've time for just a couple of questions, if you don't mind, Lady Swift.'

'Brevity is my middle name, Mr Flint.' She ignored Clifford's raised brow. 'Please, can you tell me what you saw?'

'Now, come, come, Lady Swift. That's a barrel's worth of questions and no mistake. I thought you just wanted to know one thing?'

'And what one thing did you suppose that was?'

His jowls wobbled as he huffed indignantly. 'I've no idea. All I know is I heard a woman scream and ran upstairs to see what had happened. I saw the crowd gawping, er, I mean hovering outside the room and hurried in to take charge.' He sat back in his chair. 'And you know the rest, and more I would say, seeing as you were already there. Mr Clifford too.'

'We were. But where had you come running from?'

'From the cobble yard where I was checking the beer and ale delivery. One has to be very careful about these things.' He pointed to the black-beamed ceiling. 'The Eagle is a sixteenth-century coaching inn, you know. I'd have thought a house as grand as yours might have had a cobble yard by the old stable buildings?'

'Maybe. But it's at ground level. And you said you "ran upstairs" when you heard the scream?'

'Ah, now that's easily explained. Your yard'll be different, you see.'

'Not yet. Keep going, please.'

'Well, the one here has a cellar underneath it.' He threw her a smug smile. 'Beer is kept in the cellar but titled ladies wouldn't usually wish to be bothered with such details.'

'So people often say. But' – she leaned forward on her elbows, which made him shrink back – 'I'm still rather new at this titled lady thing so I'd be delighted to accept your invitation.' She jumped up.

Flint rose less enthusiastically. 'Begging your pardon, but I wasn't offering a tour of the cellar. No, no, no, that wouldn't do at all. Not safe for patrons. And too, er... sticky for ladies. Now, if you'd be so good as to let me be about my business.' He yanked the door open. 'I'm glad to have been of help.' He paused. 'And I think you'll find, Lady Swift, that the police have already made sufficient progress without you looking into things. No offence intended, of course.'

She smiled sweetly. 'None taken again, Mr Flint. But what progress?'

He hesitated. 'Well, I want to make it clear from the outset that I'm only repeating what I've heard, but it's common knowledge. That Lord Davencourt fellow has had the finger pointed at him as the one going down for it.' He held up his hands. 'But, like I said, it's not my opinion, just what I heard. I would never besmirch the reputation of a gentleman. Especially a lord.'

Eleanor bit back her defence of Peregrine. *It's not the time or place, Ellie.* 'Speaking of going down,' she said. 'I wish to speak to Mrs Harris, after she fainted in front of us all. She's a fellow member of the Women's Institute, you see. It would be horribly churlish of me not to pass on my good wishes after her ordeal.'

'Ah, no can do, I'm sorry. I've given her a couple of days off. To recover like.'

'Exemplary management, if I might say, Mr Flint. So very caring of you. Then I shall leave you to your paperwork. Good day.'

He opened the door hurriedly. 'Please do come again soon, Lady Swift. Your patronage is always welcome. And, of course, you too, Mr Clifford. However, please also be clear that as manager of the Eagle, I must insist again that my staff are not to be questioned over this unfortunate incident.'

He closed the door firmly behind them.

13

'Dash it, Clifford!' she whispered as they rounded the empty reception desk. 'I didn't factor in Flint being so obstructive.'

Clifford nodded thoughtfully. 'A little too obstructive, I felt.'

'Me, too. However, despite his obstructiveness, he didn't mention anything about me visiting the crime scene.'

Clifford's lips pursed. 'I surmise he imagined it was inherent in his remark about the hotel's good name?'

'Well, he needs to be much clearer.' She set off determinedly across the lobby.

Clifford gained access to the murder scene with his usual mysterious flair for breaking and entering as Ellie kept watch. The room itself seemed colder than the rest of the hotel, as if it knew a woman had died there only a short while before. A vase had been placed on the fireplace, bearing a single long-stemmed white flower with a soft button of sunshine yellow at its centre.

'Clifford, look at that.' She pointed at the gilt mirror as tall as she was. The entire glass section had been covered with sheets of paper. 'Why would someone have done that?'

'Likely because several superstitions surround mirrors hung in a room where a person has died, my lady. The majority have withered over the decades. However, clearly not the notion that if one were to see one's reflection in such a mirror within a few days of a person passing, it would be a most ominous portent.'

'Marvellous,' she muttered. 'And I thought it was gloomy in here before I asked.'

He pulled out his pocket watch and tapped it. 'I think we must hurry. Not only before we are discovered but also because you have another appointment.'

'I know. Let's recount what we both remember quickly.'

'Then, shall I begin out in the corridor? At the point of your hasty refusal not to heed my plea—'

'Oh, save the telling off, please, Clifford.'

'Very good.' He took a few strides backwards to be in the doorway. 'You and I were among the first on the scene to my recollection. You came in before me.'

'Yes.' She looked around the room. 'The first thing I saw was the housekeeper – Mrs Harris, I now know – standing at the far side. I assumed she was the one who had screamed. Then I saw Beatrice with Bertie and wondered what on earth they were doing here. And what Beatrice was shielding Bertie's eyes from. And then I saw Mrs Harris faint, I think. I would have rushed to help, but I'd already seen poor Daisy lying there in front of me, by which time you had somehow reached her and were checking her pulse.' She shivered at the memory.

'Are you alright, my lady?'

Eleanor took a long breath. 'Fine enough, thank you. Now, I remember people coming in behind me. I turned around at the noise, I think.' She frowned. 'Lady Davencourt and Sir Grainger among them.' She shook her head. 'Everything happened so fast, and I was preoccupied with poor Daisy.' She gathered her thoughts. 'Either way, then two members of staff, waiters I think, went and helped Mrs Harris.'

Clifford nodded. 'They helped her into a chair and then

asked if anyone had smelling salts and, rather fortuitously, someone did.'

'That's right. Then Flint barged in.'

'To take charge, as he has just declared, my lady.'

'Well, he failed spectacularly in that regard to my mind. He went to pieces.'

'Tsk, a gross omission in his hotel training of how to manage a murder,' Clifford said wryly. 'However, before he entered, what precisely do you remember seeing?'

She closed her eyes. 'Poor Daisy, lying so deathly still. Bits from her handbag scattered nearby.' She opened them again. 'No, not nearby. Scattered all about, now I think of it.'

'Not surprising. I imagine when she was grabbed around the neck and—'

'Yes, yes. Her handbag and its contents would have gone flying when she tried to loosen her scarf as the attacker...' She shuddered. 'Moving on, I remember the room being too gloomy to see details clearly until you turned on that tall lamp.' She hugged her shoulders. 'Then I realised how young and fragile she looked.'

Clifford scanned her face in concern. 'My lady, we needn't—'

'It's alright, thank you. Let's get it over with.'

'Mmm. In which case, maybe we should consider the contents of the lady's handbag, seeing as you now remember it differently?'

She shrugged. 'I can't see that it's important?'

'The devil, my lady, is often in the details.'

'True. Right.' She closed her eyes again. 'I saw her brown purse and a comb near the handbag. And a little further away, a small travel mirror, I think.' She opened her eyes, a puzzled expression on her face. 'And...'

Clifford arched a brow. 'My lady?'

'I'm trying to remember if there was anything else.' Her eyes widened. 'There was! Although it was the only thing on the floor further away than the rest, so I imagine it was just something someone had dropped earlier.'

'Nevertheless, what was it?'

'I noticed it briefly out of the corner of my eye when I first entered, but had more important things on my mind!' She tapped her forehead. 'It was lying on the opposite side of the room to where Beatrice and Bertie were standing.'

'And the item itself?'

'It was some sort of disc. Perhaps that explains why it was further away if it came from Daisy's handbag as it could have rolled for a while once it hit the floor. It wasn't very big. Maybe an inch or two across. And it must have been made out of something shiny. I remember it glinting in the light. Metal, maybe?'

Clifford strode over to the area Eleanor had indicated and examined the floor. She joined him. After a few minutes, he straightened up.

'Whatever it was, it seems to have gone. Perhaps if we asked the chief inspector to let us see Miss Balforth's handbag? It might have been placed in there by one of the policemen.'

'Or even if he could get us a list of its contents, I should be able to recognise it from the description. But what do you hope to discover?'

'Until it is discovered, my lady, I have no idea.'

Something tugged at her thoughts again but refused to formulate into anything tangible.

She turned in a slow circle. 'No, there's nothing else I remember noticing.'

'Really? Nothing?' He tucked his jacket tails up and dropped to his haunches only a pace away. 'Because Lord Davencourt is not inconsiderable in size. And he was kneeling just here.'

She groaned. 'Clifford, I know what you're thinking.'

'Likewise,' he said gently. 'But, my lady, discounting Lord Davencourt's presence won't change his situation.'

'Strange place to be waiting for the tea you ordered,' a strenuous voice called from the doorway. 'And how did you get in here? The door has been kept locked since the murder.'

'Ah, Mr Flint. Again.' Eleanor winced discreetly at Clifford.

The manager strode into the room. 'Lady Swift, with every ounce of respect I can muster, I shall have to ask you to stop whatever shenanigans this is.' He gestured towards the door. 'I am running a hotel, and a busy, highly respected one at that. Not a pantomime show!'

'Quite.' She rose. 'However, you promised to answer a couple of questions when we were in your office, and never did, so you can answer them now.'

Flint huffed. 'Alright. But only if you promise to leave the premises straight afterwards.'

She nodded. 'Absolutely, Mr Flint. Now, first question. When was this room last cleaned?'

He frowned. 'I do not see what—'

'Do you want me gone, Mr Flint, or not?'

'Alright. The room would have been cleaned the day before the... incident. We had a party in here and I checked it was spotless once the maids had finished.'

'I would expect nothing less of you, Mr Flint. So, my second question is this: did anyone use the room between it being cleaned and Miss Balforth being shown into it?'

'No. It was locked until needed to save extra work.'

She smiled sweetly. 'Then good day, a second time, Mr Flint.'

Passing the reception desk, Clifford stopped to pay for the tea they'd never intended to take.

The doorman nodded as he let them out under the watchful gaze of Flint, who had followed them and was pretending to busy himself with a floral display. 'Best of the day to you, m'lady, Mr Clifford.'

As Clifford drove away, Eleanor fought off Gladstone's licky welcome. 'Flint's demeanour this afternoon has made me think. But think what, I don't know.'

'Myself also. Hence...' He stopped just past the tall coach gate set centrally in the hotel's impressive facade and then reversed the car carefully underneath it and on into the cobbled courtyard.

She gave him a quizzical look.

'Mr Flint's self-professed cellar, which is too perilous and sticky for titled ladies,' he said, pointing with a gloved finger through her side window, 'is over there. Between the tradesman's entrance to the hotel and the Nest, the separate bar the general populace drink in, as you know.'

'But that's near enough I'd have thought for him to have heard the scream as he said he did?'

'Indeed. But also, near enough that it is rather odd that Mr Flint was the last on the scene, perhaps?'

'Clifford, you clever bean!'

He drove back under the Eagle's arch and turned onto the high street but slowed immediately.

'One moment, my lady.' He swung the car right to tuck it along the side of the Town Hall. 'I believe you have an unexpected rendezvous.'

In the passenger mirror, she saw a woman dart across the road to follow them.

The anxious-looking waitress they had given their tea order to appeared at her window.

Eleanor smiled at her. 'Matilda, isn't it?'

'Yes, m'lady. And 'tis terribly rude of me, I know, stopping you like this in the street, you a lady and all.'

'That's no problem. Can I help you?'

The waitress wrung her hands. 'I... I saw that poor girl. The one who was...' She seemed to lose her courage.

'Go on, it's okay.'

'But...' Her face flushed. 'I might lose my job if Mr Flint finds out I've been talking to you.'

'Then say whatever it is quickly before you get into bother.' She took in the woman's deeply troubled expression. 'Or is it something the police need to hear?'

The girl shook her head vigorously. 'The likes of me can't go to the police about a man the likes of him.'

'The likes of who?' she said tentatively, fearing the name Lord Davencourt was about to be uttered.

'The gentleman, so called, who attacked another member of staff at the other hotel I used to work at a couple of years ago.' She jumped as Gladstone let out a low growl. 'And it was over a tiny thing. 'Twas all hushed up because he's a big businessman. The few of us who knew were told we'd be dismissed on the spot if we ever spoke about it to anyone. But I can't stay quiet. Not now. Not after that poor woman was killed in... in that way.'

'What way?' Eleanor said gently.

'You know. Strangled. That's what he did to John, the waiter at the King's Arms. Just lunged at him and put his great hands around his neck. John was almost unconscious by the time they pulled the madman off. He had bruises on his throat for a week!'

Eleanor's breath caught. 'You're sure he was the same man as the one at your previous hotel?'

'Sure as I'll be penniless if I lose this job at the Eagle. I had to tell you, m'lady.'

'You did the right thing. Now, what did he look like?'

The girl gave a brief description of the man before hurrying back to the hotel.

In the Rolls, Eleanor threw her head back against the

passenger seat. 'Oh, Clifford! Is it just me, or is there only one person you can think of at the Eagle that day that fits that description?'

He nodded as they continued down the high street. 'Most regrettably, yes.' He tightened his gloves against his fingers. 'The very gentleman you are currently going to meet!'

14

'Come!' Sir Grainger's booming voice penetrated the oak door of his study.

In the corridor outside, Constance squeezed Eleanor's arm and opened the door. 'Hello, Father. It's Eleanor. I'll leave you to it.' She ducked quickly off down the corridor.

'Leave us to what, exactly?' Sir Grainger rose from behind his desk.

Unlike Eleanor's late uncle's study, which she had lovingly left intact with its floor-to-ceiling bookcases bursting with well-read tomes and sentimental photographs, the room Eleanor stepped into was almost clinical in comparison. Stark pale-grey walls stared back at her, the oak shelves housing only regimented slate-coloured files. The only personal touch was the large-framed portrait of Sir Grainger beside his wife, with Constance and her sisters sitting cross-legged at their feet.

'Good afternoon, Sir Grainger.' Eleanor crossed the room. 'I hope you will forgive my perhaps unusual request.'

'I did when I agreed to see you.' He hooked his thumbs into his waistcoat. 'In principle, anyway. Although "unusual" would not be my first choice of description for the request. However, good afternoon, Eleanor.'

She took the seat he waved her into. 'You know, Sir Grainger, I'm so honoured Constance asked me to be a bridesmaid. She is so looking forward—'

He snorted. 'If you have been sent by my daughter to try to turn my mind on that bounder...' He dropped into his high-backed leather chair to regain his composure. 'On Peregrine, please do not waste either of our minutes. It is he who needs to redeem himself. If he can.'

'Agreed,' she said, hoping it would take the wind out of his sails.

It did. He frowned, running a hand down his thick whiskers. 'Then I am all the more mystified as to the purpose of your visit.' He gestured across his desk. 'But since business does not wait for general niceties to be exchanged, might I hasten you to the nub of whatever the matter is?'

'Of course.' She watched his face discreetly. 'It's about Miss Balforth, the woman who was killed.'

His brow furrowed. 'Well really! What sort of topic is that for a young lady? But doubtless my daughter has put you up to this. Whatever the meat of it is.'

She nodded. 'Initially, yes. But I'm going to be completely truthful with you, Sir Grainger, in the hope that you will see the true position.'

He leaned forward. 'Of what?'

'Your daughter's future happiness.' Ignoring the frown this was met with, she added, 'And justice. Whatever you might think of Peregrine at this moment – and I can't blame you for being horrified to learn of his previous engagement – he deserves truth being his jurors, not supposition.'

'There is no supposition in recognising the behaviour of a cad. Nor that of a wretch who thought Constance need never know of his disgraceful past.' He stood up and walked stiffly to the window, hands on his hips. 'To my mind at this point, justice is being served. And most appropriately.'

'Actually, any of us could have ended up being the one under scrutiny over Miss Balforth's death.'

He spun around.

She shrugged. 'We were, after all, in the right place at the right time.'

His mouth opened, but then slowly closed again.

'If you think about it, Sir Grainger,' she pressed on, choosing her words carefully, 'on paper, you and I have just as much to suggest we might have done the unthinkable. For me, Constance is the best and dearest friend I have. As a brides-maid, seeing all the anguish she is going through, why if I was standing in someone else's shoes, I could consider that sufficient motive for murder.'

She watched him retake his seat, deep in thought. Finally, he looked up. 'And what exactly would you consider incrimi-nating on my part?'

'Oh gracious, I didn't mean that. But as Constance's friend, I have come to discreetly warn you of some malicious chatter. Chatter that implies you might be seen to have thought it better if Miss Balforth was out of the way, so to speak.' She mentally crossed her fingers. It was a lie, but in a good cause.

He held her gaze. 'As I asked, what could there be specifi-cally to incriminate *me*?'

'Only the abiding love of a father desperate to see his daughter married to the man of her dreams. Which you couldn't allow her to do if a breach of promise had been proven. And, also, a loving husband's desire...' she faltered.

He waved a hand. 'To fulfil the equally desperate wish of my wife, yes.'

She didn't miss that he hadn't said 'the desperate last wish'.

He sat back and steepled his fingers. 'Eleanor, I have been in business too long and negotiated with too many shrewd and ardent men not to see that you are far from the average female. Surprisingly, however, you are at least genteel enough not to mention the most obvious reason I might be considered a suspect for Miss Balforth's murder.'

'Peregrine's fortune?'

He shook his head. 'How wrong I was! Yes, Eleanor, Peregrine is a very wealthy man. And I will admit, I was far from unhappy at the prospect of Constance having a secure financial future. And if the breach of promise case had been proven, Miss Balforth would have walked off with money that should have rightly gone to my Constance!' He slapped his desk. 'I am not a young man. I need to make sure my family is taken care of if I should not be here. Bertie, the only salvation to my business continuing to provide for my family, is a mere child. And a singular one at that. I cannot fathom how he will ever take over the business when he seems incapable of even uttering a word!'

She changed tack. 'Do you like the Eagle Hotel?'

He frowned in confusion. 'What? It's convenient enough.'

'But you see, that's the trouble. We've come full circle to my argument. It's so convenient we were all there at the time Miss Balforth was killed.'

'There is nothing peculiar in a businessman meeting another business associate. Everyone dines there of an evening.'

'Indeed. And I hope your meeting went well.' She collected her things as if about to leave. 'But maybe it was interrupted by the terrible incident?'

He eyed her suspiciously for a second, then shook his head. 'No. The man I was hoping to meet managed to elude me entirely.'

'Oh dear. So much for gentlemen being forthright with each other. Couldn't he have just called off your meeting if he had changed his mind?'

'We hadn't arranged to meet, in fact. I was passing the front of the hotel, saw who I thought was him clearing the top step and I hurried in after him.'

'Poor fellow must be hard of hearing then,' she said sympathetically. 'Or maybe you didn't think to call after him?'

He hesitated. 'I did, but it was noisy and he didn't hear me. The Eagle is very busy at that hour.'

'Of course.' She slipped her gloves on and rose. 'Sir Grainger, unorthodox though it has been, it has also been a pleasure.' She went over to the portrait. 'Constance is a lucky girl to have a father who cares so much for her reputation.'

He joined her. 'Although she believes I care nothing for her happiness now.' He waved her down. 'Oh, don't try to refute it. Her emotions will not let her see what I do. Which is the truth about her fiancé.'

'If you really believe Peregrine killed Miss Balforth, is there not an inch of you that sees that it would only have been for love, so that he might still marry Constance? And if he did kill Miss Balforth, why has he not invoked his right of "Trial by Peers"?'

That drew Sir Grainger up short. 'I did not know he hadn't. And, anyway, you have jumped to an erroneous conclusion. I do not believe Peregrine guilty.'

She gasped. 'You don't!'

'No. In my estimation, he has proven himself far too weak-willed to do such a thing. The man has no fire in him.'

'Well, in some ways, that's heartening to hear, Sir Grainger.' She walked to the door. 'By "fire" do you mean a fearful, or unpredictable, temper? Funny, I've never imagined you considered violence an admirable quality.'

'I think no such thing!'

'My mistake.' She took hold of the door handle. 'By the way, why did you switch from holding your business meetings at the King's Arms to the Eagle?'

Sir Grainger's cheeks flushed. A muscle twitched in his jaw

as he stepped to the middle of the rug. 'What exactly has that to do with this conversation?'

'I just wondered if it had anything to do with the attack you made on—'

He held up a hand. 'Stop! I do not know where you have found out about... that. But whoever informed you, informed you wrong. It was entirely the other way around. Wretched waiter suddenly went berserk. I... I was merely defending myself.'

She cocked her head to one side as if considering his reply. 'Mmm. In that case, there won't be any harm in my mentioning it to the inspector in charge of Miss Balforth's murder investigation, will there?'

'Eleanor!' He flushed. 'I... I have nothing to hide, but if you go to the police, Constance is bound to find out. Not,' he added hurriedly, 'that there is anything untoward for her to find out.'

'Well, I certainly shan't be the one to tell her. However, Peregrine's "disgraceful past", as you put it, appears not to be the only one that has come to light.'

Sir Grainger slammed his fist onto his desk with such force, she jumped. *I can see why Constance was frightened when Sir Grainger threw Peregrine out, Ellie!* He composed himself with an effort.

'I think we are done here. Good day, Eleanor.'

She nodded. 'We are. Thank you for your time. Please understand, I only came out of friendship for Constance. It is a shame that despite our very candid conversation, however, we are none the wiser as to who did kill Miss Balforth.'

Sir Grainger stepped to the fireplace and wrenched on the bell pull. 'Perhaps. Perhaps not. You've heard the expression, like father like son? Not so in the case of the Davencourts. Peregrine may not have had the backbone to do what was necessary, but his mother, that's a different matter!'

15

_____

'What do you mean, that isn't what it was invented for?'
Eleanor's eyebrows rose. She was standing in the corridor
outside Henley Hall's kitchen.

Clifford pursed his lips. 'My lady, the official term "brunch"
reserves its usage for a meal taken so late in the morning that it
shows a disgraceful disregard for the household's scheduling.
Being, as it is, a replacement for both breakfast and lunch. Not
an _addition_ to the two.'

Her stomach let out a low gurgle. 'Can I help having a
healthy appetite?'

He sniffed. 'Hardly germane to our discussion.'

'Squabble, Clifford. We're not discussing, we're squabbling.'

'Ah, in that case...' He mimed rolling his sleeves up.

She was still laughing as she stepped in through the kitchen
door.

'Good morning, ladies. How are we all?'

'Fine, as the sunshine itself, m'lady.' Her cook bobbed a
curtsey along with the housekeeper and two maids who had
shuffled into a line in front of the six-ovened range.

Eleanor sniffed the air. 'Something smells divine, if too

unusual to put my finger on.' She gestured around the room. 'How busy you've all been, as always.'

Neat piles of folded laundry lay on the table, trays of chopped fruit covered the side tables, rows of polished silver filled the nearest oak dresser, and a vast rack of pristine dishes stood draining beside the deep ceramic sink.

The back door flew open to reveal her gardener's rear view struggling to pull off his thick wellington boots by pressing his heel to the edge of the top step. 'Ah, that's got him,' he grunted. As he turned, Eleanor saw his arms were filled with four small wooden crates.

'Morning, Joseph,' she said enthusiastically, for it was a very rare thing to see him in the house at all.

'Oh lummy!' he muttered, staring at Mrs Trotman. 'Umm, morning, m'lady. Permission to say how sorry I am, Mr Clifford?'

Eleanor's brow furrowed as Clifford nodded.

'Granted, Joseph.'

Her gardener gave her a wan smile. ''Twasn't my idea and apologies in advance, m'lady.' Joseph set down the crates and shuffled backwards. 'Grew them for the table, not the glass whatnots.' The door clicked closed behind him.

Eleanor looked at her butler in concern. 'Is he alright, Clifford?'

'He is in sturdy health and fine... spirits.' He peered into the first crate and then cocked his head at Mrs Trotman. 'Carrots? Please reassure me, otherwise.'

Eleanor's cook smiled back innocently. Mrs Butters shushed Polly at the giggle she let out. Ever delighted that her staff were enjoying a mischievous moment, Eleanor felt bad that she might be spoiling their fun.

'I'll, er, return later, I think.'

'Not necessary, my lady.'

With the merest twitch of Clifford's white-gloved finger, the ladies moved away to reveal the range and the floor around, which bore a remarkable resemblance to a chemist's laboratory.

'Distilling time!' Mrs Trotman said proudly.

'Oh my!'

Three enormous copper stills spanned the entire stovetop. They each had an elaborately domed lid that featured a large temperature gauge at the base, and then at the top tapered into an artfully curved pipe that arched down to an equally shiny copper drum standing on the floor.

Eleanor shook her head. 'So, this is how you conjure up all those wonderfully moreish but lethal concoctions that have us partying way past the small hours?'

Clifford coughed as he caught Eleanor's eye. 'And grasping for a raft of headache powders on finally rising in time to watch the evening curtains being drawn, my lady?'

Eleanor joined in the ladies' laughter. 'So, dare I ask what delights await us this year?'

Mrs Butters bustled over. 'Trotters has come up with a whole new selection. Gooseberry gin, apricot rum, rhubarb brandy—'

'And carrot and turnip tipple,' Polly and Lizzie chorused.

Clifford closed his eyes and pinched the bridge of his nose. 'Then, my lady, I respectfully give two weeks' notice.'

'Nonsense! You enjoy it as much as we do. Now, to business!'

Furnished with the perfect cup of tea by her housekeeper, Eleanor took the notebook Clifford held out. 'Oh, this isn't my usual one?'

He lowered his voice. 'Forgive my presumption, but I conjectured when you next meet with a certain chief inspector, you might not wish him to discover your plans for the Women's Institute rally? Assuming that is, he, ahem, cosies up sufficiently to see your notes.'

She failed to keep her cheeks from colouring at the image of the dashingly attractive Hugh sitting that close to her. The ladies approached the table.

'We've been ever so busy 'bout the rally,' Mrs Butters said.

'Really? You are too wonderful for words.' Eleanor motioned for them all to sit. 'But I didn't mean to burden you with helping me.'

'Ach, it's no burden, m'lady,' Lizzie said, her Scottish burr all the broader with the excitement.

'No, 'tis such fun, your ladyship!' Polly breathed, nodding vehemently.

'Right, to report,' Mrs Trotman said once they were settled. 'We've all got bushels of notes and ideas about our own area, but you'll only be wanting the short versions, m'lady.'

Eleanor was amazed. 'You've divided yourselves out to take an area each?'

Mrs Butters chuckled and spun each of their pads around so Eleanor could see the meticulously written list on the first page of each. 'We might have had a bit of expert guidance with that.'

All eyes slid to Clifford.

'Thank you,' Eleanor mouthed to him.

Twenty minutes later as the teapot was drained a second time, she clapped her hands, wishing she could draw her entire staff into a grateful hug. 'I don't know how to express my gratitude to you all. You've managed to secure nine, ten, no, eleven suitable vehicles for the floats. And come up with the best eye-catching banner designs imaginable. Not to mention already having made a box of the most striking rosettes in the perfect police dark blue!'

Mrs Butters beamed. 'And Joseph has promised summat special too. Enough of his precious greenhouse roses'll be blooming just right to decorate the big policeman's helmet for the front float.'

Eleanor was too overwhelmed to trust herself to reply for a moment.

Mrs Trotman pushed her pad forward. 'You need this list as well, m'lady. If it suits, of course?'

'I'm sure it does.' Eleanor took the pad and began reading down. 'A grouping of the Women's Institute members for each float?' She frowned. 'But can't they all simply herd onto whichever one draws up closest to them at the start?'

Her cook and housekeeper gaped at each other. 'Only if as you want the police to be called,' Mrs Trotman said, 'to come break up the fights among the very bunch of bonnets who are supposed to be championing women joining the force!'

Eleanor caught sight of Clifford's pointed nodding. 'Ah, not always the most harmonious group of ladies, then?'

Her cook and housekeeper shook their heads.

'Then jolly good thinking, thank you.' She gestured at Mrs Trotman's pad. 'Alright if I rip these pages out then, to add to my pack of notes?'

But as she reached forward, Clifford's gloved hand got there first.

'If I might be permitted to carefully extract said pages instead, my lady? In the meantime, perhaps you would care to partake of brunch?'

In the morning room, Clifford wheeled over a trolley bearing six silver-domed hot plates. He lifted each of the first five lids in turn. 'Aged nettle-wrapped cheddar and chive potato scones, miniature scotch eggs, sage and thyme sausage pinwheels, black pudding with watercress relish and oven-fresh honey and walnut bread.'

'Too heavenly! But what's under the last one?'

She lifted it tentatively as he held it out to her. 'Ah! My investigations notebook and your best fountain pen. Thank you. Perhaps you'd be good enough to scribe while I munch? Then if Hugh happens to be "cosied up", as I believe was your shockingly inappropriate term, and happens to see, he'll be fooled into thinking I've learned the art of being neat.'

'Highly doubtful, my lady.' He turned to the first page and grimaced. 'Unless, that is, we might consider starting afresh, minus whichever spider you dipped in ink to make the original suspect list?'

She waved an airy hand, savouring her mouthful.

His pen moved across the page with mesmerising flowing strokes. 'Right. Starting with Lady Davencourt. Now, the chief inspector had little to nothing tangible on the lady in regard to Miss Balforth's murder, unless I am mistaken?'

'True. However, when Hugh asked her if she recognised Daisy laid out dead on the carpet,' – she shivered – 'Lady Davencourt said no. But now I remember I'm sure she *did* recognise her. It took me seeing her wearing that same look again at the interview for it to finally strike me.'

'Which look, my lady?'

'I can't be sure, but I'd say... triumphant? She had the same look when she thought she'd put Hugh well and truly in his place. Which she hadn't. But back at the Eagle when she first saw Daisy's body it was even stronger. In all the confusion, I hadn't quite registered it before.'

'Interesting. Because you and I had no idea who the poor lady was at that time. Might she have seen a photograph of Miss Balforth, however?'

'Hardly. Why would she have one of a working-class girl like Daisy? More to the point, where would she have got it from?'

'Mmm. Might Lord Davencourt have shown his mother a picture of his' – he gave a sharp sniff – 'former fiancée?'

'Unlikely. And do you need a handkerchief?' she said impishly.

'Touché. What of Lady Davencourt's explanation of her presence at the Eagle?'

'Total fiction! She said she was there to arrange a room for one of the wedding guests. An earl's wife arranging things like that? I don't think so!'

'I concur. It is unlikely in the extreme that Lady Davencourt would be making reservations herself. But surely such a shrewd lady would have created a far stronger alibi as the first step in planning a murder?'

'Not if she didn't plan it in advance. Seldon's pretty sure it was a spur-of-the-moment attack.'

'In that case,' – he adjusted one perfectly aligned cufflink – 'I might be able to make a few enquiries.'

'From whom? Surely not another of your dubious contacts?'

He tutted. 'Sorely maligned contacts. In some cases, perhaps. I was, however, referring to the head butler at the Davencourt residence.'

'But he won't betray any confidences, will he?'

'Certainly not.' His lips quirked. 'But he and I are old acquaintances and, as the upper classes are so fond of saying, staff do gossip so among themselves.'

'Enough said, you scallywag. Come on, let's do Sir Grainger quickly since it's too hideous that Constance's father is a suspect as well as her fiancé.'

Clifford rose to help her with a second serving, then returned to her notebook. 'The summation of your thoughts from interviewing him, my lady?'

She sighed. 'That when all this is over, I shan't be welcome at the Grainger house, whatever the outcome. I'm surprised he didn't throw me out, in truth, despite my most tactful questioning.'

Clifford busied himself with his notes.

'I was very tactful!'

'And what did your impeccable tact allow you to glean, my lady?'

'I'm pretty sure he was lying about being there to meet a business associate.'

'And did your diplomacy also allow you the opportunity to slide in a question about the attack that the waitress, Matilda, spoke to you of?'

'No, but I did anyway. Naturally, he denied it.'

'And suggested it was, in fact, the other way around?'

'Spot on! But I didn't believe him. I think we'll have to call for Hugh's help in investigating the matter. Although Matilda said it was all hushed up, he might be able to dig up something more on it.'

Clifford looked up from her notebook. 'I agree we need to confirm the matter before we can proceed any further.' He cleared his throat. 'Speaking of Lord Davencourt, our last suspect...'

'Which we weren't.'

'Quite. There, ahem, seems to be nothing written under his name?'

'I know, but what's the point? We both know we could fill the page with damning observations. At least I have an entry for him.' She frowned. 'What's the name of that female statue holding a set of scales outside every law court?'

'It is commonly agreed that she is Justitia, introduced by Emperor Augustus during his reign, which began in twenty-seven BC.' He let out a small sigh. 'She is the symbol of justice, my lady.'

'And Hugh's boss has loaded her scales entirely on one side. The side against Peregrine! Even Hugh isn't looking for any more suspects because he can't. So, I need to balance Hugh's boss' bias against Peregrine with mine. That's only fair, isn't it?'

'Ahem, your being a friend of Lord Davencourt's precludes my ready concurrence that the two balance out. With apologies.'

'Understood. However, I shan't give up on my belief. So please feel free to declare *out* now if you wish.'

He hesitated, then shook his head. 'With grave reservations, I declare *in*, my lady. If largely to prevent you investigating alone.'

Her heart swelled. 'Thank you, Clifford. And, actually, Sir Grainger also declared he believed Peregrine innocent.'

He arched a brow. 'May I inquire why?'

'Interestingly, he used exactly the same phrase as Lady Davencourt. He said Peregrine was too "weak-willed" to have done such a thing. Whereas his mother!'

He tapped the notebook. 'Perhaps, therefore, my previous suggestion that Sir Grainger and Lady Davencourt decided to join forces to remove this obstruction to both their families' futures may have some merit?'

She nodded. 'It might indeed. Now, for the moment, I propose we skip any more talk of Peregrine and introduce a fourth suspect, Horace Flint.'

Clifford thought for a moment. 'I do agree that Mr Flint appeared to be hiding something, but not necessarily connected with the murder.'

'True. But I don't trust him, so stick his name down for now.' She pushed away her empty plate. 'I shall ring Hugh and ask him to check out Sir Grainger's alleged attack at the Kings Head and anything he can dig up on Flint, too.' Her eyes widened. 'Of course! I almost forgot. Flint insisted the room had been kept locked since the murder, so what happened to that dice I saw? If anyone could have gained access to the room, it was probably Flint. As the manager, he must have the key.'

Clifford's brow creased. 'Indeed.'

She shrugged. 'I've no idea if it's of any significance, but I'll ask if Hugh can also let me see the contents of Daisy's handbag, as we said. If, that is, it doesn't offend my butler too much that I'm breaking off part way through a meal to telephone?'

He sighed. 'After partaking of brunch, my lady, what could it matter?'

Out in the marbled hallway, the telephone exchange seemed to take an age to connect her. Finally, the deep voice that always delighted her ears came through in a hushed tone.

'Eleanor, are you alright?'

'Fine, Hugh. But I need your help... if it's still on offer?'

'Absolutely, if we're discreet, which you have rarely managed in my experience.'

She laughed. 'You rotter.' Aware he was taking a risk in even accepting her call, she hurried on with her requests.

The muffled sounds of something she couldn't place came through and then silence.

'Hugh? Are you still there?'

'Yes,' his voice came back. 'But I've just been handed a report that may make those requests rather null and void.'

She took a deep breath. 'And why is that?'

'Because, well, I'm sorry, Eleanor, but as well as Miss Balforth's fingerprints on the murder weapon – which I expected, as it was her scarf – there was one other.'

She gasped. 'You don't mean—'

A long sigh came down the phone. 'Unfortunately, I do, blast it! The other set of fingerprints were—'

'Peregrine's!'

16

Eleanor hung the handset back on its cradle a second time and stared glumly at her butler's reflection in the gold-framed mirror above the hall table. She'd rung Peregrine immediately after ending her phone call with Seldon.

'Dash it, Clifford! Peregrine is his own worst enemy. What was he thinking?'

'I fear I couldn't answer without speaking out of turn, my lady.'

She shrugged. 'You're entitled to your opinion, but aren't you going to ask what his explanation was just now for his fingerprints being on Daisy's scarf? And not telling Seldon?'

'That he felt confessing to putting his hands around Miss Balforth's neck – even if it was in an attempt to loosen the scarf that had strangled her – sounded too incriminating to own up to?'

'Uncannily perceptive as always.' She sighed. 'He also said he didn't consider that fingerprints might become an issue.'

'To be fair, that is still far from an everyday part of police investigation methods, as we have noted in previous cases. And he was in shock.'

She smiled. 'Ever Mr Even-Handed.'

'"Doubt is not a pleasant condition, but certainty is absurd."'

'Oscar Wilde?'

'Voltaire, my lady. Only last evening, the eminent philosopher reminded me so. Therefore, might I be so bold as to suggest you write Lord Davencourt a brief missive?'

'Saying what? That I want to bang his head repeatedly on something extremely hard for making such a mess of everything?'

'If you wish.' He held out his fountain pen.

She stared at him for a moment, and then the penny dropped. 'Ah! A letter would be a plausible ruse for you to have to drive to Davencourt House and speak to the butler personally.'

'Whom else could you entrust to deliver such a private, and evidently unladylike, message? And who else to receive it?'

'Excellent plan! And while you're doing that, I'll bicycle into the village and find Mrs Harris. As Flint informed us earlier, she should still be off work. Then I'll grill her on exactly what she saw at the Eagle without Flint being able to stick his nose in.'

A short while later as she urged her bicycle down Henley Hall's tree-lined driveway and out under the arch of its imperious gates, Gladstone let out a series of excited woofs beside her. He was securely restrained in his smart dog trailer, which Joseph had built as a surprise after too many afternoons of her feeling guilty at leaving her eager bulldog behind. Painted to match the olive green of her cycle, the sidecar never failed to draw waves and giggles wherever the two of them ventured out.

Mindful of her precious cargo, she carefully navigated the hairpin bends of the narrow lane down towards the village.

Verdant hedgerows of blackthorn and hazel peppered with
vibrant-red rosehips and sporadic swathes of blackberries
bordered the road. Her cycling adventures had taken her across
the world through deserts, mountains and vast forests. Despite
this, pedalling through Buckinghamshire's green and wooded
countryside still filled her with wonder.

At the bottom of the hill, she passed Little Buckford's
village common, ringed with beech trees dressed in their early
autumnal best of bronze, yellow and gold leaves. She slowed on
reaching the pond and bent to ruffle Gladstone's ears to distract
him from the gaggle of ducks crossing the road. Ducks passed,
she pushed on into the high street of seven small shops, presided
over by the medieval flint church of St Winifred's.

A huddle of women with shopping bags gossiping outside
the butcher's directed her through the village and out along a
cobble lane. At the end, a short uneven path led to a tiny stone
cottage with a roof badly in need of re-thatching. The narrow
stretch of ground that ran down the right side of the house was
marked out with overgrown vegetable beds, through which two
scrawny chickens were listlessly picking.

In the absence of a knocker, she rapped on the front door.
After a long wait, she frowned. It couldn't have been a fruitless
journey? In a village as small as Little Buckford one's business
and whereabouts were usually known by the whole community.
Surely the women who directed her would have said if her
quarry had been out and about? She knocked again. But again,
only silence answered.

From where she was standing on the stone porch step, she
could see clearly through the one window into what appeared
to be the only room. Mrs Harris' entire daily life must have
unfolded at either the small square wooden table or at the
ancient-looking treadle sewing machine. Two low-backed
wooden chairs sat on either side of the coal-less – and log-less –
fireplace, a man's hat on one. A pipe and tankard sat on the

mantelpiece. A long simple bureau had been placed widthways like a shop counter, with a small area left behind it. Over the mantelpiece hung an embroidered sampler.

Embarrassed she'd peeped through the window, she hurriedly skirted around the lean-to, towards the back garden, calling out as she went. 'Hello? Mrs Harris?' But all that greeted her was a near-empty coal bunker and a line of drying washing.

She was just beginning to doubt she was at the right house when her eyes fell on a burgundy housecoat that seemed familiar. She risked having no idea what to say if anyone were to appear and challenge her and nipped over to the washing line. There was no mistaking the Eagle Hotel's emblem on the collar.

With one last effort, she knocked on the back door before peeping through what she'd thought would be the scullery window, but it merely gave onto the back of the same room she'd seen from the front. A small butler sink and a two-ring burner had been hidden from her view by the bureau, which she now realised had been positioned to do just that. Probably so Mrs Harris could wash in private, there obviously being no bathroom.

All the more grateful for her luxurious home, she returned to the front and remounted her bicycle, Gladstone woofing a welcome from his passenger seat. Back on the high street, the bulldog barked again, this time more urgently.

'What is it, boy...? Oh gracious!' she gasped as a pair of hands flew out and grabbed her handlebars, jerking her to a halt. 'I'm so sorry, Mr Brenchley. Are you alright?'

The owner of Little Buckford's general store nodded slowly, the ever-present crease in his earnest-minded forehead all the deeper. But his warm brown eyes smiled back. 'Right enough, m'lady. Been a fair while since you attempted to run me down with your bicycle.'

Beside him, Mr Penry, a heifer of a man in a pristine striped butcher's apron, chuckled. 'Fret ye not, m'lady. Would take

more than your bicycle wheel to chop Arthur here into anything
fit for one of your Mrs Trotman's casseroles. Even at the fair
speed you manage with your hairy beast of burden alongside
you.' He ran a hand over Gladstone's head, which earned him a
slobbery lick.

She smiled, delighting as always in the meandering cadence
Penry's Welsh roots lent his every word. 'Gentlemen, forgive a
possibly foolish question, but why were you standing in the
middle of the road?'

Brenchley slid his hands into his brown shopkeeper's overcoat. 'Because even being so impolite as to be hollering after
you, m'lady, hadn't worked the first time.' He pulled out her
favourite sage silk scarf. 'You dropped this when you flew
through here earlier.'

The two men exchanged a look.

Penry tried a nonchalant tone. 'Obviously, it must have
been on a very important errand to have trussed your thoughts
up tighter than a chicken ready for roasting?'

She hid a smile at their nosiness, but more so at their lack of
subtlety. 'Oh, just a short trip to offer my best wishes to someone. And thank you for the scarf.'

'Ah,' Penry said. 'Shame you'll have to make the trip again
then.'

'Remarkable! How could you know that, I wonder?' she
teased.

Brenchley elbowed Penry in his ribs. 'Oh, 'tis but a small
village, m'lady, and folks, they will go a'chattering.'

'Without needing any encouragement, course,' Brenchley
added hastily.

'So,' Penry said, 'can we pass a message on to Mrs Harris?
Save you another trip, as it were?'

'No, thank you. But I'm pleased to hear she's been out and
about. It's a sign she's not too upset by the events at the Eagle.'

'A terrible business, m'lady.' Brenchley looked thoughtful.

'Mrs Harris has called into t'shop, right enough. Not quite herself, though, I'd say.'

'Poor thing,' Eleanor said sincerely. 'Still, at least she has her husband to make sure she's alright.'

'There's no Mr Harris,' a female voice said from behind.

Eleanor turned to see two felt-hatted ladies, who blushed at having given away that they'd been eavesdropping.

Eleanor nodded to them. 'Hello, ladies. I didn't realise Mrs Harris lives alone, bless her.'

'Another husband lost to the war by all accounts,' Brenchley said.

Penry nodded. 'And never has she visited my shop without reminding me how lucky I am to have come through unscathed, unlike her poor other half.'

One of the women nodded. 'She keeps that cottage like a shrine to her late husband. She needs to move on. He ain't coming back, is he?'

'Least she was given a roof over her head,' the other woman said a little snidely.

The other nodded. 'That cottage was left to her by her aunt Ida. Lovely woman, she was. One of the cheeriest souls you'd ever meet. Still, some folk keeps different habits, don't they? Always t'otherside of the holly bush, as it were.'

At the assembled company's collective nod, Eleanor wished she wasn't so baffled by the local expressions. Evidently, her face gave her away.

Penry leaned in. 'Meaning a bit... prickly, m'lady.'

'Bet Hartbridge wasn't too sad to wave farewell when she took the cottage here,' one of the women said.

The men both looked uncomfortable at this. 'Best not let Father Time steal a march on you, ladies,' Brenchley said firmly.

With a nod and a smile to Eleanor, the two women reluctantly moved off.

'I don't know that other lady they mentioned,' Eleanor said. 'Bet Harbidge, was it?'

Penry chuckled again. 'Beg pardon, m'lady, but it was *Hartbridge*. And 'tain't not a lady, but a place.'

'Nigh on twenty miles east,' Brenchley added, gesturing way past the church. 'Over the border, 'tis, mind, so... you know.'

Deciding she would ask Clifford later what that might mean, Eleanor smiled brightly. 'Well, I shall endeavour to call on Mrs Harris another time. Thank you again for my scarf. Oh, and a bone for Gladstone as well, I see. Too kind.'

Penry beamed, then ran a slow hand over the bulldog's ears. 'He'll be good company for wherever it is you're off to now, perhaps, m'lady? Not too far, is it?'

She hid another smile at their clumsy attempts to hide their nosiness again. But living in a village like Little Buckford meant that your business was everyone's business. However, as her business involved someone who didn't live in the village, she jumped back on her bicycle and wished them a good day. Setting off towards Henley Hall, she hoped she would have more luck with her next interview!

17

'Eleanor, you really are every inch as unorthodox as everyone says!' Beatrice, Constance's eldest sister, glanced at Clifford, where he stood respectfully out in the hallway. She patted the intricate pleats of her blonde chignon. 'But if it will help Constance, I suppose you'd best bring your butler in as well.'

'Thank you. And it will, without question.' Eleanor settled onto the nearest of two sapphire-blue velvet settees and muttered, 'One way or another.'

Clifford stepped in, bowed, and closed the door. The room's bird-print drapes and matching cushions gave the silver silk-damask-wallpapered space a cosy family feel, one echoed in the proliferation of framed photographs of Beatrice with her sisters and husband and son filling the mantelpiece and the upright piano. Eleanor winced.

Unfortunately, Ellie, your visit is to do with family, but not in a cosy way.

Beatrice's brows came together as she took a seat on the opposite settee. 'Constance said something about having asked you to investigate? But what on earth could she have meant? Investigating is surely the job of the police?'

'It should be,' Eleanor said ruefully. 'But even the best-intentioned members of the force have their hands tied on occasion and unfortunately Detective Chief Inspector Seldon has had to bow out.'

'Well, to be honest at the Eagle after... after it all happened, he did seem rather out of his depth. He must have asked me to calm down a dozen times!'

Eleanor's gaze slid to Clifford's. He gave an imperceptible shake of his head.

He's right. Best not to say that you know Hugh. Beatrice might be guarded in what she says and unintentionally miss out something important.

She smiled instead. 'I heard somewhere that chaps find us a little tricky to handle if we're feeling... emotional.'

'Well, if I'd realised how quickly turning on the waterworks was going to have him leaping for the door, I'd have started crying from the outset.' She stared at Eleanor. 'But what can you do alone?'

'Alone? Nothing. That's why I asked that Clifford join us. I'm helpless without his unwavering logic and infuriatingly methodical approach to everything.'

He bowed. 'Too kind, m'lady. But they would be grossly insufficient without your equally unwavering illogicality.'

'And infuriating impulsiveness, I know.' Eleanor laughed at Beatrice's bemused look. 'It's complicated. The short version is that, somehow, I've found myself mixed up in a few other such matters rather recently, and Clifford and I turned out to be quite the team.'

Beatrice stared between them. 'At what?'

'Solving murders.' The harshness of the reality behind Eleanor's words silenced the room. Even Clifford paused in setting out the tea things.

'It was murder, wasn't it?' Beatrice said in a trembling voice. 'I really can't believe it, still.' She looked up sharply as

Clifford offered her a filled cup and then melted to the side of the room.

Eleanor nodded vehemently. 'Yes. And, right now, Constance feels we are all she has. Peregrine too, in fact.'

Beatrice bristled. 'So, you've spoken to him? Well, I can't imagine what he had to say for himself. My poor baby sister! It's too awful of him.'

'You don't... you don't think Peregrine is responsible for Miss Balforth's untimely death, do you?'

'Well, in a roundabout sort of way, yes. If he hadn't consorted with the girl, to say nothing of becoming engaged to her, none of this would have happened, would it? He and Constance would still be planning to glide down the aisle on Saturday as the newly wedded Lord and Lady Davencourt.' Her eyes flared. 'He had us all fooled. The whole family adored him from the start.' She ran a finger along the arm of the settee, something in her tone making Eleanor's skin prickle. 'We've always been so close as sisters, you know? All three of us. But Constance and I particularly so.' She laughed mirthlessly. 'Something about the eldest mothering the youngest, probably. Constance arrived just after my eighth birthday, you see. She was such a happy, jolly little thing. So full of life. And she's never been anything else... until *now*.' Beatrice broke off with a sniff and reached for her tea.

The anger in that one word made Eleanor frown. *Does Sir Grainger's volatile temper run in other members of the family? Would Beatrice have done the unthinkable to protect her younger sister's happiness?*

Eleanor grimaced in sympathy. 'I agree getting engaged to Miss Balforth might not have been Peregrine's best decision.'

Beatrice put down her tea. 'Well, let's hope it was his worst and there are no more skeletons waiting to leap from his wardrobe!'

'I'm sure there aren't. Now, to business. Please tell me

everything you saw at the hotel that day, no matter how unimportant you think it is. Just let everything tumble out. No need to try to be ordered or organised about it.' She waved an encouraging hand, ignoring Clifford's imperceptible shudder.

'Right, what do I remember?' Beatrice took a moment to select a walnut-topped chocolate from the silver-tiered stand. 'I'd come back from the railway station rather flustered. Bertie had been getting restless waiting at the Eagle for his papa to join us for an early supper, you see. Bertie's a delight, of course, but it can become difficult when he has an attack of the fidgets.' She let out a long breath. 'Especially in public. He's rather... unpredictable.'

Eleanor smiled. 'I understand how he feels, poor little chap. Sitting waiting for anything makes me want to leap up and scream.' She pretended to whisper behind her hand as her butler poured her tea. 'Clifford hasn't noticed, of course, but I think I might not have been at the head of the queue when patience was being handed out.'

His lips quirked. 'Or indeed, in the line-up at all, my lady.'

Beatrice giggled in surprise. 'Well, it's sweet of you to be so understanding of Bertie. Many people aren't. Which is why I thought distracting him with watching the train steam into the station and then trying to spot his papa among the passengers was a good idea. Except, Frederick wasn't on the train.'

'I hope he was alright?'

'Just caught up with work, I discovered later. As he too often is.' Beatrice sighed. 'So, Bertie and I went back to the Eagle. I settled him on one of the seats inside the door of the lounge with his latest favourite pastime of coin rubbing. He is obsessed by details, you see. The more intricate, the more fascinating he finds them, especially letters and numbers. Once he was absorbed, I crept off into one of the two telephone booths. They're just across from the reception area. I quickly called Frederick at his office to see if he was still intending to join us.'

Out of the corner of her eye, Eleanor caught Clifford pull his pocket watch from his waistcoat and tap it. She nodded. 'What time was that?'

Beatrice shrugged. 'Honestly, I couldn't be at all precise. Frederick's train was the express from London, but it was ten or fifteen minutes late coming in. Then the walk back to the hotel with Bertie could have taken anywhere between ten and twenty minutes.' She smiled wearily. 'We did have to count every single railing we passed. Twice. Then stop to study an unusual silver-coloured gate latch. He's like a magpie over shiny objects. And then I had to settle him into his coin rubbing, so I couldn't say timewise.'

'No matter. Go on with everything else you remember, please.'

'But that's just it. There isn't anything else, really. I'd just finished my telephone call when I heard the most fearful scream. I dropped the handset and ran as fast as I could to see who needed help. You arrived almost immediately after me.' Beatrice glanced at Clifford, a look Eleanor couldn't decipher crossing her face. 'And, now I think about it, your butler too.'

'Mmm, yes. But when I saw you in the room, Bertie was there as well. You said you left him in the lounge coin rubbing, wasn't it?'

'Yes. That's the thing. He just appeared.' Beatrice paled. 'He must have heard the scream and followed everyone out of the lounge. I should never have left him alone. He's too young not to have' – she pressed her handkerchief to her mouth – 'his mama when he needs her.' She looked away, but not before Eleanor glimpsed another look she couldn't fathom flash across Beatrice's face. 'But we all do things on the spur of the moment we're not proud of.'

An uncomfortable feeling pricked at Eleanor's skin again. She peeped over to where Clifford now stood a few feet away. Behind his back, she caught the telltale twitch of one hand tapping the palm of the other. Something had unsettled him too, it seemed.

'It was an upsetting experience for everyone,' Eleanor said gently. 'Take a moment to recover.'

Beatrice stood and went over to the long windows that looked out on the colourful flower borders. 'At least I shielded Bertie's gaze so he wasn't staring at the... the dead woman.'

Her words made Eleanor's hands fly to her temples. Something in them had transported her back to the awful scene. She scrunched up her eyes, but nothing came. Sensing Clifford had appeared at her side, she whispered, 'It's alright, thank you. But please remember that exact phrase for later.'

As Beatrice turned back to Eleanor, Clifford paused in pouring fresh cups of tea for them both.

'Ahem.' He nodded at the long bird-print curtains.

'Well, look who it is!' Eleanor said brightly, fearing this might be the end of her chance to find out what else Beatrice knew. 'I think a certain little man has come to join us. Hello, Bertie,' she called out.

After a beat, the curtains twitched and a tuft of Bertie's blond curls appeared. Slowly, he emerged and slid over to stand in front of Clifford. Taking great care to line the toes of his buckled sandals against those of Clifford's impossibly shiny shoes, he craned his neck to look up at Clifford's tall frame. The two of them held each other's gaze impassively, Bertie imitating the perfect butler stance.

As Beatrice moved to call him away, Eleanor flapped a quieting hand. She dropped her voice to a whisper. 'I've always wondered if anyone could beat Clifford's maddening ability to maintain that inscrutable look of his. Bertie might just be that man.'

He was, it transpired. The clink of cups was the only sound until the mantle clock struck three. Clifford's lips twitched. 'Touché, Master Wilton.'

Beatrice gasped as Bertie briefly smiled back. The young boy crouched down and traced the intricate weave of each of Clifford's shoelaces.

'Ah,' Clifford said. 'Most discerning of you. Patons shoelaces are indeed the strongest and finest laces a young gentleman could ever require. Guaranteed never to break, no matter what the situation.'

Eleanor's heart swelled with affection as her butler looped up his jacket tails and sunk to his haunches to be in Bertie's eyeline. Reaching into a pocket, he held up a spare set, a slim band of dove-grey paper keeping them in meticulous order. Then with a magician's flourish, he dropped them into his other hand and closed it. Bertie's gaze never left the laces. Clifford then opened both palms to reveal... nothing!

Eleanor and Beatrice gawped. Bertie, however, simply shook his head and moved around to pull out the laces from Clifford's side pocket.

Clifford clapped. 'Bravo, Master Wilton. I believe you have earned them.'

With a nod, Bertie closed his hand tightly around his shoelace prize.

'What do you say, Bertie?' Beatrice called over. 'Not that we ever hear it,' she added despondently to Eleanor.

Bertie stepped over, this time to stare up at Eleanor. 'Bravo, madam!' Bertie called.

Eleanor looked down at the feel of something being slid into her palm. 'Oh, Bertie! Thank you so much. One of your wonderful rubbings in exchange. Thank you.' She made a show of putting it carefully into her pocket.

He skipped off, leaving his mother with her eyes welling up.

'Oh goodness! He so rarely says anything and never, ever, when there are strangers present.'

Eleanor threw Clifford a grateful look. 'Let's finish up our conversation so we can leave you to relax. Plus, I hate to mention it, but time isn't exactly on our side. Not if Constance is going to have her wedding day as planned.'

'For her, I would do anything,' Beatrice said grimly.

Including murder? Eleanor mentally shook her head. Beatrice wasn't supposed to be a suspect! She glanced at Clifford, whose look told her he was having the same thought. He arched one brow. *He's right. Why not?*

She realised Beatrice was waiting.

'Sorry. Just run over the whole episode in your mind once more, if you would? Is there anything you've missed out? Something that maybe felt too unimportant to mention? Or that you'd forgotten?'

Beatrice rubbed her cheeks. 'Right, was there anything else? I said about going to the station. Running when I heard the scream. Then seeing you in that dreadful room. Hiding Bertie's eyes from the... the body. The police telling us we needed to go into the lounge.' She rolled her eyes. 'Bertie, as ever, not cooperating and running to the other side of the room before I could catch him and drag him out. Then waiting until that inspector arrived from Oxford.'

'And telephoning Frederick? Did you speak to him?'

'Yes. I was actually just replacing the receiver when I...' Her brows knitted. 'That was strange, now that I think of it.'

'What?'

'It might be nothing. You see, I'd all but forgotten that when I went to telephone, the first booth was in use, so I went into the second. You know how they have that sort of frosty glass between for privacy, but it has the hotel name cut out of it, which is ridiculous because you can glimpse the other booth through the lettering?'

'Yes. Go on.'

'Well, it's just struck me that when the scream rang out, I instinctively ran in the direction it came from. As did everyone who heard it. We ended up in... that room, as you know. But the man in the other telephone booth, why, he didn't move at all!' She frowned. 'Goodness, and now I think of it, he wasn't amongst us all in the lounge after the two policemen rounded us up.'

Eleanor's pulse quickened. 'You're sure he wasn't?'

'Absolutely. We sat there for what felt like hours, staring round at each other. We were all wondering what on earth was going on while waiting for that inspector to drive down from wherever it was.'

Eleanor nodded at Clifford as he opened her notebook, pen poised. 'Beatrice, think, please. What did the man in the telephone booth look like? In as much detail as you can remember.'

'Goodness, it was only a glimpse. It was mostly the back of his head. I do remember he was wearing a hat pulled down low over his face. But then he turned and I caught sight of' – she shivered – 'his piercing black eyes.'

18

As the front door closed behind them, the silence of Henley Hall's marbled entrance hall was pierced by a cacophony of laughter rolling out along the corridor from the kitchen. Eleanor shrugged off her coat into Clifford's waiting hands and spun around to stare at him pleadingly.

'Whatever the ladies are up to—'

'Warrants no censure. Quite right,' he said with uncharacteristic lenience. 'A well-earned sherry to take up with you, my lady?'

'Not without being let in on the secret, of which you are clearly a part?'

'Perhaps later? Since you do not have much time.'

'Hang on! Up where? And why don't I have much time?'

'I believe you are expecting a visitor for whom you will no doubt wish to change before meeting in' – he pointed to the tall grandfather clock in the wood-panelled alcove – 'a mere forty-seven minutes.'

She shrugged. 'No point. I've been shamefully decked out in this very set of less-than-fashionable togs on many an occasion when we've met up.'

At his arched brow, she threw her arms out. 'Alright. I'll hurl myself into some semblance of a dress, but that will only take five minutes.'

'Ah, Lady Swift's five minutes. Peculiarly identical to most people's thirty.'

She tutted. 'Oh, stop it. I've acres of time. And I'm dying to know whatever the lark is, so lead on, please.'

'If you insist on visiting the kitchen now, my lady,' Clifford boomed through cupped hands as he strode ahead.

But the sight that met her couldn't have been further from what she'd expected. Her staff were nowhere to be seen. Also, the main table was covered in a bright-white sheet. And in the centre of the room, something was staring back at her, wild-eyed, a long streak of pink flapping excitedly.

'Gladstone!' She choked on her laughter. She sank to her knees and held out her arms to receive her bulldog's exuberant welcome. 'What on earth are you wearing?'

Clearly enjoying being the centre of attention, Gladstone spun in an erratic circle, showing off the all-encompassing knitted navy-blue creation he sported. This made his tiny domed headwear swing down sideways on the silky ribbon tied under his chin.

'Clifford! It's a—'

'Policeman's outfit! Helmet, jacket and trousers.' Mrs Trotman stepped out of the pantry, followed by Eleanor's other three staff. 'Butters made it, m'lady, to cheer you up about the nasty business you've got caught up in again with Mr Clifford. Only we've been doubled over with laughing.' She pushed the housekeeper forward.

'Beg pardon though, m'lady, didn't mean to overstep. We were just concerned as you've already got so much on your plate, what with the Women's Institute rally. Thought a bit of fun might be a bit o' fresh air for you. I hope 'tisn't too much?'

Eleanor shook her head and wiped the tears from her eyes,

still holding her sides. 'Ouch! It's far from too much. It's hilarious. He's even got a row of shiny brass buttons along his tummy!'

Lizzie linked arms with Polly. 'You'll ne'er peel that off him, m'lady. He's totally daft for a wee bit o' dressing up.'

They all watched as the bulldog continued his excited, lumbering circles. Even Clifford failed to hide his amusement.

'But we've been busy with more besides.' Mrs Trotman grabbed one corner of the sheet, the other three following suit. 'One, two, three... ta-dah!'

'Oh my!' Aside from the neat piles of beautifully sewn rosettes, folded banners and posters, their notepads lay in a row, displaying a long line of ticks on each of the lists. She turned to her butler. 'Clifford, surely this level of dedication deserves—'

'Ahem.' He stepped to her side, bearing a small silver tray of four sherries and two elderflower cordials for the young maids.

'Perfect. Thank you all so much. A toast then.' She paused as everyone took their respective glass. 'To more women in the police... Gladstone!'

The bulldog let out a loud woof and shot out of the back door faster than she'd ever seen him move. They all stared at each other.

'Silly thing.' She shrugged. 'Where were we? Oh yes, to more women—'

'No! Thief! Stop!' The cry came from outside.

Eleanor hurried out the back door and careered into something athletically solid.

'I lugh!' She rubbed her jaw gingerly. 'Gracious, sorry about the sherry down your jacket. Lovely to see you, albeit a surprise at the tradesman's entrance?'

Seldon ran a hand through his tousled chestnut curls, clearly embarrassed. 'Eleanor, it's unforgivably rude, I know. Not only am I early, but I just saw the disappearing form of what seemed to be...' He frowned and shook his head. 'Whatever it was, it stole my bag. I thought I might rescue it and then appear, more appropriately, at the front door.' His hand reached towards her cheek, then pulled back as Clifford ushered the gaggle of whispering ladies inside with a flick of one gloved finger.

Seldon scanned the side of her face anxiously. 'That was quite the collision, sorry.'

'No harm done, unlike your jacket. Slip it off and come in and join us all in a sherry while Mrs Butters works her magic before it stains. Clifford will retrieve your bag.'

He hesitated. 'It's important. It's—'

She tutted. 'Don't fret. I promise you he'll have it retrieved before you've finished your first sherry with the ladies.'

He laughed. 'Alright. But drinking with your staff again!' His deep chuckle tickled her ears as he followed her inside. 'What's the occasion?'

She jerked to a stop in horror, making his now waistcoated form bang into her.

This isn't the time or the best way to tell him about the rally to get women back into the police force, Ellie!

Clifford reappeared and gestured them into the kitchen. 'Perhaps, if I might suggest, a more appropriate part of the house for your guest, my lady?'

He gave her a knowing look as he took Seldon's jacket. She looked around in amazement. How her staff had cleared all evidence of the rally so quickly, she had no idea. And how they had filled the kitchen with all manner of supper-type preparations in which they were now deeply engrossed was nothing short of a miracle.

Clifford coughed. 'Joseph is on the task, Chief Inspector. He will retrieve your stolen item. In the meantime, perhaps you'd like to retire to the snug?'

Seldon nodded, and they trooped in to the snug. He settled down opposite her and opened his familiar police notebook. He sighed heavily. 'Yet one more session feeling awkward with you, arguing about unseemly matters.'

Clifford melted out the door.

'I've no plans to argue, Hugh. And more talk of feelings, Chief Inspector?' she teased gently. 'What's happened to the policeman who said he had no time for them on an investigation, I wonder?'

'Genuinely, I don't know. Perhaps it's your bewitching influence?'

They both coloured, him with embarrassment, her with delight.

'Hugh.' She gestured down her clothes. 'Really, I'm just the haphazard girl who jumped off her bicycle one day and woke up owning her beloved late uncle's enormous house. And now everyone expects me to suddenly be capable of being a proper grown up.'

He laughed, his deep-brown eyes holding hers momentarily. 'Is it wrong that I find myself hoping you don't quite manage it?'

She beamed as Clifford returned and handed Seldon his stolen property.

'Come on, Hugh, let's get the ugly business out of the way then so we don't sour too much of Mrs Trotman's special supper. She's prepared bacon-wrapped shrimps served in her divine thyme and basil baskets and the most sublime pork and creamy leek raised pie with honey parsnips to follow.'

'Supper? I didn't expect—' He broke off, eyes bright. 'But if you and Mrs Trotman insist. But first things first. You asked me to do a little digging on Horace Flint. Well, I did what I could on the quiet and came up with very little. Before he became manager of the Eagle, he was the assistant manager. And before that he worked in various public houses in Chipstone after moving from Hartbridge, where he was manager of the Bell Inn.' He shrugged. 'That's about it really. No record of anything illegal.' He handed her the battered brown-paper-wrapped item Clifford had retrieved. Curious, she opened it.

'It's Daisy's handbag!'

'As you also asked for.' He tapped it thoughtfully. 'There's not much in it though.'

'You sound surprised,' she said as she opened the bag.

'Do I? Maybe that's because, like most men, I have no idea why women need all the things they usually keep in handbags.' He patted his jacket sides. 'All men need are pockets. Nice and easy they are to use, too.'

She laughed. 'Really? Well, let's see how easy it would be to cart everything in Daisy's handbag about in your pockets, shall we?' Turning over the bag, she gently tipped out the contents and spread them over the table. 'Well, I remember this brown purse with the twist clasp, and that small folding mirror. Oh, and her comb.' She ran a finger over the next few items. 'But these must have stayed in the handbag.' She pointed to a couple of hair slides, a stub of a pencil and a handkerchief. She looked in the bag again, running her hand around the lining. 'Hmm, not much, as you said. But most importantly not—'

'Not?'

'The shiny disc I saw lying on the floor. It was apart from Daisy's other belongings. It definitely wasn't in the room where she died when Clifford and I searched it.'

Seldon nodded slowly. 'So, someone thought it important enough to risk taking it from a murder scene. But why?'

19

'Really, Mrs Butters, there's no need to keep apologising.' Eleanor regarded her unusually large breakfast the following morning. 'Hugh saw the funny side of Gladstone masquerading as a policeman by the time he left last night.'

At his name, her bulldog pawed her leg under the table, clearly hoping he might entice her to send a sausage his way.

'But I'm sorrier than I know how to say, m'lady.' Mrs Butters wrung the tea towel she held. 'Truly, 'twas all my fault.'

'Nonsense. Clifford told Hugh that he'd given his permission over the outfit being made.'

'Ahem.'

She looked up at her butler's impeccably suited form in the doorway.

'Mrs Butters, her ladyship has been more than sufficiently regaled in breakfast and every other regard, thank you.'

As the housekeeper scurried away, Eleanor gave him an admonishing look. 'Tell me, my infallible butler, how was it that you, the undisputed master of timing, allowed the ladies to unveil Gladstone's outfit just minutes before Hugh was due to arrive?'

This drew a woof from under the table.

Clifford aligned the seams of his gloves. 'I tried to delay you in venturing into the kitchen, my lady, if you remember?'

'No. You told me I had no time, knowing that would make me determined to prove you wrong.' She pointed a finger at him. 'You meticulously wove the entire affair on purpose!'

'Impossible, my lady, since the policeman's outfit was, in fact, knitted, not woven.'

She laughed. 'Well, don't tell my disgraceful butler, but just as his scallywaggery intended, I ended up having a perfectly delicious time with Hugh. It was a treat to talk so easily, since it wasn't entirely of murder for once.'

He held up two empty salvers pointedly. 'As delicious as the week's worth of breakfast subsequently devoured, perchance?' He nodded at the mantelpiece clock. 'I believe we have an appointment with Sir Grainger shortly?'

Eleanor rose. 'After what Hugh told us before he left, definitely!'

Not long later, in the Rolls, Eleanor ruffled Gladstone's ears where they lay in her lap as the last of Chipstone faded behind them. Clifford swung the car onto the main road and cleared his throat.

'Perhaps now is a good time to relay the details of the telephone call I received while you were breakfasting?'

'Yes, please, who was it?'

'Mr Pockford, butler to the Davencourt household.'

She winced. 'Bit of a risk, calling from their house telephone?'

Clifford tutted. 'No butler worthy of his uniform would ever presume to use the house apparatus for personal use.'

'Well, I wish mine would, if he needs to. So, Pockford telephoned you from where then?'

'The local inn. It transpires, after my visit, he asked the rest of the staff for any update on domestic events. He was informed by the first footman that about a week before Miss Balforth's murder, a man called whilst Mr Pockford himself had been dispatched by Lady Davencourt to complete errands in Oxford.'

'Ah! A suspiciously timely dispatch, perhaps?'

'Indeed. I arrived at precisely the same conclusion on hearing the footman's narrative relayed. Evidently, this man presented his card and said Lady Davencourt was expecting him.'

'Nothing unusual in that, is there?'

'Nothing. Except that the card bore the man's name only. A Mr Cramdon. No business insignia, no professional title, no address. All the more curious as well that Lady Davencourt not only received him but that none of the staff saw him leave, which was definitely before Mr Pockford himself returned.'

'Very odd.'

'Odder still, that a man of the same name should telephone the very next day.'

'Really! So now we need to ask Hugh to quietly use his official sources to find out more about this Mr Cramdon.'

'Already done, my lady. I took the liberty since the chief inspector mentioned last evening he would be in his office only briefly this morning. Had I come to you first, it would have been too late. He said he would investigate and get back to you.'

'Top-notch, Clifford.' She tried to keep her tone airy. 'How did he... umm sound, by the way?'

'Perhaps the best description would be... extremely disappointed' – his lips twitched – 'that I had called on your behalf.'

After several miles of hawthorn- and hazel-hedgerow lanes, and Eleanor dreaming of more evenings with Hugh, Clifford eased the stately vehicle onto a wide metalled drive flanked by immaculate grass. A smart painted sign declared they had arrived at Egglesbury Golf Course. Pulling up in front of the imposing clubhouse, he stepped around to open her door.

'Ready, my lady?'

'Always,' she fibbed.

Inside, the whippet-thin attendant in a bottle-green suit ran a bony finger down the reception desk book. 'You're too late, I'm afraid, madam, though you've not long missed him. As his opponent for this morning cancelled at the last moment, he chose to play on alone. And this being a quiet time of day, I'd say' – he looked up at the clock – 'the gentleman might have reached as far as Old Harry's Lure.'

Her butler's expression let her know that wasn't gibberish to him.

'Thank you,' she said. 'Come on, Gladstone.' She turned to go, lightly pulling on the bulldog's lead.

Clifford, however, held the attendant's gaze. 'Might one enquire if Sir Grainger is accompanied by his usual caddy this morning?'

'No. Being a particularly competitive player, Sir Grainger always prefers to be self-sufficient.' He shook his head. 'Honestly, if I had even a ha'penny for the number of times he's told me a caddy would be an unnecessary distraction!'

'Ah!' Clifford slid out his wallet. 'On that note, payment herewith for the box of golf balls it appears a certain wilful bulldog has quietly chosen as a memento of his visit this morning.'

Outside, Eleanor turned to Clifford. 'I didn't know you'd played at this club?'

'I don't, my lady.'

'Then how do you know which number hole that bizarre name referred to?'

'The elaborately embroidered emblem on the attendant's breast pocket is a pictorial layout of the course, mirrored in the bespoke reception rug.' He traced out a shape on his palm. 'The fourth fairway here, is bordered by a long sand trap, to wit, into which one's ball is lured by "Old Harry", being a common moniker for the devil. Simple.'

'Well, that's precisely how I feel, dash it! I'd never have worked that out.'

With Gladstone puffing through his jaw-clenched prize of boxed golf balls, they hurried on towards a distant sweeping copse of trees.

A moment later, Clifford pointed left down an immaculate grassed slope. 'The start of the fourth hole.'

She shielded the unusually bright September sun from her eyes. 'Well, I can't see Sir Grainger down there. Nor anyone within shouting distance. It really *is* a quiet time to play. Maybe he's got further than the attendant thought? Let's head to the fifth...' She broke off and stared forward intently. 'What's that bit of coloured cloth flapping down there in the sand?'

He quickly handed her a set of miniature field glasses.

'Oh gracious, Clifford! Someone's fallen.' But as she said the words, an icy feeling washed over her.

She was already half running, half sliding down the slope before Clifford could reply, Gladstone panting along not far behind her. At the edge of the sand trap, she jerked to a halt as Clifford caught her up. Her hand flew to her mouth. The motionless form of Sir Grainger lay face down, a deep gash to the back of his head, which was thick with crimson blood. Nearby lay a bloodied golf club.

Clifford dropped to his knees beside the prostrate figure.

She bit her lip. 'Don't say he's dea—'

'No. Alive. Unconscious. But breathing. Shallow, however. We need help.'

A sudden movement in the bushes made Eleanor stiffen. Beneath a heavy-brimmed hat obscuring most of the man's face, a pair of piercing black eyes stared out at her. They held her gaze for a moment before the man turned and darted deeper into the undergrowth. Eleanor spun back around.

'Quick! Man stealing away over there!'

Clifford hesitated.

She stared at him and then groaned in anger. 'You're right. We're needed here more. Leave him. Go for help. I'll attend to Sir Grainger.'

As Clifford sped off, she marshalled her nursing training from the war and looked over the wound. It was deep enough to need pressure to stem the bleeding. Equally, she knew it might obscure a skull fracture, which would not take direct pressure without the potential risk of worsening the injury.

She tapped her forehead. 'Check for changes in breathing. Monitor pulse. Assess alertness.' Placing one hand carefully under Sir Grainger's mouth, she frowned at the shallowness of his breath. But it was regular. Switching to taking his wrist, she felt for his pulse, which took too many worrying seconds to find. But then there it was. Stable, if dauntingly weak.

'Sir Grainger, can you hear me?' She bent close to his ear. 'It's Eleanor, Constance's friend. Let me know you can hear me.' Only silence came back in reply. She swallowed hard.

Stay focused, Ellie.

She laid a clean handkerchief gently over the wound on his head. 'I'll just chatter on, Sir Grainger. You're going to be fine, I'm sure. But do forgive me holding your hand.'

The sound of deep wheezing heralded the arrival of help of sort. A balding man in matching sweater, plus fours and socks puffed over to her.

'Your man told me to tell you...' His eyes widened. She followed his gaze to the now blood-soaked handkerchief. 'I say... I... I think I might just...'

'Pass out,' Eleanor finished for him as he toppled backwards like a rag doll. 'Marvellous!'

She jumped as Clifford appeared at her elbow.

'A vehicle to take Sir Grainger to hospital will be here in moments, my lady.' He quirked an eyebrow and nodded at the fallen figure a few yards away.

'He fainted.' She turned back to her patient, his breathing now even shallower. 'Stay with me, Sir Grainger. Stay with me...'

20

———

'You should have gone straight home, Eleanor,' Seldon gruffed. The concern in his eyes deepened as she tried to hide another shiver. He glanced over his shoulder at the man in the brown suit scouring the sand trap where Sir Grainger's body had lain. Behind him, five uniformed officers walked slowly in a fan-shape across the golf course's fourth hole, sweeping their heads left and right. Clifford was deep in conversation with a sixth, pointing to where the attacker had disappeared into the woods.

'What good would that have done, Hugh?' she said firmly. 'I wouldn't have found any clues at home as to who dealt Sir Grainger such a malicious blow to the head, would I?'

'True, but just for once, you might have put yourself first.'

She hid the smile his tender tone had brought on by rubbing her hands over her cheeks.

He sighed. 'Well, at least you did find Sir Grainger's pocket watch and snuffbox next to the poor man. Maybe you'd like to return them to... what is it?'

'I'm sorry, Hugh, was I frowning? It's just that no one looks at their watch and takes snuff at the same time, do they?'

'Mmm, I see what you mean.' He glanced over at the sand trap again. 'In fact, who takes snuff when they're playing golf?'

'Especially alone!'

He tapped his chin. 'So, whoever attacked Sir Grainger was probably going through his pockets when he was disturbed. But why? What would he have been looking for?'

She shrugged. 'You'll have to ask Sir Grainger that same question if... *when* he regains consciousness.' She nodded towards the sand trap. 'Your man wants you, but he's trying not to notice.'

Seldon's brows flinched. 'Notice what?'

'That you've been "questioning" me for ages' – she gestured to the open notebook in his hand – 'but haven't written down a single word.'

'Blast it! That's Morrison. Thankfully, he's a decent man.'

'I know. You brought him in before on another awful case, not long ago. But you don't need life made more difficult by your men ragging you about me.' She felt her cheeks colour. 'Not that there's any real ammunition for them to, of course.'

His lips parted but then met again with no words escaping. Running a hand around the back of his neck, he took a deep breath, then turned on his heel towards the sand trap.

'Morrison,' he called, 'can you handle it from here? It's been quite the ordeal. I should probably take the, umm, witness home.'

'No bother there, sir. We'll be about an hour, I'd say. I'll join the beat-boots and make sure they finish their sweep thoroughly.'

Clifford materialised at Eleanor's side. 'Uniformed officers,' he said in reply to her puzzled look.

Seldon hurriedly flipped his notebook closed as his second-in-command appeared next to him.

'The lady did a remarkable job until the doctor arrived, sir,'

Morrison said. 'By all accounts, if it hadn't been for her, we'd definitely be looking at murder.'

Seldon grimaced. 'We may still be yet. Sir Grainger's in a very bad way.'

'Well, I'll make sure we leave no stone unturned while' – he looked away, his face deadpan – 'you escort the lady home.'

'Excellent work, Morrison,' Seldon said stiffly. 'About an hour, you said?'

As Morrison joined the uniformed officers on the fourth hole, Clifford stepped forward. 'Chief Inspector, if I might be so bold, you are very busy and Henley Hall is not close. If I may, I know a place much nearer where her ladyship can recuperate.'

Seldon nodded. 'Certainly. Lead the way.'

Under the cover of a ring of ancient vibrant spindle trees, Seldon hovered as Eleanor settled herself at the small rustic picnic table. Clifford had whisked them to a nearby picturesque village she'd never heard of, led them to the green, and then disappeared across the road without a word. The table and bench seat she sat on were speckled with the russet-pink leaves that fluttered down around them with every sigh of the autumn breeze.

Seldon finished wrestling his long legs underneath the other end of the bench seat. 'How was Miss Grainger when you telephoned her before we left the golf club?' He grimaced. 'Sorry, stupid question, really. How would anyone be on hearing their father had been brutally attacked and is hanging on to life by a thread.'

She nodded glumly and cradled Gladstone's head where he had scrambled up between them to lie against her shoulder. 'Constance took the news badly, naturally.' A flash of anger suffused her face. 'If only I'd got there earlier, I might have stopped whoever did it! Dash it, it's my fault for always arriving everywhere later than I intend.'

Seldon looked at her in concern. 'Eleanor, Sir Grainger wouldn't be here at all if it weren't for you. And, selfishly, I can't tell you how glad I am that you were too late to even meet the attacker, let alone wade in as you inevitably would have done.'

'That's sweet of you to try to make me feel better, Hugh, but what if he doesn't pull through? It will finish Constance's mother off for sure. And likely tip the rest of the family over the edge too.'

'Then how about we don't think about it? Not now, anyway. You had a terrible shock finding Sir Grainger like that. And then you ran yourself ragged on the golf course looking for clues, and bravely called Constance, so at least she heard the dreadful news from someone she knows.'

Her head fell to her chest. 'Not that I found anything like the right words to break it to her.'

He reached around Gladstone and lifted her chin between his thumb and forefinger. 'Eleanor, the fact that you were the one to call must have helped enormously. Rather than her hearing it from a' – he pointed at himself – 'hopelessly insensi-tive chief inspector who's probably grown horribly more blunt about delivering such news than he realises. Wishing you could turn back the clock won't bring you any peace of mind.' He coloured and hurriedly pulled his hand away.

She managed a wan smile, her stomach skipping from his all too brief touch. 'You sound like Clifford. Managing to wrap up a telling off in a raft of wise and concerned words.'

'No.' A lock of hair swung across his brow as he shook his head. 'I could never begin to match that man's ability in that field.' He ran an awkward finger along the edge of the table. 'One last try, Eleanor. What would it take for you to do as I ask just this once and go home to rest?'

'Daisy Balforth not to have been murdered and Sir

Grainger to still be blithely teeing off in over-patterned tweed trousers.'

He held his hands up in surrender. 'Alright. Back to business then.'

He opened his notebook as Clifford arrived bearing a loaded wooden tray. Gladstone eyed the offerings eagerly and let out an expectant woof. She and Seldon leaned forward in surprise. Among the mismatched tea things was a large plate of glossy jam tarts and a selection of generous cake slices arranged on an old-fashioned china stand.

Seldon spun around in his seat, scanning the tiny row of thatched flint cottages set back from the green. 'There's no teahouse, or even a village store here that I can see?'

'Indeed, there is not, Chief Inspector,' Clifford said enigmatically, holding out the tartan blanket he had looped over his arm.

'But then how?' Seldon waved his hand. 'On second thoughts, don't bother. More of your usual wizardry, I expect.'

A few minutes later, Eleanor realised she was way more wrung out than she'd wanted to acknowledge. The soft picnic rug Seldon gently tucked around her shoulders felt almost as comforting as she imagined his arms would have been. And the dash of warming brandy Clifford added to both of their cups of tea finally halted her shivers.

'Thank you, both. I'm absolutely fine now.'

The two men frowned.

'Yes alright,' she conceded. 'Perhaps that whole episode at the golf club was a tad more upsetting than my stubbornness would admit. But, look, here I am doing the proper ladylike thing of being swathed in luxurious warmth, surrounded by a royal amount of fussing. So, no more pulling faces, you two.'

'Umm, Clifford?' Seldon said. 'You wouldn't grab a lump of oak or whatever we're perched on, and join us, would you? We, well, we need you.'

Clifford's hand strayed to his perfectly aligned black tie, the sure sign that he was uncomfortable with the request. But the light in his eyes showed he was delighted Seldon had asked. He arched a brow in her direction. 'Hardly the place of a mere butler.'

Seldon shook his head. 'You're hardly a mere butler, old chap.'

Over her third cup of tea Eleanor shook her head. 'I know. But he might be able to, mightn't he?'

Seldon frowned. 'Hopefully, yes. But in truth it's unlikely Sir Grainger could identify his attacker even if... I mean, *when* he comes to. Whoever whacked Sir Grainger around the head would have jumped him from behind, I would have thought, given his injury.'

'He had black eyes, though! Like the man Beatrice described as seeing in the telephone booth at the Eagle Hotel.'

Seldon's hand poised over his notes. 'Are you sure?'

'Definitely, I saw those clearly enough. The rest of his face was obscured by the wide brim of his hat and his turned-up collar though, dash it!'

'Nevertheless, excellent observation.' He glanced across to Clifford. 'So maybe Mrs Wilton's mysterious man does exist?'

'Let us hope so, Chief Inspector.' Clifford's brow flinched. 'However, if that is the case, I concur with Mrs Wilton that he was not among those Sergeant Brice and Constable Lowe escorted to the lounge.'

Seldon nodded. 'And he didn't get sent in to see me either.' He pushed the plate bearing the remaining slices of cake closer to Eleanor.

Clifford picked up the two forks he had been using as improvised tongs and selected a slice for her. 'Chief Inspector, might one enquire as to whether you believe the attack on Sir Grainger is related to the murder of Miss Balforth?'

'You can. But I haven't a concrete answer. Certainly not one based on tangible evidence. Honestly, though, I feel it could be.' He glanced at Eleanor and held up a finger. 'Yes, Lady Swift, I said "feel", but you needn't comment on it.'

She hid a smile. 'No problem. I'll save it to tease you with later. Given the gloomy pall we're all huddled under it doesn't feel appropriate at the moment. Despite this wonderful tea and unseasonably sunny day.'

Seldon sighed. 'Well, the only slightly good news is that if the two are related, then Sir Grainger will certainly drop further down the suspect list or off it altogether.' He ran a hand around the back of his neck. 'It's best if I'm seen to undertake the investigation into Sir Grainger's attack as a completely separate matter from Miss Balforth's murder, which it may well be. My boss won't argue about that. It does mean, however, that you will be the ones focusing on Miss Balforth's murder as before. Only if these two events *are* related...' He avoided Eleanor's gaze.

Clifford nodded. 'Noted. I will prevail upon her ladyship to take the utmost caution.'

Seldon grunted. 'If you can.' He cleared his throat. 'Now, I haven't had time to tell you until now, but I have the information you asked for on the man who called on Lady Davencourt.'

Eleanor's eyes brightened. 'The one who only left his name on his card? Well done you for digging that up.'

'No digging at all, actually. George Cramdon is well known throughout police stations in the area. He's a retired police officer, actually. Turned...?'

'Private detective,' Clifford said as Eleanor shrugged.

'Got it in one! Cramdon was forced to leave under a cloud. Nothing was ever proven, but there were those who swore he spent more time working for the other side than for us. Here's the address he operates from, but watch your step, he's a nasty piece of work. One thing is certain, though. He will have appealed to Lady Davencourt because he'll be discreet no matter how unsavoury the job is he's been given to do.' He waved at Clifford. 'If you could translate.'

Clifford bowed and turned to her. '"Discreet", my lady, is taking care that you—'

She laughed. 'I know what discreet is, thank you!'

Seldon's handsome face broke into a smile. 'Well, then please be discreet when we communicate next.'

'Of course. I—'

He held up a hand. 'And please promise me we'll speak every day.'

She beamed, taking the elbow he offered. 'Oh, if I absolutely must!'

21

The bleached-red door opened a crack.

'Mr Cramdon, I presume?' Eleanor said.

Dark eyes stared at her suspiciously from a heavily lined face above a worn brown jacket. 'Supposing you're right? What then?'

Without waiting for an invitation, she stepped inside the drab room that matched the drab second-floor corridor of the equally drab building.

'I can see we are going to get on famously, Mr Cramdon. Your reputation precedes you.'

Cramdon scowled and waved her towards a worn desk and leather chair. Two small mismatched tables sat either end of a wide blue rug, these being the only other furniture in the room. Clifford followed her in and stood to one side.

'And what reputation would that be?' Cramdon walked to the desk, trying hard to hide an obvious limp.

'Oh gracious, one marvellous enough that the widows of earls will engage your services.'

'I see, so that *is* the game.'

His inflexion gave away what she'd suspected from his first

words. He knew who she was. Which meant he also knew precisely why she'd come.

She shook her head as he offered his chair. 'I've been sitting beside a hospital bed all morning. Rather stiff now.'

'As you wish.' He heaved a hip onto the edge of his desk and looked them both over. 'I don't normally see clients here. For obvious reasons.'

'Well, forgive my disagreeing, but I think it's perfect.' She gestured around the room. 'Very professional, uncluttered and... extremely discreet.' His brow creased. 'Which is obviously why you're intrigued as to how I found you – since you don't advertise your address anywhere.' She paused until he nodded. 'I clearly have connections in the police force you left.'

He looked up sharply. 'Whatever you've been told, I was set up. Nothing was ever proved.'

She shrugged. 'Maybe not. But, still, you have my sincere admiration since it's quite the test starting again in a new life.'

'Oh. And you'd know about that because?'

'Because I used to spend my days haring across remote spots around the world, more latterly in the South African bush, dodging wild animals and fatally spiteful plants. But now' – she lowered her voice – 'I'm supposed to be cutting it as a titled lady.'

Despite himself, Cramdon folded forward with a wheezy laugh. 'And how's that working out for you then, Lady Swift?' He gestured at Clifford's pursed lips and laughed again. 'Not too good, I see.'

She waved a hand airily. 'Not too good indeed, Mr Cramdon. Whereas you appear to have done well with your new enterprise. Except, it means you are no longer empowered by the law. So, in the matter that you undertook recently for a certain party, you may well already be an accessory to murder.'

He ran his tongue down the inside of his cheek. 'Cor

lummy, you don't muck about, do you? Straight in for the kill, eh?'

'Not me, Mr Cramdon. You see, I take a very dim view of murder.'

Anger flashed across Cramdon's face. 'As do I! So, watch what you're saying.'

Clifford stepped in front of him.

'Alright,' Cramdon snarled. 'Call your terrier off. We're not fighting on different sides.'

She recalled Seldon's words. *There were those who swore he spent more time working for the other side than for us.* 'That's good to hear.' She waved Clifford down. 'Now, we know you visited Lady Davencourt.'

His face remained deadpan. 'And supposing you're right?'

'There is no suppose. But there is the question of what you were then asked to do by Lady Davencourt that ended in someone taking a young woman's life so early and maliciously.'

His already black eyes seemed to darken. Then, almost immediately, they lightened again. He ran a gnarled finger over the desk's tooled-leather top. 'Seeing as I don't know no Lady Davencourt, what's that to do with me?'

'You disappoint me, Mr Cramdon. You told me all the rumours I'd heard about you were lies. An innocent man doesn't lie. And you *are* lying. I know you were hired by Lady Davencourt to follow Daisy Balforth.' *Okay, that's guesswork, Ellie.* 'And I can prove it.' *Now you're lying, but it's in a good cause.* 'I'd think very carefully about your loyalties. Are they to your client? Or to yourself? Because one of you is going to end up in the dock as an accessory to murder or worse, I guarantee it!'

For a moment he held her gaze. Then he slid off the desk and walked unevenly to stand behind his chair. 'Tell me what you want,' he sneered, 'and then perhaps you'll be good enough to leave me in peace.'

'Deal, Mr Cramdon. So, why were you following Daisy Balforth?'

'My client engaged me to do so. And since you have already alluded to who that was, I shan't need to betray my professional confidence in naming them.'

'As you wish. But you'll only have to say it in court, as you well know. So, there's no point in playing coy now.'

He scowled at Clifford. 'Does she ever give a man a fighting chance?'

'A great many, Mr Cramdon. Only you missed yours.'

Cramdon shook his head resignedly. 'Alright. But it doesn't leave this room unless it needs to, alright? I ain't about to take the fall for something I didn't do. Again.' He took a deep breath. 'Lady Davencourt hired me to find Daisy Balforth on account of the breach of promise lawsuit. She told me she believed it was merely an attempt to extort money from her son. I found her easily enough. And in good time for Lady Davencourt to meet with the young woman.'

Eleanor shared a look with Clifford.

'I can't imagine that was a comfortable meeting? Bit like a cat tearing into a mouse, I expect.'

Cramdon shrugged. 'I wouldn't know.' He looked at her belligerently. 'That all?'

Eleanor tutted. 'Only it isn't, is it, Mr Cramdon?' She felt her way. 'You found out... that Daisy Balforth had asked Lord Peregrine Davencourt to meet her at the Eagle, didn't you? And there's only one way you could have done that, since I know he received that communication in a letter. You must have intercepted his post.'

He shrugged. 'So? No crime in that. Least not one committed by me, per se.'

'Clifford, is that Latin for "one can still go to prison for coercion and corrupting another to commit a crime on one's behalf?"'

'Most assuredly, my lady.'

Eleanor tutted. 'Pretty is she?'

'Who?'

'The postmistress. I assume you bribed her to let you know if Daisy Balforth sent any letters or telegrams to Lord Davencourt. Just curious, did you use charm or cash?'

'You are impossible,' he grunted.

'So I'm told.'

He drummed his fingers on the desktop, then looked back up at her, his eyes glowering. 'Alright, I paid the postmistress at Lady Davencourt's behest, so what? She let me know there was a letter from Miss Balforth to Lord Peregrine.'

'Which you opened!' Eleanor failed to hide her disgust.

'No. The postmistress did. Then she read it out to me over the telephone.'

'So, what else was in the letter?'

'Nothing. It was just a request that Lord Davencourt meet her at the Eagle and that it would be to his advantage.'

'On the day, and at the time, she was murdered?'

His eyes darkened again. 'Yes.' He waved towards the door. 'Now, we're done, Lady Swift.'

In the Rolls, Eleanor leaned back in her seat as Clifford pulled away. 'Do you know, even if Lady Davencourt turns out not to be the murderer, I don't envy poor Constance inheriting her as a mother-in-law.'

His lips quirked. 'There is a reason for the dowager house being significantly distanced from the principal residence on most estates.'

'Well, let's hope the one at Davencourt House is in another county for poor Constance's sake. Anyway, the evidence is quite black against Lady Davencourt now. She not only hired a private detective and instructed him to bribe others, she also met with Daisy before she was murdered.' She slapped the dashboard, making Clifford wince. 'Which is why she recognised Daisy the minute she saw her at the Eagle!' She frowned. 'But do we really think Lady Davencourt would have killed, or had Daisy killed, because she believes Peregrine is too weak-willed to have done the necessary himself?'

Clifford turned to her with a horrified look. 'Do the "necessary", my lady? Rather uncharacteristically indifferent in one's delivery, if you will forgive my observation. Too many penny dreadfuls devoured, perchance?'

'I only meant "find a way to stop Daisy blackmailing him". But what about the black-eyed man? Where would he fit into all this? He's been spotted at two crime scenes now.'

'Perhaps he is also in the pay of Lady Davencourt? I'm sure you came to the same conclusion as I that Mr Cramdon might indeed be our man.'

'Despite his limp? The man who ran away from us at the golf course was very able-bodied.'

'A limp can be faked, as we have found out previously.'

She nodded. 'True. Then Cramdon might have killed Miss Balforth on Lady Davencourt's instructions. And if Sir Grainger had discovered Lady Davencourt's involvement in Miss Balforth's demise, that might also explain Cramdon being ordered to try to silence Sir Grainger. Again, on Lady Davencourt's instructions.'

He hesitated. 'I sincerely hope, my lady, that your hospital visit this morning did not bring back disturbing memories from your nursing days during the war?'

She shook her head but looked away.

He sighed. 'That's a "yes", then. Perhaps later, a chess match into the small hours, with the most fiercely competitive of opponents and one glass of port too many might be in order?'

She smiled. 'That sounds like heaven.' She glanced at him

appreciatively. 'Don't you ever dream of being served by another, Clifford, rather than always serving—'

'That's it!' He braked hard, jerking her forward. 'Apologies, my lady, but we must return to Mr Cramdon forthwith.'

As she hammered on the private detective's faded wood door once more, Clifford stood to one side.

'I've nothing else to tell you,' Cramdon's gravelly voice called as the door creaked open slowly.

She shook her head. 'Oh, but you do. I've just realised you must know one last piece of vital information since Daisy didn't serve the breach of promise lawsuit herself. Peregrine told me her lawyer acted on her behalf.'

'So?' He shrugged. 'That's what lawyers do.'

'Name and address. Now.'

At his thunderous look, she held his gaze.

'Mr Cramdon, as you followed Daisy, you must have either witnessed her meeting with her lawyer or been paid to track him down by Lady Davencourt. So, no more games or I guarantee that it *will* be you in the dock, not your employer!'

Scowling, he pulled a battered notebook from his jacket pocket, scrawled on a page and held it out. 'Some people doubt my honesty, but good luck getting any out of him!'

She looked confused. 'But he's a lawyer?'

He laughed mirthlessly. 'And farthings are still money even when they're as bent as hell.' He jabbed a finger at the paper. 'Just like he is.'

The door closed without ceremony.

22

From across a street in yet another unfamiliar part of Chipstone, Eleanor glanced around in confusion in the leather-worker's shop Clifford had insisted they visit. His aim became clearer, however, when she noticed that it gave an unrestricted view of the very lawyer's office they had come to visit.

Ah! Spy out the lie of the land first. Get to know your quarry. She turned back to the counter.

'But bespoke design adds an elegance all of its own.' Clifford tapped a roll of soft lamb hide with his pince-nez. 'Especially with such fine material as this. And, ahem, elegance has still proven quite the elusive beast on occasion, one might agree?'

The eager craftsman's eyes lit up above his bristly white moustache as he looped his thumbs under the bib of his waxed apron. 'Sir couldn't be more right! I mean,' he spluttered, 'in regard to owning a unique piece, not umm' – he waved an embarrassed hand at Eleanor's sage tweed ensemble – 'not in the matter of a lady's wardrobe. Maybe as I'll just fetch some more samples.' He scurried away between the two partitions into the workshop she glimpsed beyond.

As he returned, Clifford shook his head. 'Apologies. I may not have been clear. Her ladyship requires a *complete* set of accessories.' He slid a folded piece of paper across the table.

The craftsman opened it, his eyes widening at the money enclosed. 'Why, sir, this is too much.'

Clifford tapped his nose. 'Perhaps. But perhaps not for some information also about your' – he nodded towards the lawyer's office – 'neighbour.'

The man frowned and then his face cleared. 'Of course. You mean Fisher, the legal weasel?'

'Is that his courtroom moniker?' Eleanor said innocently. 'I'm not really up on such things.'

'Naturally you aren't, madam.' His whiskers quivered. 'No upstanding persons are.' He swept the rolls of leather to one side before leaning his elbows on the counter and lowering his voice. 'And no upstanding person has ever crossed *his* doorway, I can tell you. Most especially not him!'

Eleanor leaned her elbows on the counter, mirroring the craftsman. 'Fascinating. One always considers a man of the law to be the epitome of moral virtue.'

He snorted. 'He's the epitome of something, madam, but not anything one could articulate in front of a lady. If you saw some of the rum goings on over there, like I do when I'm finally upstairs after a decent day's toil tucked under my belt.' He shook his head vehemently. 'What I see is no way for a legal man to be behaving.'

'Rum goings on, are there?'

'A rougher rabble I ne'er did spy than those who creeps in and out of his office. What lawyer lowers his blinds of a daytime as often as that one unless he has much to hide? Answer me that.' Before she could, he rumbled on. 'And then a few months ago he's added to it all by having another no-good-looking gentleman calling when any decent law-abiding lawyer would have long shut up for the night.'

'Most inconsiderate,' Clifford said, without looking up from his slim leather pocketbook over which his fountain pen danced in graceful, flowing strokes. 'Have you seen the gentleman in question since last week's tail twitched free her last hair?'

At Eleanor's questioning look, the craftsman laughed. 'Your man means Friday. End of week like. Though, in truth, 'twere a week ago since he last called, I think.' The leatherworker scowled. 'Ne'er did see the man's face, as he had such a passion for overblown hats. Still, shouldn't grumble over short blessings. Least now he's stopped calling, I've got some peace.'

Clifford nodded. 'Which we shall leave you in.'

As the bell dinged behind them, Eleanor turned towards the decrepit office front opposite. She squared her shoulders. 'So, Clifford, let's go see a legal weasel about a murder!'

A few moments later, she sat on one side of a plain wooden desk, distracted by her host's heavily pomaded, tobacco-coloured hair.

'Come, come, dear madam. As a lawyer,' Fisher purred through thin lips as he ran a long fingernail across the letters after his name on the engraved brass desk plate, 'I couldn't possibly say.' He smiled like a snake eyeing a mouse. 'You must know a legal man's word is his bond.'

She smiled sweetly. 'Oh quite, Mr Fisher. Especially the words he must have declared when swearing his judicial oath.'

His serpent's smile widened. 'That is the province of judges and magistrates only, I'm afraid. Not humble barristers, such as I.'

'I do know that, actually.' She omitted to mention it was only because Clifford had imparted a few pertinent aspects of the English legal system in the twenty strides it took them to cross from the leather shop. 'Which is handy. As you might otherwise be rumbled more easily.'

'Rumbled?' He rose with a pompous dignity, which was rather diminished by his slight, unimposing frame. 'Not a legal term with which I am familiar. And I am' – he gestured along the spines of the embossed tomes half filling the left-hand wall – 'entirely conversant with every aspect of our eminent law. So, I couldn't possibly be accused of any *actus reus. Res ipsa loquitor,* my dear madam,' – he ran the tip of his tongue over his bottom lip – 'as we lawyers say.'

She tutted. 'I shouldn't bother to try to blind me with fancy words. My butler reads the heaviest of Latin texts just for fun.' She pulled a face. 'Deathly things to my mind, but he devours them like hors d'oeuvres.'

Clifford fixed Fisher with a withering look. 'Perhaps, rather than try to bamboozle her ladyship with legal terms – used, I might add, incorrectly in the context of this discussion – you could simply detail the *corpus delicti.* Which' – he took a step forward, clearly discomfiting Fisher, who shrunk away – 'has two equally applicatory legal definitions, does it not?' He turned to Eleanor. 'Firstly, the facts which make up an offence. But also secondly, the body of a person who has been killed unlawfully.' He spun back to the lawyer. 'Like a certain young lady was at the Eagle Hotel!'

'It's no use threatening me,' Fisher spat.

'Gracious!' Eleanor waved a hand. 'Such accusations. We are merely enjoying a discussion on the finer points of law.' She adjusted the pleats of her skirt. 'Do continue. It's quite engrossing. And I've the whole afternoon at my disposal.'

'Well,' said Fisher, sliding around the side of his chair, 'thankfully, I haven't.'

'Then let's move to the meat of our business proper, shall we?'

He smiled thinly. 'I've no business with you, madam. None whatsoever.'

'Unlike you had with the aforementioned *corpus delicti,* I

believe the term was. Or the now tragically deceased Daisy Balforth, being one and the same.'

Fisher merely folded his arms in reply.

'Why deny you were acting on her behalf? Unless you served the lawsuit in disguise?'

He tutted. 'A man of my professional standing has no need of such concealments. Besides, as my client has now passed,' – he held up a hurried hand – 'if I have understood you correctly that said person is deceased, then the breach of promise is void. Luckily for Lord Davencourt.'

'But not for you.' Eleanor smiled. 'Since no one has mentioned a breach of promise. Nor Lord Davencourt.'

Fisher waved an airy hand. 'An... an educated guess, nothing more.'

'Far more than educated, I'd warrant,' Clifford said. 'And whoever Miss Balforth's legal representative was, he clearly based the breach of promise case against Lord Davencourt on Lord Northcote's.'

Despite himself, Fisher failed to hide his surprise at Clifford's knowledge. 'You are well versed. Lord Northcote's case was indeed a landmark. But as I've said, a lawyer's word is his bond and client confidentiality is sacred.'

As he spoke, Eleanor's eyes were drawn to the tall filing cabinet behind him. And more specifically to the manufacturer's silver trademark disc riveted at the top. Something nudged at the edge of her memory, but it was too blurred to recognise what. She tried to focus, but was abruptly called back to the present by Fisher clearing his throat noisily.

'So, I believe we're done here.'

'Pity.' She shared a look with Clifford. 'Because it appears you've lost.'

The snake smile re-emerged. 'Forgive me, I must have missed you throwing down an elegant lady's gauntlet at the start. I had no idea we'd gone into battle. Not very sporting of you, since I therefore had no chance of winning.'

'Oh, I didn't mean we've beaten you.' She rose. 'No, I meant you've lost the last shred of hope you had that you won't be next. But' – she shrugged at Clifford – 'we tried, didn't we?'

'We did, my lady.' Her butler escorted her to the door.

'Wait!' Fisher called out anxiously. 'Next for what?'

She half turned back. 'Come, come, Mr Fisher. A lady's word is her bond also. You must know that. But Daisy Balforth was brutally murdered. And now a recent attempt has been made on another's life. It seems someone is trying to eliminate loose ends, perhaps.' She shook her head. 'You're a braver man than I took you for. I'd hate to have to lay odds on whether you survive the week.'

His face paled as he shrunk back against the wall. 'Get out. NOW!'

As the Rolls cleared the outer reaches of Chipstone, Eleanor caught Clifford glancing at her. She sighed. 'It's a dangerous game Fisher's playing, whatever it is. Wouldn't you agree?'

He nodded. 'Possibly fatal.'

She sat back in her seat. 'Hmm. As much as I disliked Fisher, I don't see him as a suspect. I can't work out why he would have murdered Daisy.'

Clifford swung the Rolls right. 'Suppose, my lady, his aim had been to kill Miss Balforth all along? Once the breach of promise had been successful and Miss Balforth dispatched, he would somehow have pocketed the money from Lord Davencourt. Not wishing to malign the lady, but Miss Balforth might have been easily hoodwinked by legal jargon included in any contract between her and Fisher.'

'Good theory. But Daisy died without succeeding with the

breach of promise lawsuit. Peregrine hadn't paid her a bean since their original agreement to call off the engagement, so why would Fisher kill her before he even got the money?' She flung out her hands. 'And if Fisher *wasn't* Daisy's killer, just her legal representative, what is he scared of? Or more correctly, *who*? It doesn't add up. Not Peregrine, since Fisher faced him happily when he brandished the lawsuit. Lady Davencourt? Seems a bit far-fetched. Beatrice?'

'Seems even farther fetched, my lady. Mr Flint, perchance?'

'Maybe, but we haven't anything on him to support that. Dash it, Clifford. Meeting Fisher has confused me even more.'

'Perhaps Mr Fisher is scared of Mrs Wilton's mysterious man with the piercing black eyes? Who might also be the man from the golf course and the man Mr Fisher's neighbour told us visited Mr Fisher late at night?'

They stared at each other. 'Cramdon?'

She nodded. 'Possibly. Either way, I believe it's time we found out more about our Miss Daisy Balforth.'

23

The outskirts of Chipstone struck Eleanor as run-down as they had done on the previous occasions she'd ventured beyond the limits of what Clifford deemed was suitable for a titled lady.

'Poor Daisy.' They inched around a black, oily puddle that stretched the entire width of the street. 'She looked quite the delicate flower to be living amongst such deprivation.'

Clifford nodded as they turned to the avenue they sought, another dirt road with dilapidated and overcrowded terraced housing. Instead of heading down it, however, he led her on past.

'Fortunately, number thirty-three is the last in the row, my lady, which means we can skirt around and arrive at the quieter end.'

She looked from side to side. 'But just look at all the curtains twitching and the front steps suddenly needing to be swept! We aren't going to get in unseen, even with your infalli-ble, if questionable, lock-picking skills.'

He nodded thoughtfully. 'Indeed. Our usual disgraceful method of entry will need a creative adaptation.'

Number thirty-three was not only the last in the row, it was also the narrowest, barely wider than its weather-beaten brown door and cracked window. A brick archway led to a tiny unfenced rear strip of garden.

'She ain't in!' a hoarse voice called as they stepped onto the weed-filled path to the front door. 'And she ain't gonna be neither.'

Having spun in a circle, Eleanor was none the wiser where the owner of the voice was hiding. A moment later, a flurry of grey-and-white feathers fluttered from above. She shielded her eyes against the sun and peered up into the shadows. In the roof over the room that spanned the archway, a series of slates had been removed.

'A pigeon loft, my lady,' Clifford whispered.

A head poked further out of a window.

'Thank you,' Eleanor called up. 'But we can manage.'

The head popped back in. Clifford started counting slowly to ten. At eight, the voice returned, this time behind them.

'Well, if you're certain as you can manage. Though manage what, I won't ask. I'm not nosey like some of 'em around here who can't mind their own business.'

A woman swamped by a faded-blue housecoat with greying wisps poking from her tightly knotted headscarf stood on the path. Clifford doffed his bowler hat with a flourish, his tone tipped with silk.

'Then, since we are here on an important matter, we are grateful for you being the very essence of discretion, dear lady.'

The blush this drew to the woman's otherwise pallid face made Eleanor bite back a smile. It was a rare thing to see her butler use his charm, but the effect was always remarkable. And endearing to watch. The woman patted her covered hair.

'Well, that's me all over, ain't it? Whatever it was, you just said. And don't worry, I wouldn't say nothing to no one about you being here. Best keep your own counsel around these parts.' Her lips almost disappeared with the narrow line they formed.

'They got nothing from me when they came. Police, that is. Terrible business for poor Daisy, though. Fancy someone up and doing for her in cold blood?' She stared between them questioningly. 'But her landlord has already shown somebody the place. Strange he should waste your time, letting you have a look as well? Not that you seem the types to rent in this sort of neighbourhood, of course.' She ran an appraising eye down Clifford's long suited form. 'Pity.'

'Oh, we're not here to meet the landlord,' Eleanor said. 'We're here to... ah, to try to help a friend of Daisy's. A friend from years back, actually.'

The woman shrugged. 'I wouldn't know anything about that.'

'You said, "Had shown somebody around" though? Was Daisy moving out, then?'

The woman's eyes roved enviously over Eleanor's smart tweeds and shoes. 'Hard to say. Course my head's so full of how to make ends meet, it gets muddled. 'Specially with my husband's blinking pigeons costing such a pretty penny in food every time they flies home from racing halfway around the country. So, like I said, I wouldn't know anything, see?'

Clifford slid his wallet out nonchalantly. In one deft movement, he rolled a half-a-crown coin along the back of his hand before letting it drop neatly into the woman's apron pocket. 'I'm sure, madam, Miss Balforth was very grateful for your prudent neighbourly watch on her home when she was out.'

The woman's face lit up as he dropped in another coin to join the first. She eagerly grasped both prizes.

'You can't be too careful. Not around here. And with Daisy living alone. Mind, her being so quiet, I wasn't always sure if she was in or not. Even with the walls being about as good as made of paper.'

'Not many visitors then?' Eleanor said.

'Never. Just came and went on her own.'

'And how had she been lately? Anything different in her manner in the last month?'

The woman nodded pensively. 'Since you've asked, she'd been agitated. Unusually like. At first, I thought she'd been talking to my neighbour next along and taken her side over summat against me. I should have known better, though. Daisy wasn't that sort. Softer than butter left on the range, she were.'

'But she didn't let slip what might have been bothering her?'

'Ne'er a word. But it weren't a month ago it started. More like two. In fact, it definitely were because I first noticed it the morning after we had that terrible rain. Right when the barley were due to be cut.'

Clifford gave her an appreciative smile. 'July fifteenth. What a splendid memory you have, dear lady.'

She beamed. 'Well, I've got a good head. That's how I knew summat was wrong with Daisy. And that were at the time she changed her evening habits, too. Not my place to have said anything to her, but a girl as flowersome as her, out at night alone!' She folded her arms. 'Not right. And not safe, neither. 'Specially from all the tongues that would have been wagging, making up stories about what she were doing. But stopping out until even the chilled leftovers is cold will do that, you know.'

Clifford caught Eleanor's eye and mouthed, 'Overnight.'

'Ah! Perhaps Daisy was moving into her new home, wherever that was?'

The woman frowned. 'Don't think so. She ne'er took anything with her.'

'What a pity,' Eleanor said. 'I so hoped we might find something to make sure no one else who was close to Daisy would have any trouble.'

The woman looked at her sharply. 'I don't like the sound of that! Why, I shared a wall with her. You can take a look in her place for yerselves, if it'll help. Only got to give her lock a good double thump from underneath and it springs wide. She always did it in winter when the hoar was thick on a clear night on account of the hole for the key being iced up.'

'Oh gracious, we couldn't!' Eleanor said with a convincing gasp.

The woman shrugged. 'Ain't gonna matter to Daisy, now, is it? But what about me? I got a right to be safe in me own bed at night, ain't I?'

'Masterfully engineered, my lady,' Clifford said in a low tone as Daisy's front door closed behind them.

She groaned. 'Hardly my finest hour, putting the fear of God into an innocent woman.'

He shook his head. 'On the contrary, you made the lady's afternoon with a story she can retell for months.'

'Then let's get done and out before we have the whole street descend on us.'

They both blinked hard, willing their eyes to hurry and adjust to the gloomy interior.

'Goodness, Clifford,' she whispered. 'It's just a single rectangular room.'

'Far from unusual, my lady. One down, one up.'

She nodded and looked around. In front of the fire, a worn chair with a broken arm was draped in a holey patchwork blanket. Beneath the window there was a small table with a stool underneath. The paint on the walls – originally blue, she hazarded – was now flaking, except on the right-hand wall where it had been superseded by a large patch of damp.

Clifford pointed to the ladder-style steps in the corner, then ran a finger around his collar. 'Perhaps you might be so kind as to take the lady's, ahem, bedchamber.'

'Of course.' She hurried over, but paused as he held up a hand.

'Remembering the walls are "about as good as made of paper", evidently.'

With a nod, she nipped smartly but quietly up the rungs. As her head poked through the hatch in the floor of the bedroom, she felt a wash of sadness. A bare iron-framed single bed with plain, grey bedding stood against one wall, the brightly patterned scarf looped around the only pillow adding a splash of much-needed cheer. A doorless wardrobe tucked under the steep slope of the ceiling had six hooks screwed to the back panel, home to two faded dresses, a blouse, skirt and cardigan. A tired pair of cheap shoes and a basket of underwear was tucked below.

As she stepped off the last rung, she looked around, trying to get a feel for the pretty young woman whose life had been taken so brutally. A row of dog-eared books without jackets were piled on the meagre windowsill, a postcard sticking out of one. She pulled it out but the back was blank. The other side showed a colour-tinted photograph of a high street rather like Chipstone, only even less glamorous. *Hartbridge, 1908.* She assumed Daisy had used it as a bookmark.

Dropping it back down, she glanced around the rest of the room. A small, blue threadbare rug offered some comfort and colour, as did the chipped rose-patterned jug and mismatched washbowl on the nightstand. A tall jar filled with dried wild-flowers on the tiny table gave the space a hint of desperate optimism.

A peep under the bed revealed nothing, as did running a hand underneath the mattress. There was nothing stashed behind the wardrobe and the nightstand cupboard held just two candles set in milk bottles and a near-empty box of matches.

'Hopeless,' she said as she re-emerged in the downstairs room. 'What did you find?'

Clifford held his hands out. 'Beyond the general necessities needed to mend items of clothing and eat cold suppers, nothing.'

Eleanor tutted. 'I owe Sergeant Brice an apology, then. When Hugh said Brice had been the only man free to give the place a once-over, I was sure we'd uncover something he'd missed.'

'Not an unfounded judgement, my lady. I confess I antici-pated one of us might stumble upon a hidden photograph of Lord Davencourt or some such.'

'Not the letters, though, since she took those with her to the Eagle.'

'The specific purpose for which we are still in the dark about.'

After a last glance around the room, they nodded to each other and reluctantly went out through the door. But as Clifford yanked it shut and made sure it was secure, Eleanor felt an uncomfortable frisson that they were being watched.

'Well,' came the neighbour's hoarse voice from behind them, 'can I cosy up to Wee Willie Winkie knowing the rooks won't be gathering afore cocklight?'

'Go to sleep and wake up alive in the morning, my lady,' Clifford translated.

'Oh gracious, yes,' Eleanor said rather over-brightly, still feeling bad for having frightened the woman unnecessarily. 'There's nothing to suggest anyone had been marauding around poor Daisy's house. Nor that they would bother you next door.'

The woman nodded slowly. 'Course, they say trouble follows trouble, but sometimes it follows summat else too.'

Eleanor cocked her head, puzzled. 'Such as?'

The woman flapped her apron pocket in reply.

Clifford dropped a coin in as before, but withheld the second half-a-crown. 'Miss Balforth was a vulnerable young woman. And alone in the world, it would appear. She should be resting among angels, not looking down on wolves.'

The woman's shoulders fell. 'I wasn't trying to prey, only to help. She was a rare'un. Beautiful inside and out, she were.'

Clifford gestured to the left cuff of her housecoat. She fumbled in the folds and then, with a bashful gasp, pulled out the other coin and slid it into her apron pocket.

'What have you remembered that you thought might be helpful?' Eleanor said.

'Oh, it was about me warning Daisy about *him*.' She pointed just beyond the hedge.

Eleanor lowered her voice. 'Another neighbour?'

'Oh no. They're a rummy bunch in parts but not the kind rough enough to hurt a woman like Daisy, thank God.' She shook her head. 'But *him*. He looked a bad 'un. Hanging around outside. Hiding like, lurking in the dark. Then when Daisy went out in the evening, I swear it was his shadow, not hers, that followed.'

'And what did Daisy say when you warned her?'

'That she ain't seen or heard no one. And no one had bothered her like, neither.' The woman pursed her lips. 'I could'a been wrong, I suppose.'

'But?'

'But I don't believe I was. I got good eyes in me head, I have. It's always me as spots them pigeons coming home, long afore me husband.'

'Then I'm sure you're right about the man you saw. When was that?'

'A while back now. Right around the time she started acting like the sun would never shine for her no more, as I mentioned afore. Haven't seen him since, though.'

Clifford nodded. 'Lastly, dear lady, what did your flawless powers of observation spot about the man who was lurking?'

'He was too... careful, like, for me to get a good look at him.' She ran her eyes up and down Clifford's long frame again. 'A deal shorter than you, though. Sort of squarer, at a push, I'd say.

Course his hat was yanked down so hard, and his neckerchief up so high over his mouth 'n all. But what with the air being so bad often, 'tain't nothing unusual around here. Mind you, you could still see something of his eyes. And what eyes they were! Could have gone right through your soul!'

Eleanor and Clifford exchanged a glance. He threw the woman a smile.

'Dear lady, you have done Miss Balforth a great service. Cosy well with Wee Willie Winkie in good conscience.'

The woman blushed. 'That I will. But I wish I'd gotten a better look at him who was lurking seeing as you're trying so hard to... to... what was it you said you was doing again?'

Eleanor beckoned to Clifford.

'What we said we were doing was leaving you in peace. Thank you. Come on, Clifford, we need to see a lady about an old friend.'

24

Clifford's tone was no less adamant as he gave Gladstone's lead an encouraging jiggle and lengthened his stride to keep up with Eleanor's determined pace.

'Forgive me, but I do not believe this area of Little Buckford is any more suitable for a lady than the one we just left in Chipstone.'

She pointed over her shoulder. 'Then you should wait in the Rolls, as I suggested.'

'Not an option, my lady, because then you will be out of my sight. And as I have yet to see Prudence walking beside you...'

She laughed. 'Well, luckily, I have my protective fox terrier of a butler instead. And' – she tapped the basket he carried which bore a selection of provisions they had called into Penry's Butchers and Cartwright's General Stores en route to purchase – 'I also have a peace offering.' She pursed her lips. 'Going back to the conversation with Daisy's neighbour, though, the man who was stalking Daisy could have been Cramdon, I suppose. Most men look fairly similar in the fog with a hat pulled down over their face. And he does have black eyes.'

Clifford shook his head. 'Miss Balforth's neighbour said the man you refer to had not been stalking Daisy recently. And Mr Cramdon only visited Lady Davencourt a week or so before Miss Balforth's death as far as we know. One assumes, therefore, that Lady Davencourt only hired him to find Miss Balforth a short while before she was killed.'

Eleanor frowned. 'If that supposition is right, it seems to put Lady Davencourt in the clear. In so far as she has no connection with our hatted stalker.'

His brow furrowed. 'Unless, of course, Lady Davencourt knew of the breach of promise before it was actually served and hired Cramdon some time ago. Perhaps he was recommended to her by one of her acquaintances who had used his "services" previously?'

'Mmm. Which means she might have met him elsewhere to start, not at Davencourt House. Perhaps she only met him there recently as an emergency?' She looked thoughtful. 'Unless, that is, Daisy was being stalked by *two* men?'

Clifford raised a brow. 'Men, my lady? It is fairly easy for a woman to pass herself off as a man on a dark, foggy night, especially when heavily covered by a cloak and hat, as you yourself well know.'

She laughed. 'Okay, Clifford, I may have passed myself off as a man before when abroad, as you've mentioned previously. And, yes, it's not that hard.' She pursed her lips. 'Which means, I suppose, it's not beyond possibility that our stalker, or one of them at least, could have been Beatrice? Ah!' A familiar cottage came into view. 'Maybe the occupier can throw some light on the mystery.'

'Hello, Mrs Harris. How wonderful,' Eleanor said as the dour woman she remembered from the Women's Institute meeting opened the door.

'Don't see what's so wonderful 'bout it if my only chance

to catch up on a mountain of chores is interrupted.' Mrs Harris' tired face twisted into a scowl. She pulled her front door to behind her and folded her arms over her worn grey cardigan.

Realising she wasn't going to be invited in and would have to conduct the conversation on the doorstep, Eleanor hung onto her smile anyway. Clifford, however, gave a sharp sniff, loud enough to be heard over Gladstone's soft growl to himself. She raised a finger to quieten them both.

'My apologies for calling unannounced, Mrs Harris. I only meant it's wonderful you are home. For two reasons, actually.'

Mrs Harris pursed her lips. 'Oh, and them's reasons for me to be excited about your visit, are they? 'Cos if not, the laundry, cleaning and dishes – to say nothing of the chickens – have all got calls on my time. But, of course, you wouldn't know about chores, raw knuckles or swollen knees from scrubbing all day.' She jerked a chin in Clifford's direction. 'Seeing as you've got people to do all that for you, being an important titled lady 'n all.'

Despite the woman's scorn, Eleanor detected just as much sadness as bitterness behind the words.

'Mrs Harris, I am acutely aware of my privileges and am beyond grateful every day for them. And the best, in truth the only, way I've found to offer any kind of repayment is to help people whenever and wherever I can.'

'So?' Mrs Harris looked at her suspiciously. 'What's that to do with me? I ain't no charity case! I've got a job. Keeps my head above water all by my own, I'll have you know.'

'And you have my utmost admiration,' Eleanor said genuinely. 'Especially since the war, it really can't be easy at all. But I haven't been clear. I'm not here to offer my help, but to ask for *yours*.'

Mrs Harris sneered. 'Now, how could the likes of me possibly help the likes of you?'

Eleanor sighed. 'This has nothing to do with class or upbringing, so I hope a great deal.'

Mrs Harris' expression didn't change. 'Well, if it's about the rally I'm afraid I don't have time, Lady Swift.' She turned to go back inside.

Eleanor stepped forward. 'It's not help with the rally I need. At least not today.'

This made Mrs Harris pause, hand on the doorknob. 'Alright, if you must. I'm listening if you're quick about it. What's it to do with, then?'

'With the poor young woman who died at the Eagle.'

Eleanor immediately regretted her direct approach, as Mrs Harris shook her head forcefully.

'Nope! Don't want to talk about that, thank you very much.' Her already drawn face paled. 'Bad do all round and no mistake. Fancy you coming here expecting me to rake up the very picture I've been trying to stop filling my head.' She pulled her cardigan tighter. 'Shame on you!'

Eleanor held up her hands. 'You're right. And I'm sorry. But Daisy was a young woman. Younger than I am, I believe. And someone cruelly stole the rest of her life from her.' She fought the croak in her voice. 'No one has the right to do that.' Gladstone pressed his muzzle into her hand with a soft whine.

Mrs Harris looked away.

Eleanor spoke gently. 'I just want to know if you saw someone at the Eagle who we think was there on the day Daisy died.'

'How should I know? 'Tis a busy hotel.'

'I appreciate that, but please try. He might have been wearing a hat pulled down low, by all accounts. And he had piercing black eyes.'

'By all accounts?' Mrs Harris said sharply. 'Been bothering lots of folk about this then, Lady Swift? Rummy sort of conversation for someone of your standing.'

At Eleanor's dignified silence, the woman's shoulders jerked defensively. 'Nope. Ain't seen anyone fitting that description.'

'You're sure?'

'Sure as I am the cleaning and chickens won't even get short shrift after I've been wasting my time out here.'

'Perhaps helping bring justice for Miss Balforth might not feel like you've wasted your time? If you'd take a moment to ponder...'

Mrs Harris yanked an off-white handkerchief from her cardigan pocket and dabbed at her mouth, no longer making eye contact with Eleanor. 'I said I ain't seen no one like that! Besides, I ain't one to tattle. How's it going to sound if folks who come to the Eagle get wind that the staff are shouting their business all over the place? I'd be lucky to get as far as being hauled over the coals afore I was booted out of my job on my ear. And how would I make ends meet then?'

'Nobody wants to get you into trouble, Mrs Harris. But maybe you can think of something you saw that might help identify the person who killed Daisy?'

Mrs Harris twisted the handkerchief in her hands. 'Why would I know owt about summat so terrible?'

'Because you're a member of the housekeeping team. Which means, as I've learned from my staff, you have a keen eye for detail. Mr Flint must think so.'

At the mention of the hotel manager's name, Mrs Harris shrunk back into the house.

Eleanor tried again. 'Mr Flint gave you the time off to recuperate, didn't he? He must appreciate your commitment and loyalty, then.'

'Maybe.' The now familiar acerbic tone resurfaced. 'But he certainly ain't going to appreciate me talking to you 'bout... that day.'

'Then I shall leave you be.' Before Eleanor could go, something through the window caught her eye. She blinked. Or was it the *lack* of something?

Mrs Harris followed her gaze.

Eleanor quickly looked away. 'Like I said, it can't be easy. Especially without him here to help you.'

'Him, who?'

'Your husband.' Eleanor felt a wash of compassion for the woman. 'It takes a long time after someone precious has gone for it to feel any easier, doesn't it?'

'Pfff! Pretty words, Lady Swift. But since you don't know what it actually feels like—'

'Don't I?' Eleanor said sharply. 'Well, Mrs Harris, let's just agree on how little we know of each other's pasts, shall we? I only hope you have plenty to draw comfort from after however many years it is you've been a widow.'

'Eight, if you must pry. He were taken early by the war.'

Eleanor shook her head. 'I wasn't prying. Just doing a very poor job of passing on my belated condolences.'

'That's what it were, was it?' Mrs Harris scowled. 'Like banging on about Daisy being so young. A hard life adds nothing but unkind years to a face and don't I know it!'

The door slammed behind her.

As she turned left out of the gate, Eleanor noted the hand darting back out to grab the basket of provisions from the doorstep. She smiled at her butler as he rejoined her. 'Thank you for leaving it, Clifford, even if we didn't get what we came for.'

'Perhaps we did, my lady.' Without pausing, he peered over the end of the straggly hedge bordering the narrow stretch of ground that ran down the side of Mrs Harris' cottage. At her puzzled look, he motioned they should keep walking.

'I confess I left the basket partly as a diversion, so I might have one more moment to peruse the contents of her bonfire.'

'I wondered where you'd nipped off to. Your latest hobby, is it? Let me guess, a study of incendiary rapidity depending on the intricacies of bonfire construction or some such?'

He tutted. 'Hardly, my lady, although it's a fascinating subject. Gravity, in fact, provides the key element for efficient convection which together with the number of oxygen molecules dictated by the surface area of the fuel—'

'Alright, clever clogs, thank you. Then why were you keen to nose over her bonfire?'

'Because I noted an odd smell, and that, on our initial way past, the flames were tinged with an unusual blue hue. But it was only whilst standing on the lady's doorstep that I was able to place the smoke odour that reached my nostrils.'

'That's because you were sniffing so hard at her being impolite to me.'

His lips pursed. 'Being *rude* if you will forgive the correction. I concede, however, that the lady is indubitably daunted by your position.'

'And embarrassed about hers.'

'Quite.'

'And fears Flint would dismiss her for talking about the murder, do you think? He made no bones to both of us over how fiendishly he's trying to keep it all quiet.'

'True.' He looked thoughtful. 'But we were both surprised at his generosity. Giving Mrs Harris any leave at all to recuperate seems out of character, let alone several days. So, whether that means she knows something or Mr Flint is hiding something, one could conjecture equally on both. However, if it is the latter...' He arched one brow.

'I know. It sounds like a repeat of the incident the waitress told us about involving Sir Grainger at the King's Arms.' She bit her lip. 'I still can't believe that he would hurt a woman, though. He dotes on his wife and daughters. I've seen it myself.'

Clifford shook his head. 'Regrettably, that is precisely what is oft said by the horrified loved one of those who have stooped to violence. The basic tenet of Robert Louis Stevenson's novella of 1886 would never have captivated the nation's imagination otherwise.' At her inquiring look, he added. '*Dr Jekyll and Mr Hyde.* Dr Jekyll being a loving family man, but his alter-ego, Mr Hyde, a violent monster.'

'Hmm. Dash it, Clifford! Aside from unintentionally trampling on the sensitivities of a widow, did we learn anything just then?'

'Yes, we did.'

They carried on down the dirt track back to the Rolls. Clifford pausing as Gladstone jerked to a stop to sniff something frightfully interesting. To him, anyway.

'Well? Come on, Clifford. You can delight in pointing out I'm the blunt brick who missed whatever you gleaned.'

His eyes twinkled. 'If you insist. From my vantage point behind you on the doorstep, I was able to view all but one small section of the downstairs room. For a long-grieving widow, so incensed by your, ahem, indelicate mention of her deceased husband, Mrs Harris has not a single photograph of the gentleman that I could observe.'

'Clifford, you clever bean!' She continued on towards the waiting Rolls. 'That's what was bothering me, but I couldn't place it. When I peered through her windows on my previous visit, there were signs of a man living, or having lived, there. A' – she tapped her forehead – 'tankard and pipe on the mantelpiece. A man's hat on one of the chairs and so forth. But no photographs. And today there were still no photographs. But there was also—'

'None of those things you mentioned. Which brings us back to my assessment of the lady's bonfire.'

'Go on.'

'Mrs Harris was burning, among other things, a bundle of clothing and two leather items, one possibly a man's belt.'

'Was she now? Right, come on! Notebook and conjecture aplenty over lunch. I'm ravenous.'

Twenty minutes later, the telephone jangled on its cradle as Clifford held the front door open for Eleanor. He stepped briskly across Henley Hall's marbled floor, signalling to Mrs Butters who had appeared from the kitchen corridor that he would answer it.

'Little Buckford 342. Lady Swift's residence... Ah! One moment, please.' His inscrutable expression gave nothing away as he held it out to Eleanor.

The deep voice that rumbled out of the mouthpiece made her heart skip. 'Eleanor?'

'Hello, Hugh. How are you?'

There was a short pause. 'All the better for hearing your voice, in truth. But I'm afraid this isn't a social call. I... well, the truth is I'm mortifyingly embarrassed.'

'Good.'

'Eleanor!'

She laughed. 'You look better with colour in your cheeks. I've said so before.'

'This is serious. I've committed the ultimate presumption for which I apologise profusely.' Intrigued, she stared into the hall mirror, waiting for Seldon's next words. 'The thing is, Eleanor, Sir Grainger has recovered consciousness, but the blasted matron at the hospital refused point blank to let me or any of my men see him as he's so weak. So, I lied and said that a woman who knew how to deal with delicate cases would come on my behalf.'

She gasped. 'You rotter, Hugh! I can be delicate. Well, if I try.'

'No, Eleanor. I don't mean I lied about your lack of delicacy, although actually that is a good point.' He hurried on. 'I meant I lied about who you are.' He coughed. 'Since you aren't, thank goodness, the female police officer that I pretended you are.'

Her jaw fell slack. 'You said I was a *policewoman*?' In the mirror, she could see that Clifford had half turned to hide that his shoulders were shaking with amusement.

'I know. And, look, you don't have to go. In fact, it seems a terrible idea now.'

'No, it isn't. I'm just glad Sir Grainger has regained consciousness. I was about to discuss Mrs Harris' sudden strange predilection for bonfires with Clifford, but that will have to be put on hold. I'll set off immediately.'

'Thank you. But for Pete's sake, you need to go gently with him otherwise matron will have my guts for garters!'

25

If it hadn't been for the shroud of familiar greying whiskers covering the pallid cheeks, Eleanor wouldn't have recognised the father of her best friend. Sir Grainger lay, eyes closed, tightly wrapped in a burgundy silk dressing gown, his bandaged head propped up against several pillows.

Beside him, the stern-faced matron glanced through the glass panel in the double swing doors at Seldon, who was trying to hide his frustration at having been relegated to the role of observer.

'I confess I did not realise they had' – she looked Eleanor up and down in disbelief – '*women* in the police. Still, the chief inspector gave his word you know how to handle patients in such a fragile state.'

'Umm, oh absolutely.' Eleanor pulled out the official note-book Seldon had given her. 'I was a nurse in the war before... before I started working with the police. I'll be very gentle. And quick.'

'Five minutes then.'

'Ten will do nicely, thank you. So I can let him rest between questions, naturally.' Eleanor smiled firmly and stepped over to stand at the end of the bed.

Matron's brows met as she consulted the fob watch hanging from her uniform. 'Very well. But I shall be back on the dot.' The statement sounded like a threat rather than an agreement. Eleanor winced as the matron's unrelenting tone echoed around the corridor as she passed Seldon. 'And I can see you from my desk, Inspector, just so you know.'

Throwing him a sympathetic look through one of the round glass panels, Eleanor gathered her thoughts and turned to Sir Grainger. Up close, she swallowed hard. Far from the strident, formidable man she had encountered previously, he seemed a frail and reduced figure of his former self. She took in his sunken cheeks, the deep creases around his eyes and the blueish half-moons beneath.

How vividly a face can act as a telltale barometer for one's entire physical state, Ellie.

'Sir Grainger?' she called gently. 'Matron said you were awake.'

He grunted as his eyelids flickered. Slowly, he opened his eyes and blinked repeatedly, rubbing his lips together as if trying to find an ounce of moisture.

'Nurse?' he managed in a cracked voice.

'No, Sir Grainger. It's Eleanor. Constance's friend.'

He shuffled himself further up his pillows with difficulty and a great deal of grimacing. Leaning forward, he frowned at her. 'Eleanor! What... what the deuce are you doing here?'

She winced at the weakness in his voice. 'It's complicated. But it's also imperative to catching the person who attacked you. And I haven't long.'

He shook his head, but obviously regretted it as he held a hand to his left temple.

She tapped the back of the chair. 'May I?'

He nodded weakly. 'If you feel it necessary. And please

forgive any unfounded terseness. I... I don't think I'm quite myself. Yet.'

'Not by a long way, I would imagine. That was a hideous attack. I couldn't believe the size and gravity of your wound when we found you on the golf course.'

His mouth fell open. 'It was... you?'

'And my butler. We were there to question you, I shan't lie.'

He groaned. 'Eleanor, why am I now caught in the dilemma of wondering if I should countenance you being Constance's friend?'

She held her hands up. 'I can't help you there, Sir Grainger.'

His hand strayed to the bandage around his head. 'Although...' He paused again. She had to lean closer to catch his words. 'I am immensely grateful for what you did for me. I had no idea it was you the doctor meant. He said if it hadn't been for the remarkable young woman who attended to me, I might not be...' He swallowed hard.

She smiled. 'Be feeling even this bright? Now, let's crack on with the questions I'm here to ask on behalf of the police, since Matron is too fiendishly ferocious to let the chief inspector ask you himself.'

'Terrifying woman.' He shuddered. 'What questions?'

'First off, did you see your attacker?'

He scowled, but evidently even that was too painful to bear as he laid his head gingerly back on the pillow. 'No. Not so much as a glimpse. More's the pity. Because if I had, I would have swung the first golf club, I can tell you!'

She winced to herself, hoping this wasn't further proof of his volatile temper. *Then again, if someone had tried to kill you, Ellie, you'd feel the same!*

He raised a hand slowly. 'Wait. I remember *hearing* something, though.' He closed his eyes for a moment.

Maybe Matron was right, and this is too much for him, Ellie?

He reopened his eyes as if he'd heard her. 'I'm fine... I

remember starting to turn to have a firm word with whoever it was. I mean, it would have been poor form for someone to have entered the sand trap whilst I was hitting out.'

'Ah yes, that was made abundantly clear to me on a previous occasion where I was questioning a gentleman over his golf game.' She hurried on. 'Can you think of any reason you might have been attacked?'

'No.'

'You seem very sure.'

'Well, what else have I had to ponder on while lying here like a wretched invalid?'

'True. And just before you were attacked, were you examining your watch? Or taking snuff?'

He frowned. 'What odd questions. And the answer to both is no.' He lapsed into a fit of coughing.

So, Sir Grainger's attacker was looking for something, Ellie? But what?

She rose to pour him a glass of water from the carafe on the bedside table.

'Thank you.' He took several long sips.

Retaking her seat, she held his gaze. 'Now, before we move on, and not just because I fear the wrath of Matron, are you feeling sufficiently strong to answer more questions?'

'If you think we're achieving anything, yes.' He stiffened. 'Although...'

She sat straighter. 'You're correct to be hesitant, Sir Grainger, because I need to ask you a difficult question. About the matter you made very clear to me you did not wish to discuss when we were in your study at home.'

He groaned. 'Eleanor, this is hardly the time. Taxing a man in his hospital bed. Besides, you gave me your word you would not mention it to Constance or' – he closed his eyes – 'my poor wife.'

'And I shan't. The promise I never actually articulated in

your study still stands. But in that very same conversation, you told me how important it was that you made sufficient provision for all the members of your family. Especially as Bertie is only five and a... unique child. And with Constance's marriage to Peregrine in question...'

His jaw tightened as he heaved himself off his pillow. 'It is more than *in question*. It is off since no one has informed me that the bounder has found a way to redeem his disgraceful behaviour. Not that I am convinced there can be any such thing. A secret engagement to a chorus girl! Unforgivable.' His head fell back, as if exhausted by the effort.

Chorus girl? Eleanor filed away that he knew more about Daisy than she'd thought.

'Sir Grainger, forgive my bluntness, but you have little option but to be entirely honest with me.'

'I've no reason to be dishonest,' he said with a glimmer of the somewhat pompous businessman she'd met before.

'Only that you fear incriminating yourself further over the murder of Miss Balforth, perhaps?'

He stared at her. 'Further? Eleanor, what is this!?'

'Your one opportunity to come clean about the incident at the King's Arms where a member of staff was attacked.'

He pulled the collar of his dressing gown more tightly around his neck. 'I have nothing to say on the matter.'

'As you wish. An unwise decision, though. If,' she said, standing up, 'you'll forgive the observation, as my butler would say.'

'Unwise? Why?' he said sharply.

'Because someone tried to kill you. And they very nearly succeeded.'

'I know. But for you're having attended to me—'

'Which will be a waste of my efforts.'

His eyes jolted wide.

'*If*, Sir Grainger, they succeed next time. And I believe there will be a next time.'

Swallowing hard again, he waved her back into the chair. 'But that... that incident at the King's Arms. It... it was a long time ago. I'm not that person anymore. I have...' He sighed. 'Eleanor, this is really difficult for a man to admit.'

'Perhaps less so if he can believe I'm not here to judge him. Only to help catch his attacker.'

'Very well,' he said reluctantly. 'I have medication to control the fire that suddenly rages in me on occasion.' He tapped his forehead. 'Something in my mental wiring is wrong. Very wrong.'

'But with medication?'

'It is entirely controllable.'

'Entirely? Really?'

'Really, Eleanor, yes. After working through a few different medications and the dosage being adjusted by my doctor, I am no longer the monster that might otherwise surface.'

Even though her experience of drugs was largely limited to her time as a nurse in the war, she still doubted if there was a medication quite as powerful and effective as Sir Grainger was making out. However, in his weakened state she felt she really couldn't push him much further. She tried to keep her face neutral as he held her gaze.

'What I did,' he said weakly, pausing for breath. 'What the creature in me did in the King's Arms' – he covered his mouth with one hand – 'was beyond deplorable.'

She reached out and patted the other arm he was anxiously running back and forth over his blanket. 'Thank you for being so honest. I appreciate that it is far from an easy thing to admit to.'

'I've never admitted it to anyone.'

'I know. Including the chief inspector who interviewed you at the Eagle the day Miss Balforth was murdered.'

'How... how could I? It would have made me look deeply
suspicious.'

'Quite correct. Except that withholding the fact you were
involved in the incident at the King's Arms didn't make you
look deeply suspicious. It made you look deeply *guilty*.'

He gasped.

'Sir Grainger, do you recognise the man you can see
through the glass panel of the doors, standing in the corridor
over there?'

He shuffled awkwardly around on his pillow and peered
over to where she gestured. 'Eyes haven't quite caught up yet
after that wretched blow to the skull. Who is it?'

'Chief Inspector Seldon. He was the one who found out the
details about the incident at the King's Arms.'

With a groan, he lay back down.

She looked his face over, concerned again that he wasn't
strong enough for the emotional turmoil she was putting him
through.

But you've a killer to catch, Ellie.

Her breath caught at the sound of Matron's vociferous tone
out in the corridor. 'One more minute at most.'

Sir Grainger nodded towards the doors. 'How long before
the inspector marches in and arrests me?'

'All the time in the world if you're innocent.'

'Which I am.'

*It seems unlikely, Ellie, that he is guilty after being attacked.
But there is always the faint possibility it was a set up to deflect
suspicion. A set up that went wrong with an overly enthusiastic
accomplice yielding the club!*

'Then tell me anything you remember either side of Miss
Balforth being killed, please.'

He gave this careful consideration. So careful, in fact, she
worried Matron would return and scupper his chance to
answer. Finally, he replied, 'I followed the man I thought was

my business associate inside the Eagle. I failed to then find him, because it was the wrong person entirely. Then I heard the scream that drew everyone to the room where the girl had been killed. And then I was herded into the lounge area.' He snorted. 'Where Lady Davencourt made a scene, as one could have predicted.'

'Good recollection. And what about when you were in the lounge?'

He frowned. 'What about it?'

'Only that Constable Lowe mentioned to the chief inspector that you didn't stay in the lounge.'

Ever since Seldon had come around with Daisy's handbag, she'd been waiting to ask Sir Grainger why he'd really left the lounge. Because that meant he'd have had time to somehow slip into the room where Daisy was murdered and grab that elusive silver disc.

Sir Grainger eyed her in exasperation. 'As I said, nothing escapes you, does it?'

To her ears this sounded more like a plea than a defensive retort.

He sighed heavily. 'Alright, I've another confession. But it's the very reason I didn't mention the previous incident at the King's Arms. I realised when I was trapped in that infernal lounge at the Eagle with everyone that I had forgotten something important.'

'Ah! To take your medication?'

He nodded. 'Yes.' He grasped his head at the evident sharp pain this drew. 'Which is why I didn't tell the inspector.' His gaze shifted to the double doors. 'I couldn't say, "I'm a monster without it. Oh, and, by the way, the young woman who has been murdered in the very hotel I'm standing in, I dearly wished her dead!"'

'And had you experienced any rage that day at all?'

'None. Genuinely. You have to believe me.'

'If you say so,' she said noncommittally.

He sighed. 'Really, it's the truth, Eleanor. And, actually, there's something I saw... well, heard while I wasn't in the lounge.'

She leaned forward. 'Go on?'

He stared at the ceiling. 'Well, when I realised I'd forgotten to take my medicine, and knowing how stressful situations can trigger an episode, I told the young policeman I needed my "heart tablets". He allowed me to retrieve them. Well, I gave him little option.'

'And?'

He held his hands up. 'The manager.'

Her eyes narrowed. 'Mr Flint?'

He went to nod, then thought better of it. 'Yes. Portly chap. Burgundy waistcoat. As I took my tablets in the reception area, I realised he was in his office because the door was half ajar. I didn't think it odd he wasn't in the lounge with everyone else as I assumed he was busy making telephone calls and doing whatever one does when someone is murdered in one's hotel.'

'And was he? Making a telephone call, I mean?'

'No, that's the thing. He was standing behind his desk, which was disgracefully cluttered to my mind. And he was talking to someone in a whisper.'

'Someone you could see?'

'No. They were obscured by the door.' He paused. 'But I could see them moving behind that dimpled glass always favoured by hotel offices. I assume they believed everyone was in the lounge.'

Matron's voice filtered in to her again. 'Time's up, Inspector!'

'Quick,' Eleanor said. 'Was the obscured person male or female, would you say?'

'Oh, it was definitely a man.'

'How can you be sure?'

'Because I heard him speak.'

The double doors swung open. Matron's voice cut through like jagged glass. 'Out with you. Now!'

'Hurry! What did the man say?' Eleanor hissed.

He leaned forward and whispered with the last of his energy. 'I'm a ghost, Horace. You can't kill a ghost!'

26

'Oh gracious, Clifford, these poor people.' Eleanor's voice was choked as they neared the end of their twenty-mile drive. She pointed through the side window of the Rolls at yet another run of derelict houses, crumbling walls and collapsed burned-out roofs littering the outskirts of the town. Rubble lay everywhere in haphazard heaps. The telltale tattered shreds of wallpaper clinging to chunks of brick, the only tentative hint that normal life had ever flourished here.

She tore her gaze away. 'You said this area had suffered badly during the war, but I hadn't anticipated so much devastation.'

'Hence my having repeatedly tried to dissuade you from coming, my lady. It is not too late to return to Henley Hall.'

She shook her head. 'Thank you for your solicitude. However, I'd be the most awfully spoiled individual if I abandoned trying to get the answer we need right now because of the discomfort of seeing other people's suffering.'

'Spoken precisely like his lordship. Your uncle was never one to shy away from the task in hand, no matter what.'

'Besides, I've seen a lot worse abroad. However, it's hit

particularly hard being so close to home. In fact,' she said as he stopped the Rolls to let a man pushing a barrow of what looked like scavenged bolts and hinges cross the road, 'we should park up and walk. Driving in such a car feels as if we're parading through these people's tragedies in a solid gold castle.'

'Admirably sympathetic of you, my lady, but inadvisable. I fear we might return to a rather reduced vehicle if it is left out of our sight for even a moment.'

She frowned. 'That's not your usual unprejudiced outlook. Poverty doesn't render people automatic thieves.'

'Categorically not. However, Hartbridge already had a chequered reputation before the Zeppelin dropped its bombs here and then crashed, both events annihilating the only factories – and employment – in the town. As well as much else, as you can see. Unfortunately, the factories were never rebuilt, leaving most of the inhabitants without jobs. Those with the wherewithal and skills moved elsewhere, leaving the less fortunate behind. Then, as oft happens, others of a more unprincipled persuasion who had exhausted their welcome in other towns, moved in.'

'To what? There aren't even half the houses left.'

'Shelter doesn't always have the luxury of being even half a building, my lady.'

Something in his tone made her recall his confession that he'd been forced to live on the streets from the age of twelve. 'I know, Clifford. Let's just find our man.' *You can work out later, Ellie, what, if anything, you can do for these poor people.*

She willingly stayed put when Clifford got out to ask directions from any of the locals they passed, as he was met with surly looks and sour replies. If they replied at all. Many simply turned away.

'Oh dear,' she said as he slid back into the driving seat a third time. 'That last man looked like he was angling for a fight.'

'Not to worry, my lady,' he said calmly as he drove onwards.

'Fortunately, angling is my particular field. Anyway, we managed to come to a gentleman's agreement.'

'Oh?'

'That I would leave with my question unanswered and he wouldn't lay hands on me. That is at least the, ahem, repeatable version.'

She slumped back in her seat, watching more tattered tragedy pass by until he slowed the car again and gestured through the windscreen.

'We have arrived, my lady.'

A ripped and yellowed newspaper caught by the blustering, northerly wind whipped across the windscreen, momentarily obscuring her view. She climbed out of the Rolls and surveyed the tall chimney breast, blackened brick wall and perilously leaning arch that were the only remnants of the building. A dilapidated sign creaked back and forth on one rusted hinge, the faded letters just legible: Bell Inn. Underneath it, turned away from them, a figure appeared to be frozen in time as he stood motionless. *Your hunch was right, Ellie! Hartbridge is somehow at the centre of everything. It's the one thing that links Flint with Daisy and Mrs Harris. Their pasts – and their secrets – are buried among the rubble of this town.*

Clifford slipped a hand into the pocket where he kept his old service revolver, while Eleanor glanced around. Having checked to see which was the best way to cut off Flint if he made a run for it, she nodded at Clifford and stepped forward.

'Good afternoon, Mr Flint.'

The figure continued to stare into the distance without replying. She tried again, louder.

'I said: *Good afternoon*, Mr Flint.'

This time the man turned his head slightly, his shoulders slumping. 'Lady Swift.'

She shared a look with Clifford. She wasn't sure how she'd expected Flint to react – fight or flight, maybe – but not this.

After all, the man in front of her was a prime suspect in a murder and attempted murder. If Sir Grainger had seen and overheard Flint in his office the evening of the murder, given that Sir Grainger was then attacked, it seemed likely that Flint might have seen Sir Grainger as well. And, even though they'd yet to establish why exactly Flint would have wanted Daisy dead, as the manager he'd had the best opportunity to sneak back into the room where Daisy was murdered and take the silver disc. On top of that, he was the only one not herded into the lounge by Lowe and Brice.

Unnerved, she tried to keep her tone light. 'Your staff at the Eagle have been looking for you.'

Flint shook his head slowly. 'It doesn't matter. Nothing matters now.'

'Mr Flint,' she said more sharply. 'Why are you here?'

He turned around. For the first time, she noticed that his eyes were black. Although, rather than piercing, disturbingly they reminded her of the eyes of the walking dead she'd seen as a war nurse. She quickly stepped to one side as Clifford pulled out his revolver, but then waved him down. The face looking back at her had no fight – or flight – left in it; it was a grey mask punctured by hollowed eye sockets. There was no sign of the usual florid, overbearing man who had forbidden her from discussing Daisy's murder with his staff.

'Why am I here?' He swept his arm around the remains of the inn. 'Because I've nowhere else to go. This is where it all started. And this... this is where it will all end.'

Clifford stiffened, his finger on the trigger. She waved him down again.

Sounds more like a prophecy of doom than a threat.

'Do you know, Mr Flint, I've thought I was near the end myself several times as well. Yet here I am. Things are rarely as bleak as they seem. But perhaps that's because I've never seen... a ghost?'

Flint stared back at her, lips parted as if to speak, but no words came out.

'"You can't kill a ghost, Horace." Sound familiar? You see, someone overheard you, Mr Flint. Although perhaps you already know that. Perhaps that's why Sir Grainger is lying in hospital right now.'

Clifford raised his gun again. 'You've still a backbone man, use it! Tell her ladyship the truth. Now!'

Eleanor nodded. 'I'll make it easy for you. You must have known Daisy Balforth from when you both lived here in Hartbridge. It's too much of a coincidence you both coming from here and her ending up dead in your hotel. But the day Daisy was murdered, as we all stood in that room where she was lying, you pretended you had no idea who she was, didn't you?'

Flint groaned. 'Yes. All true.' His jowls wobbled as he shook his head weakly. 'But I didn't kill her.'

Eleanor held his gaze. 'We're listening.'

He hesitated and then took a deep breath. 'I recognised Daisy when she came into the Eagle that... that evening. But I couldn't tell the police afterwards because I thought... I thought she'd come to blackmail *me*.'

Eleanor frowned, thinking if this were true, the pretty young woman she thought she'd got a sense of was even further from the image she'd formed. 'Blackmail you over *what*?'

'This.' He jerked a thumb over his shoulder at the ruins behind him. 'When I was the manager here, I fell in with someone. Someone far worse than I realised. But I was too blinded by the chance to make money to truly understand.'

'How did you make that money, Mr Flint?' Eleanor said, sensing Clifford had already worked it out.

'I bought contraband alcohol and tobacco. And... other things. Then sold them through the hotel.' His head fell to his chest. 'But I learned my lesson. I've never done anything like that since starting at the Eagle. And it should have been that those illegal dealings never came to light.'

'How so?'

He jerked upright and whirled an arm behind him again. 'Look at it. Gone. Destroyed. Blown to pieces! And with it, all the evidence that I'd ever done anything wrong. All the records, the contraband goods. Bang! And everything went.'

Despite the sun, a bone-chilling gust of wind tugged on Eleanor's red curls, whipping them into her eyes. She swept them aside. 'So, you moved to Chipstone?'

'Yes. After struggling here for a while. It hit us all pretty quick that we'd been abandoned. There would be no help, no money given for rebuilding. So, I left and finally got a decent job – assistant manager at the Eagle. And then I became the manager.' He held her gaze. 'I'd learned my lesson, like I said. And, in all honesty, I was glad it was over. I'm not cut out to be a criminal. Living in fear of getting caught every day.' He swallowed hard. 'I thought the whole sorry chapter had died along with the best of Hartbridge. God rest its soul.'

'But then?'

'But then, after years of peace, the blackmailing started. A... a ghost from my past turned up, recognised me and demanded money to keep quiet about the contraband goods and... and the accounts.'

Clifford looked him over with contempt. 'Which you were also fiddling?'

Hunt looked at him 'Money tastes good, Mr Clifford, wherever it comes from.'

'So, you paid the blackmailer to save your job at the Eagle,' Eleanor said. 'But did you know about Daisy's breach of promise suit against Lord Davencourt before she was killed?'

'Not a word.' He looked at her disbelieving face. 'It's the truth, I swear!'

She shrugged. 'Maybe. But Daisy never served the lawsuit

herself, did she? It was her lawyer. So, was he the one black-mailing you, if indeed that part of your story is true? His name is Fisher.'

'It wasn't Fisher.' Flint hesitated. 'It was the person who was *shadowing* Fisher the day he came to meet Lord Davencourt.'

Eleanor glanced at Clifford, receiving an arched brow in reply.

Flint shrugged. 'It's the truth. I thought he was a pickpocket at first. They're a constant menace in hotels. Summer's worst.'

Clifford snorted. 'The salient facts only, Mr Flint!'

Flint held up his hands. 'Alright. Thinking the man following Fisher was a pickpocket, like a fool I grabbed him when Fisher was shown into the private room where he was to meet Lord Davencourt.'

Eleanor frowned. 'But why was that foolish?'

'Because I didn't recognise him, but he recognised *me*. And that's when it all went to hell. And that's why when Daisy turned up that day, I thought she'd been sent to demand more money.'

Something clicked into place. 'Which is why, after she was killed, you went back and checked the contents of her handbag, didn't you? You *did* go back into that room.'

He seemed about to refute her words, but he nodded instead. 'I thought she might have had some evidence on her of the terrible things I did at the Bell Inn.' His face crumpled. 'But it doesn't matter now. I'm as dead as she is.'

Clifford stepped forward. 'If what you've told us is the truth and you are prepared to tell the police, they can protect you.'

Flint's eyes widened with terror. 'You can't protect me from a—'

'Ghost?'

Eleanor jumped as Flint gave a deep wheezy gasp, his tongue falling forward as his mouth flapped for air. He collapsed onto his knees and then sprawled into the dirt. She stared in horror at the knife sticking out of his back.

'DOWN!' Clifford shouted.

She crouched and scanned the immediate vicinity, her heart pounding. 'That... that knife must have been thrown from behind one of the piles of rubble over there. Or,' she continued, pointing, 'that half-collapsed wall. There! There he is!'

She jerked up, ready to sprint after the attacker, but swung back down at Clifford's urgent tug on her arm.

'No, my lady!'

He's right, Ellie. You need to attend to Flint like you did Sir Grainger.

She nodded. 'Then I'll stay and you go!'

Clifford shook his head. 'With no time for the usual respectful formalities, I cannot. I left you on the golf course when Sir Grainger had been attacked and I haven't slept since. And that was before I had any inkling of the cold-blooded killer we are dealing with. The pistol I brought along is no match against someone who can throw a knife from a hidden position with such deadly accuracy. We need to get to safety. And Mr Flint to hospital.'

Feeling for a pulse, she pressed her fingers harder to Flint's neck where he lay still sprawled in the dirt.

'Actually,' she said with a shiver, 'it's too late. He was right. It is the end of the line for him. He's dead.'

27

'Eleanor, what were you thinking?' They'd delivered Flint's body to Chipstone's cottage hospital, Hartbridge not having one, and Eleanor was now on the telephone to Seldon. His voice fell to a pained whisper. 'I heard from Fenton at Hartbridge Police Station what happened. How am I ever going to keep you safe if even Clifford can't?'

She sighed. 'By doing what you do every day, Hugh. Catching the bad people who hurt the good ones. Though I wish you didn't have to.'

'Well, that makes two of us. But it does nothing to stop me being wracked with worry over you.'

'Hugh,' she said earnestly, 'I'm still alive and breathing, but Horace Flint isn't. Go galvanise your men to find the monster who killed him. If it's the same man as murdered Daisy – and attacked Sir Grainger – it's you I'm worried about. The killer's obviously as cold-blooded as they come. Or a maniac. Do take care! As for me, I promise you, after I finish this call, I'm going straight home.'

With Seldon having agreed on his part to keep her informed

of progress in finding Flint's killer, she and Clifford left the hospital, both in a subdued mood.

Finally, Henley Hall's imperious gates heralded the start of the tree-lined driveway, just as a rumble of thunder sounded overhead. Clifford anxiously scanned her face as he eased the Rolls around the central fountain.

'My lady, if I might respectfully suggest—'

His words were halted by Mrs Butters flying out of the front door, her apron flapping up over her uniform as the wind whipped at it. She rushed down the steps and skidded to a halt on the gravel as she bumped up against the car. 'Mr Clifford, beg pardon for rushing in front of the mistress but 'tis urgent.' She leaned down to address Eleanor. 'Miss Grainger telephoned, m'lady. She asked for you to go straight over to her eldest sister's the minute you got back.'

'Out of the question,' Clifford said firmly. 'Her ladyship needs to recuperate this afternoon.' He turned to Eleanor. 'Please allow me to telephone Mrs Wilton on your behalf. Whatever the issue is, it can wait, I'm sure.'

But there was something in her housekeeper's anxious headshaking that made Eleanor frown. 'Did Miss Grainger say what the problem was, Mrs Butters?'

'Yes, m'lady. It's Master Bertie. He's gone missing!'

Eleanor turned to Clifford. 'Drive!'

Twenty minutes later, she ran up the steps to the Wilton residence and was ushered in by the butler. In the hallway, the last person she expected to see emerged from the nearest door.

'Hugh!'

His reply was drowned out by the feverish calling from the top of the curved staircase.

'Eleanor! My baby boy! He's gone. Vanished!' Beatrice ran down crying uncontrollably. 'He's lost... or *worse*!' she wailed.

Constance appeared, and Eleanor pulled the two women into a hug.

'Listen. None of us can help Bertie if we think like that. And there is no reason why we should. He's a very bright little boy.' She tucked a lock of Beatrice's loose blonde tresses behind her ear. 'Now, you need to tell the chief inspector everything you possibly can.' She peeped over Beatrice's shoulder at Seldon. 'Need help?' she mouthed.

'Only all you can manage,' he whispered back.

In the drawing room she'd questioned Beatrice in, Eleanor gently pressed the still-crying mother into the corner of the sapphire-blue velvet settee. Constance kneeled on the floor and wrapped her arms around her older sister's waist.

'Deep breaths, Beatrice,' Eleanor said soothingly. 'Ah!' She smiled as Clifford appeared at her elbow with a silver tray. 'And some long sips of what I imagine is a lightly fortified tea.'

'I can't be...' Beatrice sobbed, 'taking... tea. I—'

'Need to stay calm. I agree. So, drink. Breathe. And think of every little detail you can.'

As Beatrice's sobs slowly diminished, Eleanor took a seat on the opposite settee. Seldon hovered beside it until she tilted her head, urging him to sit too. Having done so, he produced his notebook and ran a hand around the back of his neck.

'Mrs Wilton, please recount everything you can, as Lady Swift suggested.'

'You should be out looking for him now!' Beatrice wrung her hands. 'Surely every minute counts?'

He nodded vigorously. 'It does. And we will.' He looked quickly down at his notebook.

Something's wrong, Ellie.

Seldon cleared his throat. 'But first I need to know if he's disappeared before and where you think he might have wandered to this time.'

Eleanor sat forward, catching the anxious tone that accompanied his words, glimpsing the man behind the overworked policeman. She turned to Bertie's mother.

'Beatrice. Where were you when Bertie was with you last?'

Beatrice wiped her eyes. 'In Chipstone. We'd gone to the little park so he could count the railings. Twice as usual, so it took a while. Then we walked the long way past the black-smith's because he loves to watch the sparks as the horseshoes are hammered. That's just at the bottom end of the high street. We were walking back up the other side looking in the first of the shop windows when I stopped to... to...' She broke off into another round of sobbing.

Eleanor reached across to pat her arm. 'You're doing really well, Beatrice. Deep breath. Keep going.'

Seldon threw her a look of gratitude while Constance stroked her sister's hair and glanced imploringly at Eleanor, who waved a quieting hand. As Beatrice took a moment to control her tears, Clifford stepped over to Seldon and handed him a leather-backed, gold-embossed photograph album and a stack of five silver frames.

'Ah! Good thinking, man,' Seldon said. 'Are there enough here?'

Clifford nodded. 'I should say plenty, Chief Inspector. Your men will be able to recognise young Master Wilton as there are many recent photographs.' He turned to Beatrice and gestured at the pile. 'With your permission, of course, Mrs Wilton?'

'Anything. Anything!' Beatrice took a long sip of tea. 'Right, I'll try again.'

'Well done,' Eleanor said. 'So, you stopped to look in a shop window? Likely the milliner's, four doors along from the start of the high street?'

'Yes,' Beatrice said in a tremulous voice. 'I was... entranced by a hat. Which makes me the worst mother in the world because when I turned back to take his hand again, he'd... he'd...'

'Likely wandered off into another shop,' Eleanor said calmly. 'So, then you searched for him?'

Beatrice closed her eyes as if retracing her steps. 'Yes. He's done it before, you see. But if you don't let go of his hand, sometimes he gets terribly fractious. So, I looked up and down the street, still standing outside the milliner's. Then I peered across the road quickly. But only quickly because even though he's wandered off before, he's never crossed to the other side. It's one of the few agreements we've managed with him. So, when I couldn't see him there, I went into every shop on the side I was on.'

'And you asked every shopkeeper?'

'Only on my side of the street to start with, as I said. I was sure I'd find him in one of them, staring at something bright and shiny. Or spinning.'

'Spinning?'

'Anything that turns, actually. Especially if he can be the one to make it spin.' Beatrice held her handkerchief over her mouth. 'But he wasn't in the first shop. Nor the last. And then I tried every one on the other side of the street and they hadn't seen him either.' Tears ran down her face again. 'Oh, Eleanor, my baby boy! Where can he be?'

'Somewhere safe, I'm sure.' But as the words left her mouth, Eleanor felt an icy prickle of dread in her stomach. She buried it and hurried on. 'And which shop does he like visiting most, after the blacksmith?'

'Usually the cobbler, because he has all those metal plate things he repairs shoes with.'

'Usually?' Eleanor said as lightly as she could manage. 'Has he been favouring somewhere else lately?'

'Did I say "usually"? Oh, actually, yes! This week he spotted something hanging outside that rather,' she hesitated, looking anywhere but at Seldon before continuing, 'lower-class shop that sells all manner of unimaginable domestic things.'

'Like pigs' trotters, potatoes and drums of paraffin?'

Beatrice nodded.

'That's the Wrights' shop. They know most of the other townsfolk, so it might be worth starting there, Chief Inspector.'

'Good idea.' He wrote in his notebook. 'Excellent. Now, Mrs Wilton, what was your son wearing today?'

'Navy velvet breeches, matching jacket, white-and-blue striped shirt and' – she wiped her eyes again – 'a little matching hat.'

'The one with the ribbons?' Constance reached for her handkerchief as Beatrice nodded.

Eleanor realised she needed to hurry things along. 'Beatrice, how had Bertie been earlier today? Was he upset about anything?'

'No. But he doesn't show much, as you've seen.'

'No tellings off while you were out?' Seldon said.

'None. Bertie isn't the kind of boy you can tell off in the normal manner of children, Inspector.'

At his confused look, Eleanor turned to him. 'I can explain all about that on our way to Chipstone.'

He shook his head. 'Thank you, Lady Swift, but I shall not require you to come along. Your butler' – he threw Clifford a pointed glance – 'can run you home in just a moment. I would like to ascertain one thing from you first though, if I may.'

Something in his deep-brown eyes stopped her from arguing.

He rose. 'Mrs Wilton, please stay calm and as positive as you can. I will ensure you are kept as updated as possible. Will you kindly permit me to speak with Lady Swift in private somewhere before I leave?'

The door closed. Alone with Seldon in the library, she was about to speak when he reached out and scooped her hands in his, taking her breath away. Pulling her close, he buried his face in her fiery curls. Everything stopped, only her heart faltering marking any sense of time passing.

He suddenly pulled his head back, his cheeks crimson. 'I'm sorry, Eleanor. That was unforgivable of me.'

'No.' She gasped. 'Just unexpected. Delightfully unexpected.'

He let out a sigh of relief, but his voice was still filled with concern. 'After your telephone call... and then seeing you so soon afterwards, I... I just couldn't help myself. Eleanor, you were only feet away from a murderer. Again! Oh, blast it!' He ran an anxious hand through his dark curls. 'Why am I too caught up with all this to do what I want to do, which is whisk you home and lock you in a safe box.'

She smiled. 'Two reasons. Firstly, you're one of the most senior policemen in the South of England, purely because you are so dedicated and good at what you do. And secondly...' She leaned forward to whisper. 'Locking ladies in boxes is against the law. Trust me, Clifford would have done it to me years ago otherwise.'

'Well, the first chance I get I shall make him purchase one just your size and shape, anyway.' His cheeks coloured again. 'Both of which are too captivating, by the way. But right now—'

'You have a murderer to catch and a young boy to find.'

He groaned. 'But no men to do both!'

Ah! That's it, Ellie.

'And since I've already sent every available man to Hartbridge to hunt down Horace Flint's "ghost" killer, as you described him, I'm stuck.'

She frowned. 'So how many men can you spare?'

He shook his head. 'I've only a couple at Chipstone Police Station left. To look for the boy, I have Sergeant Brice, and your Constable Fry from Little Buckford.' He held out his hands. 'But that's it.'

She gasped. 'But, Hugh! That's only two! And Fry only has a bicycle!'

'I know.' He shook his head wearily. 'And I'm sorry you're having to witness the sort of impossible decisions I have to make several times a day. But catching a multiple murderer on the loose has to be my priority for the moment.' This time his cheeks paled. 'I know Bertie is only young, but his mother did say he'd wandered off before and always turned up. The second I have any men free, I'll dispatch them immediately.'

She shook her head. 'Not good enough, Hugh. Not that I mean any slight on you or the police force in that.' An idea struck. 'But don't worry, I've got a solution.'

'Eleanor, whatever it is—'

'Hugh,' she said softly, 'I'm thirty-one and can make my own mistakes. Bertie is only five and I can't allow him to suffer for someone else's.'

'There's nothing to suggest he's been...' Seldon looked into her eyes and nodded slowly. 'But I can sense you're feeling that all is not as it should be. However, Eleanor, there are simply no more policemen available. The minute there are—'

She raised a hand. 'Don't worry about it, Hugh. Send Brice over to Constable Fry's police house in Little Buckford and I'll do the rest.' She smiled. 'But, unfortunately, you will have to let go of my hands long enough for me to do so.'

28

Eleanor surveyed the packed main chamber in the dim light of the gas lamps. Outside, the day had already fled and night fallen.

'Gracious, Clifford, the Women's Institute members must have each brought friends and neighbours along. What an incredible turn out!'

'Indeed.' He gestured around the room. 'And your idea to commandeer the Town Hall as a centre of operations was inspired, my lady.'

'Sometimes having a title can be used for the common good. It's certainly helped secure us use of the hall. Which hopefully won't be needed for long, for little Bertie's sake.' She offered a few silent words heavenwards.

The shrill cry of an infant jolted her back to her surroundings. She glanced at the children scattered about. 'Of course, not everyone has relatives they can leave their young ones with. But they can't go out with them in this weather either.'

'A solution will present itself, panic not,' Clifford said calmly.

The chairwoman of the Women's Institute appeared at her

elbow, re-pinning her windswept nest of greying hair. ''Tis turning into a filthy night out there. Makes searching for the young'un' right tricky.' She took a deep breath and gestured at the sea of expectant faces. 'The troops are ready for you, Lady Swift.'

'For me?' Eleanor looked around. 'You know these ladies far better than I.'

'True, m'lady, but I saw the way you commanded this very room when it was filled fit to burst the roof off that time you gave your election speech.'

'Thank you, but' – Eleanor's thoughts flashed back to the last Women's Institute meeting – '"pretty words", as they obviously sound to some ears, aren't appreciated by everyone.'

The assistant chairwoman shook her head. 'Lilith and Jane called for Mrs Harris on the way, but there were no one in and the cottage were in darkness. And,' she continued, scanning the room, ''tain't no sign of her in here, m'lady.'

Eleanor's mind flipped to the smoking bonfire at the back of Mrs Harris' cottage but she shook the image out of her mind. There were more important things to focus on right now.

'I hope she joins us later,' the chairwoman said. 'No such thing as too many hands for a terrible business like this.' She gestured to the crowd of homespun cardigan- and shawl-clad women still waiting in four orderly lines. 'Right, we'll tackle the organising together.'

Eleanor nodded and addressed the crowd. 'Ladies, thank you so much for coming out at short notice and in foul weather. As you have now heard, a young boy has gone missing. We have a description of what Bertie was wearing and a table of photographs of the little fellow for you to look through.'

All heads swivelled to where Clifford was carefully removing these from the leather-embossed albums Eleanor had taken from Seldon.

'We have Bertie's last known whereabouts, that being

outside the milliner's at the far end of the high street. I do wish we had more to go on, but—' She broke off as the couple who ran the shop that 'sold all manner of unimaginable domestic items', as Beatrice had put it, staggered through the door. They were each clasping a large box.

'Mr and Mrs Wright! Welcome,' Eleanor called.

Clifford strode over and relieved Mrs Wright of her burden. Her husband seemed stage-struck by the number of women staring at him and shuffled his feet.

'Oh, you great lummock,' his wife said gently. She pointed to the boxes. 'Lanterns for everyone. Once they're built, course.'

'What a splendid idea,' Eleanor said, concerned that to build anything would take far too much precious time. 'Perhaps the front line of ladies might make a start while we continue agreeing the best plan?'

With a nod, the women nearest fanned out around the tables where Clifford and Mr Wright were setting out rows of empty jars, candles, boxes of matches and skeins of strong-looking string.

'Ah! And sand to keep the candles upright is it, Mr Wright?'

'That it be, Mr Clifford.'

Fifteen minutes later, the lanterns were assembled and twelve groups had been created with only the minimum of disagreements and one heated refusal to 'work with the likes of her!'.

'Cousins, too,' the chairwoman tutted to Eleanor quietly.

Across from the two tables of deftly created lanterns, Eleanor drew hasty circles in bold red ink on the town map Clifford had sequestered from its frame in the main council chamber. At his shudder, she waved a dismissive hand. 'I'll buy them a new one. Now—' She looked up at the sound of familiar voices.

'Don't go wasting time fretting. Her ladyship's o'er there!'

'Let's hurry over and she'll set us to rights then.'

She waved. 'Sergeant Brice and Constable Fry. Thank you for joining us.'

'Not that 'tis a good 'un, m'lady,' Brice said, showering a spray of water from his helmet as he shook his head. 'Chucking stair rods down already it be.'

'Raining heavily, my lady,' Clifford translated.

'Pfff!' A small wiry woman turned around from one of the lantern-making tables. 'Bit of water, ain't never killed nobody. A little boy lost 'tis all that matters.'

Looking admonished, Brice ran a hand over his moustache. 'Only meant as 'tis no night for women to be roaming wild in the streets.'

Eleanor let the 'wild' go. 'Well, the sooner we're out, the sooner we're back. Now—' She frowned. 'No, stop! We need a signal. A way to call everyone back.'

'Not a problem, my lady.' Clifford pointed upwards. 'The crowning glory of the Town Hall?'

'Of course! The clock tower. Assuming you can access the bell?'

'If no questions are asked,' he said in a low tone.

'Right. Shall we say a repeated double peal means to return to base? Hopefully because we've found our little man.'

At Clifford's nod, she clapped her hands. 'Perfect, then—'

'Evening, m'lady,' her staff chorused as they arrived, along with a group of young men manhandling a variety of baskets and hampers into the hall.

'Could take a goodly part of the evening and early hours to find Master Wilton,' Mrs Butters said. 'That's why Trotters and I brought all the tea, easy munching and sweet treats we could muster from Henley Hall. With 'pologies for being so bold, m'lady?'

Eleanor smiled. 'Not at all. I'm just delighted you thought

of it. Perhaps you'd be good enough to stay and be in charge of providing refreshments for each of the groups as they return for a break?'

'It'll be a pleasure, m'lady,' Mrs Trotman said. 'And we'll swap out any spent candles too while they warm their bones. Until as someone's too tired or wet and then we'll take their place in the search party.'

'Wonderful, thank you.'

Polly put her hand up, but then yanked it back down quickly.

Eleanor nodded at her young maid encouragingly. 'What is it, Polly?'

Jiggling anxiously, the young girl spoke hesitantly. 'I just thought, your ladyship,' – she gestured at the children, now huddled in a group – 'their mothers don't want to be taking them along. I could keep the littl'uns busy here.'

'An excellent idea, Polly. Lizzie can help you, too. We've plenty of ladies in the groups at the moment.'

Eleanor consulted her beloved late uncle's pocket watch and waved at the chairwoman who nodded back.

'Ladies!' Eleanor called, grateful for the instant hush that fell. 'You each have a lantern, have studied the photos, and know the signal to return here?' At the unanimous nod, she continued. 'Excellent. Then we'll head out in three minutes.'

As the women readied themselves and gathered in their groups, Eleanor frowned. 'Clifford, we have forgotten one thing! Each group needs a runner to sprint back. No point having the bell signal organised if someone finds Bertie, but has no means of telling you to sound it.'

For the first time, her butler looked doubtful. 'No immediate solution springs to mind.'

She clicked her fingers. 'The Chippers Fort Gang! I saw their leader, young Alfie, a moment ago.'

'I'm here, miss!'

She spun around and beamed at the small freckled, redheaded boy hovering nervously nearby. He and his gang of friends had helped her on a previous occasion.

'Alfie, I can't say how pleased I am to see you.'

He looked up at her. 'Me and me gang would like to help find the little kid, miss. If as it's allowed? But not for pennies or pies, honest.'

She laughed. 'Thank you, but you know I never engage a man's service without fair recompense.' *And their families sorely need those pennies and pies, Ellie.*

The boy's chest swelled. At her hurried explanation that the gang needed to divvy themselves out, one to each group to act as a runner, he nodded and started off to assemble his friends.

'Oh,' the young lad skidded to a halt. ''Scuse me, miss, but what about stopping Old Whistles and his lot from doing their second rounds? The leeries can help by leaving 'em burning!'

Clifford clapped him on the shoulder. 'Brilliant thinking, young Alfie! I shall organise it immediately.'

As the boy sped off again, Eleanor turned to her butler and threw out her hands. 'Am I ever going to speak Buckinghamshire, dash it!?'

'Actually, partly Scottish. "Leeries" is a term for the lamplighters, as used by Mr Robert Louis Stevenson in his poem of the same name. They can assist us by not extinguishing the street lights in the early hours as they would normally do. Only part of Chipstone is thus lit, but it will still be a help.'

'Superb. And Mr Whistles?'

'The head of the Chipstone leeries, my lady. I shall track him down now and then return here.'

'Via the train station, please.'

At his quizzical look, she tapped her temple. 'It's just struck me. Beatrice said she took Bertie there to wait for his father on the evening of Daisy's death because he loves to watch the steam from the trains. Oh gracious!' Her hand shot to her mouth. 'But supposing he's wandered onto one already?'

'An option not yet considered, my lady. However, if Master Wilton is not to be found at the train station, I shall instruct the stationmaster to telephone the stations down the line. We shall have every station alerted in' – he scanned his pocket watch, his lips moving imperceptibly – 'well under an hour.'

'Excellent!'

She looked at him expectantly, but he didn't move. Instead, he peered at her sternly. In reply, she reached out both arms and mimed taking the hand of an invisible person on each side.

'Come on Prudence and Patience, let's go.'

He nodded approval and strode out of the hall.

On the top step, she ignored the sheet rain and spiteful wind whipping at her hat as she addressed the crowd of over sixty women and twelve young boys.

'Ready, ladies?'

'As always. And for always!' the women's cry split the air.

'Then let's begin!'

The women hurried off to their allocated areas while Eleanor took a moment to focus her thoughts before setting off herself into the wild weather.

Four rain-soaked and wind-battered hours later, Eleanor's group returned forlornly to base without a result and without having heard the signal that Bertie had been found. The Town Hall was a flurry of activity and a great deal of wet and steamy coats. Half the other groups had also returned and some of the women were sharing blankets around their shoulders in an effort to warm up. The ladies of Henley Hall were dispensing tea and darting about with plated offerings of sausage rolls and cake slices, topping up every cup they came across on the way.

Eleanor, trying to hide her despondency, hurried over to the map of Chipstone to see what section her group could tackle next. She was intercepted by her housekeeper.

'M'lady, even your determination needs warming on a night like this.' She pressed a cup into Eleanor's hand.

After a couple of sips and a bite to eat, she felt her optimism returning. After all, they'd only just begun...

With the areas divided out again, the search resumed. As the night wore on, the numbers dwindled. Mothers had to return home to their families and the relentless rain took its toll on some of the older and less fit women. In fact, by two in the morning, Eleanor's group had abandoned searching as well and were sheltering as best they could in the lee of an old warehouse.

'Beg pardon, m'lady, but 'tis no good,' one woman said. Her words were whipped away on the wind. She cupped her hands and raised her voice. 'We can't even see, as them lanterns keep going out.'

Eleanor nodded and gestured toward the Town Hall, tuning into the fact that, like her, they must be soaked through and frozen to the marrow.

'You go ahead. And please let the other groups know to go home. Let's just hope this rain eases off. We've a long day ahead searching again tomorrow by the look of things. I'll just—'

'Do the same,' Clifford's firm voice said in her ear. He stepped out in front of her, enveloped in a trench coat, torch in one hand.

How did he know I was going to continue searching alone?

The cold finally overcame her. 'I c-can't, Clifford,' she said through chattering teeth. 'I c-can't stop feeling that Bertie's disappearance is the k-key to both Daisy's and Flint's deaths. And the attack on Sir Grainger. Which means...'

He's in danger! And Clifford knows it too.

She shook her head, rain running down her face. 'My brain keeps prodding me as if it knows the answer, but c-can't put it into words or images I c-can recognise.' She rubbed her fore-head. 'It's like there's a locked door between me and that part of my memory and I don't have the k-key.'

The torchlight lit her butler's face with an eerie glow. 'Per-haps, my lady. But I know a man who has!'

29

'In Uncle Byron's study, Clifford?'

Her butler gestured at the door leading out of the snug. 'It is this way, my lady.'

She rolled her eyes. 'I know where it is. I live here remember!'

They'd shot back to Henley Hall, and she'd quickly changed out of her soaking clothes. After a short bath, she'd slipped on her house pyjamas and had a snack. Even though she'd eaten little since lunch and it was now the early hours of Friday morning, she had no real appetite, her insides still knotted with worry over the missing boy. She took another sip of the hot tea Mrs Trotman had passed her a moment before.

'But why have you put him in there?'

'I did not. The gentleman, having asked me about each downstairs room, chose that one himself as being the most conducive.'

She shrugged. 'Maybe he wants to channel Uncle Byron's spirit?'

Clifford sniffed. 'He is not a medium, my lady.'

She left it at that. After all, the man had driven over at a moment's notice in the middle of the night, so if he wanted to play Mr Mysterious, let him. Like her staff, she'd only seen hypnotists in travelling shows or at the theatre, but she knew the more respected ones often treated cases like shellshock, apparently successfully. How he could help her she wasn't so sure, but she was willing to try anything that might find Bertie.

At the thick panelled-oak door to her uncle's study, she bent to tighten the belt on her robe, then jerked upright. 'Clifford! I'm still in my house pyjamas!'

'So you are, my lady.'

'But you barely concede to my wearing them in front of *you*.'

'Indeed, but the gentleman asked that you were "comfortably attired". With some ladies that might mean more appropriate dress, but in your case—'

She held up a finger. She appreciated his attempt at lightening the mood, but time was precious.

He nodded agreement and opened the study door.

Inside, only two small table lamps and a floor-standing bronze lamp in the shape of a long-legged bird were lit. Her eyes ran along the three walls of bookcases, the pair of high-backed chairs and the large rotating globe wishing, as she always did, that it was her beloved uncle waiting for her. Instead, from one chair, she could see the top of a man's head, a crown of black hair sticking up. Pleased at least that her visitor hadn't had the audacity to sit at her uncle's desk, her hand brushed the marble bust of Ptolemy as she stepped into the room.

At the sound of her entering, the occupant of the chair rose slowly. So slowly, in fact, he appeared to be growing out of the seat. When he reached his full stature, which was so great it made her stare in amazement, he turned, clasped his hands behind his back and nodded. She took in his wire-rimmed spectacles, pointed beard and long black jacket over a Cardinal-red shirt and matching tie.

'Good morning, Lady Swift.' His voice was far too soft to have come from such a statuesque form.

'Good morning, Mr?'

He smiled broadly. 'Mr Yield. Vitruvius Yield.'

'Ah! Well, Mr Yield, thank you for coming. And since I am in the dark, both metaphorically and literally here, perhaps you would be so good as to tell me how we are to proceed?'

He stroked his beard. 'That is entirely up to you.'

He gestured to the other chair, but she shook her head.

'I'm probably better pacing a moment, actually.'

He nodded slowly. 'Naturally. But pacing will not work. You will have to be seated.'

She went to object, but then stopped. *Remember, he's only here to help you find Bertie.*

She sat in one of the chairs next to the globe.

'Perfect,' he said, more to himself than her. 'Then we are ready to begin your session to unlock the door to your memory.'

'Oh gracious! But do you think you really can?'

He nodded again. 'Of course.'

'I know Clifford told you, but a young boy is missing. And I'm sure my mind is trying to tell me something, but I can't quite grasp it. We need to find him before... before he comes to harm. So, what do we do?'

'Hmm. *We* do not do anything. You do it all.' He took the other seat, bending his legs out sideways so he could face her. She watched in confusion as he reached out and wheeled her uncle's globe between them. 'Since you already have all the answers you seek.'

She frowned. 'Then why can't I hear them? It's too frustrating for words.'

'Yet frustration, like pacing, will only hinder your ability to see them.'

With a quiet click, the globe illuminated, instantly drawing her eyes to it. A gentle flick of his long forefinger set it spinning.

'Concentrate on the globe, Lady Swift, not me.'

She did as he asked and watched the rhythmic revolutions of green and brown, the main colours, flash by.

His tone was soft, soothing. 'I can take you back to the time it happened if you surrender to my words. Back to the time you saw what it is you want to remember clearly. It is very important to you.'

'It is.' She felt a compunction to look up at him, but kept her focus on the globe as his finger coaxed it to keep spinning.

They sat in silence for a long moment. The almost imperceptible sway the globe induced was peculiarly comforting.

'Your butler is with you,' Vitruvius said quietly.

'He usually is.'

'And he is now. With you, standing in that room. The room you have been trying to see. Where are you?'

'I'm in the Eagle Hotel. In... in Chipstone.'

'Where you have been before. But this time it is different.'

She felt herself nodding. 'Yes. Not good, different. Bad. Confusing. Everything is too quick.'

'Time is slowing as you look around. Any sounds are receding. You are in control of what you see. You can only hear your breathing. Breathe... Breathe...'

She became aware of her chest rising, then lowering.

Vitruvius' voice came again. 'Breathe as you stand there, In that room. With your butler, Breathe. Time has almost stopped. What do you feel?'

'I feel... confused. And upset.'

'Time is slowing... Slowing. What are you doing?'

'I'm looking. But I can't see it all in one go. I want to see the whole scene like a single photograph.'

'Time has stopped now. The scene is yours to photograph. Study each part of the room. Take as long as you need.'

Her shoulders relaxed. 'I need to see what has happened. To take in everything before Sergeant Brice comes in. I know something is wrong.'

'You have time. Sergeant Brice is not coming in. He is still outside the hotel.'

'Then I can look properly. Carefully.'

'Look as carefully as you need. Time is yours. Breathe. Look. What do you see?'

'A woman in housekeeping uniform. She is standing at the other side of the room. And a woman lying on the rug, wearing a pretty summer dress and yellow scarf. There is a gold mirror and Beatrice and Bertie are standing next to it. Now I'm staring at the other woman. Because she is so still. Too still. Too young. I can't stop staring. But I can't see all of her.'

'What is in the way?'

'Peregrine. He's kneeling over the young woman.'

'What do you feel?'

'... dread.'

'What's happening now?'

'Clifford. It's Clifford. He's dropping to his knees beside the young woman. I trust him to know what to do. Now I'm turning to look behind me.'

'Why are you looking behind you?'

'Because I hear voices. And running feet. In the doorway, there are people. Some I know, some I don't.'

'Who are the ones you know?'

'Lady Davencourt and Sir Grainger.'

'What are they doing?'

'They're both looking down at the young woman on the floor. Sir Grainger is just... staring, but Lady Davencourt is... gloating. Now the woman in the housekeeping uniform is fainting. It's Mrs Harris. Her arm stretches out as she falls. She needs help, I know, but I'm not moving. Beatrice is shielding Bertie's eyes from the... the body. Now waiters... yes, two waiters are helping Mrs Harris. One of them is giving her smelling salts... no, that's wrong!' She felt a sharp intake of breath.

Vitruvius' calm voice floated into her mind. 'Time has stopped. Breathe. You are seeing something important. Imagine you can write it down. Write. Feel your fingers close around the pen. What does the pen feel like?'

'It's Clifford's. With the inscription I ordered.'

'Write.'

Feeling as if she were in two different dreams, she was vaguely aware her hand was moving as if propelled by itself.

'Time is starting again. It is no longer yours,' Vitruvius' voice was firmer. 'The scene is fading. It is not your breathing you are hearing. It is my words. Slowly, you are coming back to me. To your uncle's study. To the spinning globe. It is going to stop turning now.'

She blinked repeatedly as the swirl of brown and green gradually transformed into the map of the world she knew so well. She looked up at the long figure in the chair beside her. 'I saw it all again! Mr Yield... Vitruvius! But... but' – she tapped her forehead in despair – 'now it's gone!'

Clifford wheeled the globe back into its normal position and stood in front of her. 'In your lap, my lady.'

'My lap?'

Vitruvius nodded. He gestured over the arm of her chair.

'My notebook?' She stared at Clifford. 'But I didn't have that when I sat down.'

'Perhaps not, my lady. Nonetheless, you wrote down your answer.'

'I did?' She glanced down at her notebook, then back up at him. 'That's it?'

'What does it say?' He leaned forward.

On the page there was a single scrawled line.

Bertie wasn't looking at the body!

She stared at her butler. 'Why on earth is that important?'

30

Day was breaking as Clifford steered the Rolls around the river of murky water running down the centre of Chipstone high street after the storm of the night before. A gloomy pall hung in the air as the weak morning light was smothered by a shroud of increasingly thick fog.

Eleanor turned to him, tears pricking her eyes. 'Oh, Clifford! I was wrong about going to the Eagle. I need to be—'

'Looking for young Master Wilton?' His tone was gentle. 'And where would you look, my lady? You and the rest of the Women's Institute volunteers scoured every square inch of Chipstone and the immediate outskirts for eight hours. There really can't be many places left to—'

She gasped. 'Don't think like that! Bertie's... oh gracious, he's so little. We can't have failed him.'

'My lady,' Clifford said sharply, 'you are doing all you can and have not slept for more than three hours in the last forty-eight, I fear.'

'I bet poor Beatrice hasn't even managed three!'

He shook his head. 'Actually, her doctor prescribed a sleeping draught. The Wilton's butler informed me that Mrs

Wilton slept, if fitfully, for at least part of the night. I would have advised the same for you, but you would never have taken it.'

'True. Oh, Sergeant Brice!' She waved at Clifford to stop the Rolls.

As the car pulled up, the policeman bent down to her window, his thick moustache quivering. 'Morning m'lady.' He pointed over to the clusters of women hurrying into the Town Hall. 'No offence, but' – his chest swelled – 'I noted as to how you was running things last night and, in your absence—'

'Reopened the hall and took charge. Splendid!'

His moustache quivered again. 'Although, the umm, the chairwoman of the Women's Institute is, ah, assisting. Formidable lady. In fact,' – he nodded to the top step of the Town Hall – 'there she is now.'

Eleanor leaned out and waved at the chairwoman. 'Sergeant Brice, please give her my apologies. I have to follow up a... a separate lead as to the possible whereabouts of Master Wilton.' At Brice's expectant look, she shook her head. 'It's a long shot and probably will come to nothing, so please keep on searching. I'll be back as soon as I can.'

He touched his helmet and hurried over to the Town Hall steps as fast as his portly form would allow.

As the Rolls sped off, she closed her eyes. *Let's hope for Bertie's sake it's more than a long shot, Ellie.*

'Oh dear, dear.' An officious-looking man of middle years whipped out from behind the Eagle Hotel's reception desk. His burgundy waistcoat sported an enamel badge bearing the word 'Manager'. 'One moment, please, madam!'

Clifford stepped forward. 'This is *Lady* Swift,' he said pointedly.

The man smiled obsequiously. 'Apologies, Lady Swift. And

what a delightful early visit you have made to us. Unfortunately, breakfast is not available for another half an hour. Perhaps you would like to wait in the lounge?'

She gave him her best smile. 'I didn't come here to partake of this establishment's, no doubt, fine morning fayre, Mr?'

'Quick. Jacob Quick.'

She gestured at his badge. 'Congratulations on your appointment.'

'Oh, thank you.' He rubbed a hand over the lettering. 'It may be temporary, but, well, I am hopeful.'

'Then don't let me detain you.' She went to step around him.

Concern flickered across his face. 'Not here to partake of breakfast, m'lady? Coffee, then?'

At her head shake, he drew himself up taller. 'Then what, pray, can the Eagle offer you at this extremely early hour?'

'I wish' – she pointed – 'to view the room down the corridor there.'

His expression turned to one of horror. 'Where the young woman was...' – collecting himself, he tugged on the bottom of his waistcoat – 'was found to have passed away? Impossible. Oh dear, dear. That cannot be permitted.'

'Mr Quick. I appreciate this must sound beyond unorthodox—'

'Or possible, since I am under strict instructions from the hotel owners. So, the answer is a most respectful, but resounding no, Lady Swift. With apologies, of course.'

'Of course,' Clifford said, with far too much compliance in his tone for Eleanor's liking. 'Instead, her ladyship will graciously consent to wait until breakfast is ready.' He waved her towards the lounge, whispering when out of earshot of the manager, 'As time is of the essence and it took a while for me to pick the lock before, I suggest we find Matilda, the waitress.'

· · ·

A few minutes later, Eleanor patted the arm of the trembling young woman who had flagged them down outside the Eagle a few days before. 'Don't worry, we would never dream of mentioning it was you who let us in.'

The waitress' hand shook as she turned the key in the lock. 'M'lady, if I has to lose me job to catch the evil person who did' – she gulped – 'what they did to that young woman in there, then so be it.'

'Beyond noble, Matilda,' Clifford said. 'But you won't, on her ladyship's word.'

She nodded gratefully. 'You've only ten minutes. At the most.' She looked anxiously over both shoulders. 'The staff all learned in the first hour, he weren't born with the name "Quick" for nothing.'

As the door closed behind them, Eleanor shivered at the coldness of the room. *Death really does leave her mark.* She shook her head at Clifford. 'I'm fine, but where to start?'

He tapped his pocket watch. 'We are hard up against the clock. So, to recap, from what you said and wrote down under hypnosis, you described seeing Mrs Wilton standing over there near the mirror.'

'Yes. And she was shielding Bertie's eyes.' Her brow furrowed. 'But I still don't understand why I wrote down that he wasn't looking at poor Daisy's body, but the other way. Why is that the missing link in all this? Assuming it is.'

He tilted his head. 'Which "other way" was Master Wilton's gaze fixed, my lady? Towards the door? Or his mother?'

'No, look!' She hurried over to the gilt mirror, which was still covered in white paper. Her hands were shaking slightly as she reached out. 'Good job neither of us are superstitious. Now, Bertie was looking right into it.'

He stepped over to join her. 'Indeed. Then he would have been witnessing the scene in reverse, as it were.'

Her eyes widened. 'That's it! That's why he's disappeared for sure.' Her face clouded over in horror. 'He *saw* something. Something the murderer wants to keep hidden.' She tried to quell her rapidly rising feeling of dread.

With Clifford's help, she tore off the paper. With the glass once more visible, they stared into the mirror, noting how different the room seemed in reflection.

He sniffed. 'From the disgraceful indent allowed to form in the carpet, this has not been moved in a very long time.'

'Then what we can see is what Bertie saw. Minus all the people and poor Daisy, of course.' She bobbed down to be closer to the little boy's height.

'An extra inch taller, my lady,' Clifford said. 'I noted Master Wilton's height while he and I were engaged in our, ahem, staring stand-off.'

'Right.' Her position adjusted, she looked in the mirror again. But no matter how carefully she scanned every detail of the reflected room, nothing came to her. 'Dash it, Clifford. I can't work out what he could have seen. Especially as, apart from you stepping around me to go to Daisy's side, no one moved. At least, not that I remember. Perhaps under hypnosis, I—'

'Mrs Harris. She moved, my lady.' He tapped his chin thoughtfully. 'In fact, she fainted.'

'True. But she can't have done anything while she was fainting.' She shrugged. 'And we've no grounds to suspect her of being mixed up in this dreadful business.'

'Nonetheless, perhaps you might be so good as to recreate the lady's faint while I watch as Master Wilton would have?'

'If you think it might help.' She rose and went and stood where the housekeeper had been when she'd dashed into the room.

He took her place, crouched to his haunches, jacket tails in his lap, and stared into the mirror.

'Ready? Right then, here I am fainting.' She let her body topple forward as best she could whilst fighting the natural urge to break her fall. Still prostrate, she looked over at his reflection. 'Well, Clifford?'

'Hmm. Despite your admirable performance, regrettably, it seems going out on a limb failed us.'

'Wait!' She jumped up. 'Limb! That's it! I knew something wasn't right. Ready to go again?'

'Ready.'

This time, she threw herself forward with a little more gusto, one arm outstretched, landing with a resounding smack.

In four strides, he was beside her, his gloved hand held down to help her up. 'My lady, really.' Gesturing at the red mark on her forehead, he reached into his inside pocket and pulled out a tiny tube of ointment. 'Arnica liniment. To be applied—'

'Forget the arnica, Clifford!' She sprung up. 'We need to find Seldon. Now!'

———————

31

'Oh, please let him be here!' Eleanor rocked back and forth in the passenger seat of the Rolls, willing it to eat up the last mile so much faster than it was. But even she had to concede the fog had now fallen like a grey woollen blanket, reducing visibility to little more than the car's length.

'Faith, my lady,' Clifford said calmly. 'They did not answer the telephone, but that does not mean he isn't there. And if he is not, someone will know how we can contact him.'

But as they finally drew level with Hartbridge Police Station, Eleanor spotted a familiar black Crossley parked outside.

'Oh, thank heavens! His car's here.' Not waiting for Clifford to open her door, she sprang out and dashed up the steps.

At the reception desk, a world-weary policeman who looked as if he should have retired before she was born glanced up at her in recognition.

'Good day, Lady Swift. I hopes you don't have any more bodies for us. One's enough, beg pardon for saying.'

'Lady Swift!' a deep voice called behind her.

Turning, she winced at the dark rings around Seldon's eyes and his sallow cheeks. He strode over. 'Is everything alright?'

'Yes. And no.' She took a deep breath. 'A private word?'

'Fenton!' He barked at the desk sergeant. 'Ensure I am only disturbed for news of a sighting of the fugitive. Or an arrest, preferably.'

In a closed, musty side room with nothing more than a bare table flanked by two chairs, Eleanor shook her head. 'You need some sleep, Hugh!'

Seldon ran a hand around the back of his neck. 'I was about to say the same thing to you. And it wasn't necessary for you to come all the way out here in this infernal fog. I said I would keep you informed if I'd had any progress on catching this "ghost". Which I haven't, blast it!'

'I'm not here to harangue you for a progress report, Hugh. I would never do that.'

He sighed. 'I'm sorry.' He frowned. 'Then why are you here?'

'We rang, but there was no answer, so we had to come.' She leaned forward urgently. 'Hugh, we know who has Bertie!'

He yanked his notebook from his pocket and nodded. 'I'm listening.'

'I'll give you the short version. I saw a hypnotist—'

His head shot up. 'You what? Even for you, that's pretty unusual.'

She shrugged and waved at Clifford who had entered the room behind her. 'Speak to my butler. Unusual, but effective. Anyway, after the session, we went back to the room where Daisy's body was found and re-enacted the events from the time I entered. Do you remember, Mrs Harris fainted?'

He nodded. 'Several witnesses, yourself included, mentioned that.'

'Quite so. But it wasn't until I tried to faint that I realised I've never seen anyone faint the way she did.'

'Because,' Clifford said at Seldon's puzzled look, 'the woman never fainted.'

Eleanor nodded. 'She only pretended to faint in order to grab—'

Seldon slapped the table. 'The missing silver disc from Miss Balforth's handbag!'

'Exactly! And Bertie saw her doing it. He was looking in the mirror – not at poor Daisy's body. Remember, Hugh, Beatrice said Bertie darted across the room as everyone was leaving?'

'Yes. Go on.'

'Well, he must also have seen Mrs Harris hiding the disc so it wouldn't be found in her pocket in case the police searched everyone. So, he ran across to grab it as Brice and Lowe were herding people out. He's like a magpie with shiny objects.'

'I see.' Seldon tapped his notebook. 'So, Mrs Harris has the boy, you think?'

Eleanor nodded. 'But no one knows where she is. Her cottage was in darkness and no one answered the door last night. She was burning clothes when Clifford and I went round.'

'Which suggests she's fled or gone into hiding.' Seldon's face was grim. 'Well, a madwoman could certainly have strangled Miss Balforth. And swung a golf club hard enough to almost kill Sir Grainger.'

Clifford nodded. 'And killed Mr Flint. Knife throwing, although usually the male preserve, needs no special strength. A woman can learn the skill as well as any man.'

Seldon rose and paced the room, which given its small size and the length of his stride was more a series of switchbacks. 'If Mrs Harris is our "ghost", then she must have grabbed Bertie and then followed you to Hartbridge and killed Flint.'

'Or,' Clifford said, 'maybe she isn't the "ghost". Suppose she is in league with our ghost?'

Eleanor nodded. 'That would make sense too. Which means, with Flint dead, Cramdon is our most likely candidate. I know he cooperated when we saw him in his offices, but maybe he decided it would have made him even more suspicious if he didn't, given we already knew about his connection with Lady Davencourt?'

Clifford nodded. 'And he cleverly shifted suspicion onto Mr Fisher when we returned.'

Seldon stopped pacing and spun around to face Eleanor. 'Whether Cramdon – or even Fisher – is our ghost or not, have you any idea where Mrs Harris might have taken the young boy?'

A tentative knock on the door interrupted her reply. Seldon wrenched it open with an impatient gruff.

'Fenton! It was a simple instruction. Do not disturb me unless you have a reported sighting of the killer. Or better still, an arrest. Well, have you?' He glared at the older policeman, who shook his head. 'Then what is it?'

'A woman, chief. Asking for you.' Fenton shuffled his heavy boots. 'Insisting more like.'

Eleanor tried to contain her frustration at the interruption and not glare at him herself.

Seldon grunted. 'Deal with her, will you, Fenton? I'm tied up here.'

'If as I have to, sir.' He swallowed hard. 'But you haven't met the woman afore as I have, so don't be surprised when I'm left guarding the front desk with no head. Mrs Harris ain't one to be told— '

'Wait!' Eleanor shouted in unison with Seldon, her chair falling backwards as she jumped up. 'Mrs Harris?'

'Show her in, man.' Seldon spun the astonished policeman around by his shoulders. 'And double quick!'

. . .

'Mrs Harris. Come in,' Seldon said authoritatively. He gestured to the chair he had vacated and picked up his notebook. He waved at Eleanor and Clifford. 'No, both of you stay, please.'

Eleanor tried hard to hide her disbelief as the drawn, pinched face she now knew all too well poked around the door. The woman shuffled in wearing a worn brown coat hanging open over a patched grey cardigan.

'Thought as you might be here,' Mrs Harris said to her with an edge in her tone. 'Can't keep your nose out of a bad business, can you?' She looked at the floor. 'I might be here on account of you, anyways.'

Eleanor glanced at Seldon but said nothing. She was impressed by how well he was hiding his evident amazement at the woman's appearance.

Seldon tapped the table with his pen to get her attention. 'Mrs Harris, before you say anything further, are you here to confess?'

'Depends.' She darted another look at Eleanor, then stared back at Seldon. 'On what you are laying out for me to confess to?'

'The murder of Miss Daisy Balforth and Mr Horace Flint. As well as the attack on Sir Grainger and the abduction of Bertie Wilton.'

Her mouth opened and closed, but no sound came out.

'Your answer?' He rapped the table this time.

'No!' she breathed, eyes wide. 'Murder? Me? No. Never.' Her face suffused with anger. 'And as for stealing a little boy what's barely out of his christening robe, what do you take me for?'

'Mrs Harris, I shall ask the questions! If not to confess to murder, assault and kidnapping, then why *are* you here?'

'Because of that little boy,' she said quietly. 'I heard he was missing and my heart... it as good as stopped when I thought of... of the harm that could come to him.'

Eleanor gasped.

Mrs Harris scowled at her. 'Just because a woman ain't had a child of her own, don't mean she don't feel summat. That she don't understand the loss.'

Catching Seldon's eye, Eleanor nodded. 'That's one thing we have in common, Mrs Harris. But you said you knew the harm that could come to Bertie?'

The woman hung her head. Eleanor's mouth was dry.

'Then you must know who has Bertie. If not you, then *who*?'

The room held its breath. The woman hesitated, her face a mixture of pain and anger. She finally seemed to win the battle with herself.

'Used to work in the old mill with me and Daisy and most of the rest of the street afore it got bombed. Then he—'

Seldon rapped the table again. 'Mrs Harris, who has the boy!'

Her eyes flashed. 'That mad dog who killed Daisy and attacked Sir Grainger. He's got the boy. He... he's evil to the core.' A look of pain crossed her face again. 'I... I realise that now.'

Seldon leaned down to hold her gaze. 'Did this person kill Flint as well?'

She nodded. 'They went way back. Back to when Horace was up to his neck in all sorts of trouble.'

Eleanor's brow knitted again. 'Are you saying the man who killed Flint is the same man he bought contraband goods from when he was the manager at the Bell Inn?'

Mrs Harris looked daggers at her. 'Ain't anyone or anywhere you ain't been poking about in then, I see.'

'Mrs Harris!' Seldon barked again. 'Answer Lady Swift's question.'

She jutted out her chin. 'Yes, it was him. He had lots of people fooled about him. Including me.' Her bottom lip shook. 'I feel such a fool.'

Seldon and Eleanor shared a confused look. She turned back to Mrs Harris.

'We know that Bertie saw something in the room where Daisy was murdered. Some—' She broke off with a gasp and scrabbled in each of her jacket pockets. 'I'm wearing the same clothes as when you gave Bertie the shoelaces, Clifford!'

He cleared his throat. 'Right-hand skirt pocket, my lady.'

Reaching in, her hand closed around the piece of paper she sought. 'Bertie's coin rubbing!' She held it out to Seldon. 'I never looked at it. I just took it and slid it into my pocket, thinking it was one of a hundred he'd done. Only it wasn't a rubbing of a coin. It's of the silver disc. He was telling me in his silent way what he'd seen and found!'

Seldon was studying the paper. 'There are numbers at the top. Eight. Seven. Four. Three.' He looked up. 'The last two lines are too faint, as if the original was damaged or defaced. But the second line is very clear. Hmm, I see now. This is a rubbing of an identity tag. They were issued to soldiers during the war to make identification easier in case they were killed on the battlefield. The numbers are the soldier's identity numbers.'

She took the rubbing back and ran her finger over the paper, her eyes sad. 'You're right. I saw too many of these during my time as a nurse.' She stared at the tag again. 'The name of the soldier is quite clear. "Aubrey Paling."' Her brow wrinkled. 'So, he must be the man with piercing black eyes who seems to have been playing cat and mouse with us since poor Daisy's murder.'

Seldon nodded grimly. 'And the "ghost" I've been chasing through the ruins of Hartbridge!'

Mrs Harris' cry silenced the room. 'Aubrey Paling is no ghost. He's the devil himself!'

Seldon snapped shut his notebook and wrenched open the

door. 'Fenton! Telephone HQ urgently.' He spun around. 'Mrs Harris, where is he now?'

'I don't know.' Her pained face turned to Eleanor. 'Honestly. If I did, I'd say. I wouldn't risk that tiny boy's life. Like I'm risking mine coming here.'

The harsh reality of her words jabbed like shards of glass at Eleanor's skin. *Think, Ellie, think!* She closed her eyes, her hands over her face, forcing the last forty-eight hours to flash back in her mind's eye like a jerky, moving picture. Until, suddenly, it stopped dead. *The map of Chipstone from the Town Hall!* The map she'd drawn red circles on, each one an area to search. Clifford had been wrong when he'd suggested they'd looked everywhere. When she'd drawn those circles, despite her fears, she'd marked out the areas based on where a small, very individual boy might have wandered. *Not* where a small boy might have been taken by a madman on the run.

'That's it!' she shouted, opening her eyes and staring at Seldon. 'I think I know where Paling has Bertie. He never left Chipstone.'

He strode from the room, shouting Fenton's name. A moment later, his voice boomed out again. 'Another false sighting? Where? But that means my men are miles away on the other side of this infernal town!'

He marched back in and picked up the telephone on the table. 'Patch me through to Chipstone. Urgently.' He caught Eleanor's eye and held his hand over the mouthpiece. 'I'll do my best, but it'll take ages to round up my men from Hartbridge in this fog, get them here and then over to Chipstone. I— Brice? Oh, Constable Fry. DCI Seldon here. Write down everything I tell you. Quick as you can, man.' But after each of the orders he fired off, his frustration increased with every reply from the other end. 'But that only leaves the two of you. Again!'

'Hu— Inspector!' She held out her hand.

Without hesitating, he gave her the handset.

'Constable Lowe. Lady Swift here. Change of plan.' Only a few moments later, she nodded. 'You've got it. We'll meet you and Sergeant Brice there.' She passed back the receiver, spun on her heel and headed for the door, calling over her shoulder. 'There's no time to waste if we're to save Bertie!'

32

Before Seldon's Crossley had even reached the end of Hartbridge's high street, Eleanor was having to clear the mist from the inside of the windscreen for him. Not that her efforts made much more difference than the wipers did on the outside.

'Blasted fog!' he muttered, craning his head forward until his nose almost touched the glass.

Clifford's measured voice came from the back where he was sitting beside Mrs Harris. 'It will, at least, hinder Mr Paling as much as us if he is attempting to flee, Chief Inspector.'

'That's some consolation, I suppose.'

They lurched violently sideways as Seldon avoided another car that loomed out of the fog at the last minute.

Eleanor tried to focus on something other than their painfully slow progress. The more they knew about Paling before arriving in Chipstone, the better. She spun around to face Mrs Harris. 'When did you first meet Daisy?'

'Hartbridge. Her parents moved into the same street. Daisy was half my age, but everyone played – and courted – together in them days. Course, she was the rose and me nowt but the

ugly mare. All the menfolk would sit up when she was about.'
She let out a long breath. 'Specially Aubrey.'

'Go on,' Eleanor said. 'Anything at all you can tell us might
be useful.'

Mrs Harris hesitated, but held her hands up as Eleanor
opened her mouth. 'Alright. Daisy had a thing about being on
stage and she got work in the small theatre that used to be in
Hartbridge. Afore the Zeppelin took it like everything else, that
was. Well, Aubrey, he saw her that first time at the theatre and
then...' She broke off with a desultory wave of her hand.

'He led Daisy to believe he'd fallen for her?' Seldon asked.

'Maybe he really had.' Eleanor cleared the windscreen
again.

'Oh, he had, alright,' Mrs Harris said bitterly. 'Like a dog
with two tails when he were with her. She stole him good and
proper.'

'Stole?' Eleanor shared a glance with Seldon. 'Mrs Harris,
did you know at the time that he was mixed up in illegal
activities?'

'I knew he were supplying Horace at the Bell Inn with
smuggled goods. And all the other bent landlords in the area, if
that's what you mean.' At Clifford's sniff, she pulled a tart face.
'Everyone had to make a living best they could back then. Not
so different either now, mind.' She shot a look at Eleanor. 'For
most of us, that is. Anyhow, after Daisy stole Aubrey away, he
married her pretty quick. Only he got called up not long after.
Then she got a letter with his identity tag inside saying as how
he'd been killed. She took it bad. And so did I. Felt as if the
bayonet they said had done for him had ripped through me too.'

Seldon swung the wheel, the car lurching violently again as
a hay wagon materialised in front of them out of the fog. The
danger avoided, he waved a hand. 'Go on, Mrs Harris.'

The woman gathered her thoughts for a moment. 'Well, not
long after the news of Aubrey's death, the whole place got

blown apart by that Zeppelin. After that, there weren't no jobs, so Daisy moved to Chipstone.'

'As Mrs Paling or Miss Balforth?' Clifford said.

'Balforth. Didn't know myself until I bumped into her when I also moved that way. Would have been about five or six years back that my aunt left me her cottage. Daisy'd moved to Chipstone a few years earlier, saying she'd needed a new start. Like I didn't! I was lucky to get a job on my knees scrubbing most of the day. And then Horace took me on at the Eagle three year ago. But Daisy, course, she did better. Got work in the theatre again. She was a beauty. Talked the manager there into letting her have a go on the stage like she'd done in Hartbridge, singing and dancing, you know. Right little success she was, as usual. And that's where he saw her.'

'He who?' Seldon yanked the wheel right as they drifted onto the rutted verge. Once back on the road, he repeated the question.

Mrs Harris sniffed. 'That Lord Davencourt, that's who. Saw her swaying about in all her stage frippery and then started going whenever she were in the show.'

Eleanor's eyes widened. *She must have been spying on Daisy all those years! Talk about obsessed with jealousy!* She kept her tone even. 'And when did you realise Paling wasn't dead?'

'I'd finished a late shift at the Eagle a few months ago and when I walked in my front door, my heart stopped. There he was sitting in my parlour as large as life, grinning like he'd never been away.'

'His explanation for being alive?' Seldon shook his head at the relentless swirling fog outside.

'Said he switched identity tags in the trenches with what was left of another soldier and deserted. Then gave himself up to the Germans. After the war, he found a way back to England, changed his name and laid low.'

'So why did he return to this area?' Eleanor said.

She hugged her shoulders. 'Claimed he'd come back for me. Realised he'd married the wrong woman, and he'd loved me all along. He... he were very convincing.'

Eleanor slapped her forehead. 'Of course! You never had a husband, did you?'

Mrs Harris' voice trembled. ''Tain't easy being given the looks of a whipped horse left out in the frost. It should have been Aubrey sharing my cottage, so when I first moved in I... I set it up so it felt like he were. Folks around just assumed the rest, and I let them.'

Eleanor winced to herself. *The poor woman pretended to herself – and everyone else – that she used to be married. Even to the point of having fake mementos to the husband she never had lying around the cottage!*

Eleanor shook her head sadly. She was trying to process all this while fretting at the car's painfully slow progress. 'And you thought you'd get your revenge for originally losing Aubrey to Daisy by telling him she'd been engaged to Lord Davencourt?'

'To me shame, now, yes. Only I never intended for any of the rest to happen. Honest. Only 'bout a week later Aubrey got it into his head – probably after realising he couldn't get any money out of me – that he could get some money out of Daisy. So, he stalked her for a couple of weeks and broke into her lodgings. Only instead of money, he found letters from Lord Davencourt saying as how he agreed with her finally to break off the engagement. T'were a mistake they'd both made. That's what he'd written. Aubrey had stolen those particular letters from her and showed me.'

Eleanor's breath caught in her throat. 'So, they did end the engagement by mutual agreement!'

Seldon nodded without taking his eyes off the grey shroud beyond the windscreen. 'Whose idea was it to blackmail Lord Davencourt, Mrs Harris? Before you reply, I should advise you,

you are not bound to answer but it might harm your defence later—'

'Oh, to hang with any of that!' she cried. 'Are you going to save that little boy or not?' At his nod, she slumped back against her seat. 'Then I'll tell you everything and at least go to me grave an honest woman. Aubrey then found out about Lord Davencourt inheriting his father's estate. He told this lawyer who he'd known from way back—'

'Mr Fisher?'

'That's right. And together they cooked up that breach of promise scam.'

Eleanor nodded to herself. 'So, Fisher met Lord Davencourt at the Eagle and served him the notice on Daisy's behalf, although Daisy had nothing to do with it. And Flint was telling the truth about it being the "ghost" from his past who was following Lord Davencourt. Poor Flint. He wrote his own death warrant when he grabbed what he thought was a pickpocket.'

Mrs Harris nodded back. 'After Aubrey'd been stalking Daisy for a while, she caught him breaking in. She was too terrified to tell anyone. And when he then came up with the breach of promise scam, he told me she didn't want anything to do with it. But he put the fear of God into her and made her agree.'

Eleanor shook her head, imagining just how he'd have done that. 'The fear of the devil, more like!'

Mrs Harris shrugged. 'Anyway, he still didn't trust her. So, the night she... she were killed, he followed her to the Eagle and found out that she'd arranged for Lord Davencourt to meet her there so she could give him his letters back and then run away.'

Seldon pursed his lips. 'Which explains the suitcase.'

Eleanor spun around. 'What suitcase?'

'I sent one of my men to search Horace Flint's rooms late last evening. He unearthed a small suitcase hidden at the bottom of the wardrobe. It held a few clothes and personal belongings pertaining to Miss Balforth.'

Clifford leaned forward. 'Given by Miss Balforth to Mr Flint as the manager to place somewhere secure while she met with Lord Davencourt, in all likelihood. Because she feared she might have been followed perhaps, Chief Inspector?'

'Almost certainly,' Seldon said. 'And then I imagine Horace Flint was too scared to hand it over to the police since, I now realise, he had worked out who killed Miss Balforth.'

'And he felt too guilty to throw it away,' Eleanor said. 'Poor Daisy. She was trying to do the right thing all along.'

Seldon tapped the dashboard. 'The truth, Mrs Harris, about the night Miss Balforth was murdered.'

Her words stuttered out. 'I was working when Daisy came in. I didn't know Aubrey had followed her, I swear. I saw Horace lead her into a room, so I snuck along to see what was going on. But when I went into... that room, oh, it were too awful! I screamed. She was lying so... so still. Then I saw Aubrey's identity tag on the floor, like it had fallen out of her bag. And... and I knew.'

Eleanor took a deep breath. 'Daisy must have still loved him to have carried his tag with her always, despite everything.'

Seldon shook his head. 'It was ironic then that it should fall from her bag and proclaim to the world who her killer was!'

Mrs Harris wiped a tear from her eye. 'I pretended to faint and grabbed the tag. Then as the other staff helped me up, I hid it under the edge of the rug, thinking I'd be able to sneak back quick and destroy it.'

'But when you returned, it had gone?' Eleanor said.

'It had. I thought Aubrey'd found it so, like a fool, I asked him. He said he hadn't, and he'd kill me if I told a soul about it.' Tears fell down her cheeks. 'I was so scared. And then he shouted it must have been that bloke with the white whiskers who'd taken it because he'd seen the man slinking about in the lobby afterwards.'

'Sir Grainger,' Eleanor said.

'Oh, but Aubrey were like a mad devil by then. Had this fierce fire in his eyes and swore he was going to get the tag back, whatever it took!'

'Which is why he attacked Sir Grainger. But Sir Grainger had only left the lounge to retrieve some medication from his car.'

Mrs Harris swallowed hard. 'Aubrey fell through my door that evening, shirt covered in blood, saying as how he'd searched Sir Grainger's body but there weren't no tag on him. And then... then he asked me to marry him.'

Seldon's gaze swung away from the windscreen. '*Marry* him?'

'Yes!' Mrs Harris cried. 'But you can't even begin to know what his words meant. I'd dreamed of him being mine since ever I could remember. But' – her jaw clenched – 'I realised it were all a lie! Like everything else about him. If I'd married him, the law would have stopped me going up against him in court and telling as I knew he killed Daisy and all his other wicked deeds. He...' – a sob wracked her body – 'he didn't want me for a wife. He just wanted to keep me silent.'

'And then you burned all those keepsakes when you finally realised that Paling wasn't the husband you'd desperately wanted all those years.' Eleanor's voice was gentle. 'It sounds like poor comfort, I know, but his feelings for you must be enough that he didn't dispatch you the same way as Daisy.'

Mrs Harris shook her head. 'Thank you. But 'tis only hell that's got a place for me now. I... I tried to stand up to him when he said I needed to tell him about everyone who might have had a chance to grab his tag. When I said no, he... he threatened to kill me again.'

'You're doing really well,' Eleanor encouraged. 'So, you talked Aubrey through who was in the room. And then?' But as she asked, her stomach twisted.

'I... I remembered that little lad had let go his mum's hand

and run across the room as we was all going out. Oh, if only I
hadn't said, because Aubrey realised he must have taken the tag.
I tried to talk him out of going after the boy, but he tied my
wrists and locked me in me bedroom. But after hours of rubbing
the strings he bound me wrists with against the broken leg of
the bedpost, I managed to get free. Then I climbed out the
window onto the ledge that meets the apple tree in the back
garden.'

Seldon rapped the dashboard again. 'Mrs Harris, I am officially charging you with several counts under the Accessories
and Abettors Act of 1861.' He ran a hand around his neck. 'But,
unofficially, I am applauding your bravery for coming forward
to save young Bertie Wilton. I will mention it to the judge.'

Eleanor's face clouded over. 'What I don't understand,
though, is why Aubrey didn't let Bertie go the minute he'd got
the identity tag back?'

Seldon cleared his throat. 'Aubrey Paling is clearly the worst
kind of devil, as Mrs Harris has said.' He avoided Eleanor's
eyes. 'The kind who understands the power of a hostage. Especially a young one. And especially when he's cornered!'

33

From the shelter of a copse of beech trees high on the opposite bank of the river, the sprawling stone edifice seemed more fortress than disused mill. Eleanor stared in dismay at the nine floors of the monolithic block that rose starkly from the now low-lying fog. The sheer sides were punctuated only by small windows, the glass and wooden frames long since gone. On the far right-hand wall, a rudimentary fire escape, formed from a series of hammered-in iron rungs, ran from the roof to the ground.

She shook her head in despair. Not only was the whole building perilously dilapidated, but it offered myriad hiding places for a fugitive. Assuming her hunch was right, of course, and Aubrey was here at all.

'It's certainly ghostly enough for a ghost, Clifford,' she said in a low voice, just as a sharp wind blew her hat off into his deftly outstretched hand.

'Without a doubt, my lady. And as you noted on the way here, Mr Paling would know the basic layout of the mill here in Chipstone if he used to work in a similar one in Hartbridge.' He handed her hat back. 'The two were, indeed, owned by the same company at one time. But we do have surprise on our side.'

'True. But Aubrey still holds the most important card. Little Bertie.'

A few yards behind them, Seldon was addressing Sergeant Brice, Constable Fry and Constable Lowe. Just beyond them, the Women's Institute stood awaiting their instructions. With Clifford on her heels, Eleanor ducked through the yellowing ferns to join them.

Seldon stepped to her side and addressed the attentive women in a hushed voice, only Eleanor catching the reservation in his calm, authoritative tone. 'Ladies, I will be honest. I am as grateful as I am troubled that we are reliant on your help. But there is no choice. I am here to catch a man who has already proven he has no morals or mercy. Therefore, please understand, the only part I can allow you to play is one from a distance.'

Quiet nods ran through the crowd.

'And trust me. The safety of the young boy is as paramount to me as it is to you.' His lean face looked even more tense as he gestured to Eleanor to join him away from the other women.

She jumped in first. 'Hugh, I'm as concerned about you as you are about me. Don't waste precious seconds telling me to be careful.'

He shook his head. 'Don't fight me, Eleanor. Not this time. If you can't do it for me, do it for Bertie. Because I shan't be able to focus at all in there if I'm worrying about you. But I won't ask you to stand by and do nothing. I know that won't happen. Instead, just promise you'll still be in one piece at the end' – he ran a hand through his wind-whipped curls – 'so I can tell you what precious really is.'

'Promise,' she breathed. 'Now, you be careful as well!'

With a discreet brush of her hand, he strode back. 'Ladies. Please follow Lady Swift's lead.' He threw her a last beseeching look. 'And her circumspect instructions.' He waved to the men and moved forward.

Clifford hesitated until Eleanor nodded. 'Bertie needs you more than I do. Go! And it's my turn to insist you keep Prudence with you.'

She watched their hunched-over forms clamber down the bank to the half-collapsed bridge submersed in fog. The fog was a double-edged sword. On the one hand, it would make it harder for Paling to spot them. On the other, it would make it easier for them to step on a rotten board and plunge into the rocky river below. Once they made it safely over the bridge and reached the mill at least she knew Seldon and Clifford were armed, but it gave her little comfort. Paling could choose a dozen places to hide. Places perfect to throw a precisely aimed knife, like the one that had ended Flint's life in a heartbeat.

When the men were no longer visible, Eleanor motioned for the women to crouch low and follow her. Creeping forward to the edge of the camouflaging scrub, she swept the buildings with her field glasses, silently cursing the elements again. The fog was so dense that even the churn of the river seemed muffled. She strained to hear any noises from the mill, but her racing pulse filled her ears. Shaking her head, she took a deep breath until the pounding was replaced by her mother's calming voice. *Never fear what hasn't happened yet, darling girl. You are always strong enough, whatever it may be.*

'Thank you, Mother,' she whispered.

Signalling to the ladies to stay silent and hidden, she returned to scouring the mill. For what seemed like an eternity, nothing. Then movement! On the third floor, a man's form creeping past an opening which fell to the turbulent river below. Then another figure only feet behind. The first stood taller and waved to the other.

Hugh!

Even with the poor light and fingers of fog, there was no

mistaking his broad frame and commanding stance. In a blink, he cleared the opening and was lost from view. The second followed, the outline of his police helmet just visible before he disappeared.

Constable Lowe!

She relayed what she'd seen along the line of women as she peered harder through the glasses. A sharp cry made her throat constrict. But then the flurry of a grey heron shooting skyward from the reeds let her breathe again.

But if that startled you, Ellie... Before she could focus the field glasses, something flashed past her vision.

A roof slate. That came from above!

She scanned higher up. And then saw it. Along the knife-edge pinnacle of the mill roof, a figure held another, much smaller, by its collar as he urged it ahead of him. Fighting her rising panic, she quickly scanned the building, but there was no sign of Seldon or the others now.

You can't risk alerting Paling by hollering for Hugh. He's evil enough to do the unthinkable and throw Bertie off the roof if he needs to! And who knows if Hugh will even hear you?

Spinning around, she whispered four hasty instructions. 'But *only* if you see my sign,' she repeated.

The chairwoman yanked out several pins from her hat. 'Won't work if the wind takes it afore you get a chance, m'lady.'

'Good point.' She stared back up at the roof, driving the pins into her hat to keep it firmly in place. 'We haven't long. Six of you creep inside and try to find any of our men and let them know where Paling is. As silently as you can. They'll be safe so long as he's on the roof. The rest stay here and wait for my signal.'

The chairwoman nodded. 'Will do. But how are *you* going to stay safe, m'lady?'

Having no answer, she patted the other woman's arm and set off. Keeping low, she scrambled down the muddy bank, snagging her trouser leg on a gnarled branch. Crossing the bridge in the fog was even harder than she'd imagined. She narrowly avoided falling through the gaps left by missing planks and tumbling over the edge through those left by the missing handrails. Below, the river shot past, a roiling tide of angry water. Jumping over the last gap, she sprinted across the open ground to the mill. From there, she shadowed the wall until she reached the far corner of the building.

'Dash it!' she muttered.

Up close she could see that many of the rungs forming the fire escape down from the roof were now little more than jagged points of rusted iron. She had no idea if they were still safe to hold. If one crumbled beyond the second floor, let alone the eighth or ninth, she would almost certainly break her back plunging onto the stony ground below. Gritting her teeth, she started climbing...

She reached the third floor. *Still in one piece, Ellie. A third of the way up and clear of the fog.* She took a deep breath. That also meant if Paling looked over the side, he'd see her.

With no alternative, on she climbed. But level with the fifth floor, her coat sleeve snared on the sharp point of a broken rung. Praying the current one she was holding was sound, she held on with only one arm at a time while she shrugged off her coat.

On she climbed again. Past the sixth, seventh and eighth floors, blood now streaking her palms from the flaking iron cutting into her fingers. Light-headed, and not daring to look down, she reached the last rung of the ladder and, praying it would hold, heaved herself up and onto the roof.

'One move, copper, and the boy's dead!'

She rose slowly, hands held up in surrender. In front of her, a raggedly dressed man with the most piercing black eyes she'd ever seen held a knife to Bertie's throat. His lithe physique seemed honed more by hard times than hard work, the dark creases in his forehead accentuating his ferocious scowl. It seemed he'd either dispensed with a hat this time, or it had blown away. She silently thanked the chairwoman for her extra hat pins.

She tentatively stepped forward and then saw the rafters had collapsed, leaving a large hole that dropped dizzyingly to the bottom of the mill, nine storeys below. She forced herself to slide around it, looking at Paling, not the boy or the drop.

'I'm not the police. How could I be? I'm just a woman.'

A man doesn't see a woman as a threat.

Paling spat as he tightened his grip on Bertie. 'Don't move I said! Who are you then? And what are you doing up here?'

She stopped only a few feet from Paling and Bertie. 'I'm no one, Aubrey.' She smiled and nodded to the wide-eyed young boy. 'It's alright, Bertie. You don't need to be scared now.'

Paling pointed the knife at her. 'No one, are ye? Well, you know my name. And you made it all the way up them rungs, didn't you? I don't know no woman what could do that. What's your game?'

She kept her voice calm. 'My "game" is to see that the little boy you have here stays safe.' She held his gaze. 'He's only five years old.'

'So?' A malicious grin split Paling's face. His tongue ran along his bottom lip. 'Younger the better. More of a bartering tool if the police ever do catch me up. Course, I might decide he's more trouble than he's worth.' His eyes glinted with pure evil as he shoved the boy towards the chasm.

Eleanor's brain raced. Bertie blinked slowly at her. *He understands. But does he understand enough?* She held Paling's fierce stare. 'Well, for now, why don't you let him sit? His legs are trembling. You'll end up having to carry him otherwise, which will make escaping much harder, won't it?'

Paling scowled, but pushed Bertie's shoulder, making him bob down.

She smiled again at the young boy. 'Bertie. Paton. Bravo for being so strong. And brave!'

Aubrey shot her a suspicious look. 'I thought the boy's name was Wilton?'

She shrugged. 'Paton is his middle name.' She noted the expression of concentration now filling Bertie's face as he shuffled the toes of his leather sandals to line up with the front of Aubrey's tattered boots. 'But you didn't drag Bertie up here to discuss what he was christened, did you?'

From where she stood, she could see what Paling couldn't. Seemingly lost in his own world, Bertie ducked his hand inside his jacket, then pulled it out, his fist closed.

As he glanced up at her, she nodded imperceptibly. 'Bravo, Bertie. Won't be long now.'

Aubrey growled. 'Don't see as how you're in any position to be making statements like that. I'm in charge of how this ends, woman. I don't know what you think you're doing up here, but me and the boy—'

'Are going nowhere.'

Paling jerked around. Seldon stood ten feet away, revolver at the ready, the two policemen and Clifford fanning out behind him.

Aubrey whipped Bertie in front of him, the knife at the young boy's throat again. 'I'm telling you, I'm walking out of here, copper!'

Stay calm, Ellie. This isn't over yet. She inched forward, marvelling at how collected Seldon's tone was.

'No can do. I won't let you take the boy, Paling. But let him go and we can make a deal.'

Paling laughed curtly. 'I know your sort of deal! I give you the boy and you still take me down. NO DEAL!'

Seldon glanced behind him at Clifford, who also held a revolver pointed at Paling. 'It looks like a stalemate. So, what do you suggest?'

Aubrey dug the tip of the blade into Bertie's neck. 'Stalemate? Before a bullet reaches me, he'll be dead. How about my deal *now*?'

The murderous look in his eyes left Eleanor in no doubt. *He means it.* She inched forward again, relying on Paling seeing the policemen and Clifford as more of a threat than her.

Seldon's face blanched. He let the revolver swing on his finger as he held up his hands. 'Okay, okay. What do you want?'

'Out. I want OUT! But I don't trust you an inch. I'll talk to her.' He tilted his head in Eleanor's direction.

She waved Seldon down as he opened his mouth. 'You're quite right, Paling. You can trust me.' She glanced at Seldon out of the corner of her eye.

He nodded imperceptibly to her as she had done with Bertie.

Paling grinned in triumph. 'On the ground. All of you except her!'

Seldon gestured to his men and Clifford to do the same. Clifford laid down his revolver, one brow arched in her direction. Once they were spreadeagled on the flat section of the roof, Paling waved the knife at her.

'Listen, woman, and listen good. I want—'

She raised her hands. 'Do you know, Mr Paling, I don't care what you want.' She unpinned her hat. 'But what happens to the young boy? *That* I care about deeply.' With a deft throw, she let her hat fly out over the back of the building.

Paling followed it with his eyes. 'What the—'

A cacophony of shouts, screams and noises rent the air below. Instantly, Eleanor threw herself forward. Paling, distracted by the commotion, reacted a split second later. But a split second was all she needed to grab Bertie with one hand and push Paling sharply with the other.

Paling's face suffused with rage. He tried to stop himself from falling backwards, arms whirling, but he stayed rooted to the spot. He stared down at his feet in disbelief. 'Little bastard tied my ankles together!'

He tried to jerk them apart, but Bertie's laces held. His face a mask of malevolence, he raised the knife and flung it at Eleanor as he toppled backwards, his cry following him to the ground, nine floors below.

34

Eleanor shook her head with a grateful smile. 'No, thank you. You still understand all these ladies so much better than I. This is absolutely your meeting.' She glanced around the packed Town Hall, delighting in the warm blanket of sisterly camaraderie enveloping her.

The chairwoman of the Women's Institute chuckled. 'There's not a soul in this hall as would say you've anything but generosity and the fiercest of courage running through you, m'lady.'

The woman on Eleanor's left nodded vehemently. 'Fancy you risking your life climbing up them iron steps to save that little lad. ''Tain't an ounce of stuffy or la-di-da lady 'bout you. Even with you having a butler and everything.'

Eleanor groaned. 'Yes, but don't tell him, will you? I might just get away with not quite cutting the mustard as the lady of the manor then.' She looked down at the multitude of dressings she still sported on her badly cut fingers. 'Mind you, you should have heard the telling off he spent most of last evening dispensing to me.'

This drew more laughter, which rippled around the table until the chairwoman rose.

'Ladies.' She waved an arm over to the raft of boxes stacked against the nearest wall. 'We are here to deliver on our promise to petition for women to have the chance to join the police force again. And, along with the exceptional organisational efforts of Lady Swift, you've all worked very hard to produce an eye-catching set of materials.'

Eleanor raised her hand. 'Forgive me interrupting. I just wanted to say I was so caught up in... well, that ugly business, that in truth the planning and preparation came from my hard-working staff, not me.'

''Tain't no matter who did what,' the chairwoman said. 'But on that count, 'tis only right they have a say too, which I sorted first thing this morning.' She smiled at Eleanor. 'With a bit o' help from a gentleman who's rather partial to his long-tailed suit and telling off his mistress.' The room laughed again. 'Ladies,' the chairwoman continued, 'it struck me while I was running over everything we did for that little boy, we've no need of owt fancy to show what we women can do.'

'That's true!' a voice called out.

'We showed it t'other night. And yesterday, alright!' another replied.

The chairwoman nodded. 'And given the sombre events of yesterday, I feel a colourful rally might be inappropriate, even though, of course, the young boy was unharmed. Therefore, I propose a simple procession to the police station, wearing our rosettes and carrying those wonderful posters would be more appropriate. What do we think?'

On the steps of the Town Hall, bathed in the morning sun, Eleanor thought she might burst with pride as the women arranged them-

selves for the *County Herald* photographer. Sunday best outfits
were adjusted, neatly brushed hats pinned in place. Sliding into
the back row, she held her poster high, grimacing as her aching arm
muscles reminded her of her epic climb up the mill building.

The rows of Women's Institute members set off seven wide
and five deep, but by the halfway mark had swollen to almost
double. Their raft of unannounced supporters had not only
appeared and fallen into formation but, confusingly, most had a
rosette and a poster. Then she saw Clifford, flanked either side
by Polly and Lizzie, each holding boxes, and Mrs Trotman and
Mrs Butters waving clipboards and pens. Even Gladstone was
joining in, woofing encouragement.

By the time they reached the top of the high street, their
unified presence was so striking, the rest of the town fell back to
offer them clear passage. Horse-drawn carts were steered aside
and delivery vans stopped. Encouraged by the rousing cheers
that rang out and the lines of clapping shopkeepers who
tumbled from their doorways, the procession marched on
proudly.

Word always travelled fast in this part of the world, Eleanor
knew. So, it was no surprise to find Sergeant Brice waiting on
the top step of the police station, his walrus moustache quivering as he shuffled his boots. Constables Fry and Lowe hovered
in the open door, wide-eyed and repeatedly nudging each other.

This time, the chairwoman would hear none of it. With a
firm nod, she waved Eleanor up the steps. At the top, Eleanor
held out the petition and signatures.

'Sergeant Brice, on behalf of the Women's Institute and all
the people in support, it gives me great pleasure to present—'

She jerked to a stop at the imperious hand he held up. 'No
can do, m'lady. Begging your pardon, of course.'

'No, can what?' she said in confusion. 'We're simply asking
you to accept this petition on behalf of the—'

'Which I can't, m'lady.' He shuffled his boots again. 'I can't accept this here petition that is suggesting women be police-men. Police policy is quite clear on the matter.'

'Then police policy is an arse, Brice!' Seldon strode through the crowd, which parted like the Red Sea. He bounded up the steps and held out his hand. 'Over this, anyway.'

Brice's jaw fell slack. 'If as you're sure, chief?'

'More than sure.' Seldon clapped the sergeant on the back, his face breaking into a smile. 'But top marks for standing up to a very formidable bunch of ladies.'

''Tain't easy,' Brice mumbled.

Seldon laughed. 'No, it's impossible.' He turned to Eleanor and muttered. 'Like you.' Raising his voice, he addressed the crowd. 'Ladies of the Women's Institute, I am honoured to accept your petition. And I will ensure it is safely received by the powers that be. And furthermore, I shall make it clear that I support your aims.'

Eleanor and Seldon both covered their ears at the raucous cheer that rang as far as the Town Hall and back.

'Thank you,' she said as the roar died away, confusion on her face, 'but I thought, I mean, Chief Inspector, you—'

He held up his hand and turned back to the crowd. 'I saw for myself with the search for young Master Wilton just how feminine intuition and determination can be vital in the most difficult of matters. And, I admit, you ladies have both in buck-etloads.' He waved down the cheer that rang out again. 'But I have to be honest and add that I hold unwavering reservations about women ever being placed in dangerous situations.' He glanced at Eleanor. 'However, I hold even greater reservations about criminals getting away with crimes because we don't have enough officers. And victims of crime and circumstances getting short shrift because we don't have enough – or any – women on the force. So, we've something of a mountain to scale on both scores.'

'Send Lady Swift,' a voice yelled out. 'She can climb anything!'

Another cheer split the air.

Ten minutes later, Eleanor was still standing off to one side, delighting in watching the rank and file of the Women's Institute thank Seldon personally for his support. That more than half of them blushed as they shook his hand was making her heart swell, as he was clearly oblivious to the effect he was having on them.

Bless him, he has no idea how attractive he is, Ellie!

'Lady Swift.' His deep voice broke into her thoughts. 'I would like a word with you.' He took her to one side and lowered his voice. 'A very firm word. Blast it! Yesterday... on the mill roof! What were you thinking? Do you have any idea how much my insides churned when I ran out and saw you there?' He held each of her hands as gently as if they were butterfly wings and turned them palm upwards, running his thumb across the dressings. 'So cut and' – he swallowed hard – 'bleeding.'

'They're just fingers,' she said, trying to sound casual. 'And I was fine.'

He rolled his eyes. 'Fine? And the knife? It missed you by an inch or two, if that. You promised me, Eleanor.'

'I did. But only that I would still be in one piece which' – she patted the top of her head, wincing at the pain that shot up her arm – 'as you can see, I am.' She sighed. 'I can't help who I am, Hugh.'

'Rash. Impetuous. Impossible. A danger to yourself.' He shook his head. 'And a blessing to everyone else since yet again a murderer was only caught because of you.'

'Us, Hugh. Because of *us*.'

His eyes lit up. 'Now that is the first thing you've said that I like the sound of.' He tucked a few stray curls behind her ear. '*Us.*' His cheeks turned crimson as he realised half the crowd who had yet to disperse were watching them. He coughed awkwardly. 'Oh look, Clifford seems to need your presence.'

He led her down the steps, fighting off Gladstone jumping up to welcome him at the bottom.

She smiled at her butler. 'What ho, Clifford. Thank you for all your super-efficient, and unbidden, help at the end there. The ladies too. Now, did you need me for something? If not, I'll...' She tilted her head in Seldon's direction.

Clifford held up his pocket watch.

'Ahem, my lady. I regret interrupting the chief inspector when he was, I assume, taking you to task, as I did last night, for abandoning Prudence at the bottom of that mill ladder. However, I feel this afternoon's occasion is not one with which to confirm your reputation as the tardiest lady that ever lived?'

She looked at his watch with a puzzled frown. Slowly, her eyes widened. *Oh no!*

35

'Nervous?' Eleanor whispered as she helped her best friend from the ribbon-decked wedding car.

Constance's spirited blonde waves bobbed under her rosebud headdress as she nodded. 'Hugely! Partly because I think I'm supposed to feel very grown up, but I'm too excited for that. And partly because I'm worried I'm going to get an attack of the giggles at an inappropriate moment.'

'Pah! No such thing. Certainly not in Peregrine's book. I've seen how his face lights up when you laugh. Nothing you do will ever be wrong.'

Outside the church, a small huddle of people stood expectantly. Front and centre was Sir Grainger, who still looked tired and pale but far more like the robust businessman Eleanor knew. As Constance approached, he took both her hands in his.

'I'm so sorry for the stress I caused you, my darling. I shall be proud to call Peregrine my son-in-law for as long as I am breathing.'

'Oh, Father!' Constance's eyes filled. 'Thank you.'

He spun her around. 'You look every inch as beautiful as your mother did on our wedding day. And still does today.'

Constance's mother was seated on the bench, already dabbing at her eyes with her handkerchief. Sir Grainger whipped off his top hat before helping her gently to her feet.

'Constance, darling,' her mother said through the tears coursing down her cheeks. 'I'm here. I made it.'

As the two hugged, Sir Grainger turned to Eleanor.

'Oh dear, tears already. Still, I imagine we'll be swimming in them soon enough. But before we are, will you accept my sincere gratitude for everything you have done for my family? We are all forever in your debt.'

Eleanor shrugged. 'Thank you, but I only did what any friend would do, Sir Grainger.'

He shook his head gingerly, the injury obviously still sore. 'No, my dear girl. You did a great deal more. I will never forget it.'

The vicar appeared beside him, his white surplice fanned over his outstretched arms. 'Sir Grainger, welcome, welcome. Such a special day with so many extraordinary blessings from Our Lord.'

Sir Grainger clapped him on the shoulder. 'I rather think you'll find he had a little extra help in the shape of this lady here, who, I am delighted to say, is my daughter's best friend and bridesmaid.'

Far from seeming affronted, the vicar laughed. 'Blessings come in all shapes and sizes, Sir Grainger. You should listen more at Sunday Matins.' He looked at Constance and tapped the book he held. 'Miss Grainger, can you spare me a moment before the ceremony? There is one last quiet prayer I like to share with every bride.'

'Of course.' Constance bobbed up on her toes and hugged Eleanor. 'You couldn't just pop and give this to Peregrine, could you?' She pressed a small object wrapped in silk gently into Eleanor's hand. 'I was wondering how to get it back to him. Tell him it means the world.'

A few moments later, Eleanor found the groom alone in the vestry.

'Psst! Peregrine!'

'Eleanor!' He came over, his face split in two with a euphoric smile. 'You do know, don't you, that I'm going to marry the girl of my dreams today, thanks largely to you? We should all be shouting and whooping, so why are we whispering?'

She laughed. 'I don't know. Constance asked me to give you this.'

'Peregrine!' a familiar sharp voice called as the door opened. 'Why aren't you out in the...' Lady Davencourt, dressed in a sapphire-blue silk suit jacket, jerked to a stop. 'Lady Swift?'

'I was just going,' Eleanor said quickly. 'Bridesmaid duties and all that.'

Peregrine waved the object she had given him. 'The first of which you have executed perfectly.'

But Lady Davencourt blocked her way. 'Another modern contrivance favoured by young people? Or just more highly irregular behaviour on your part?'

'Mother,' he said gently. 'Eleanor was merely delivering back Father's words.'

Lady Davencourt stiffened, but her voice sounded choked. 'What words?'

He unwrapped the parcel and gestured for her to take the silver pocket watch now lying in his palm.

'But that's just the one he gave you on your eighteenth birthday...' She stared up at him as he shook his head.

'There's nothing "just" about it, Mother.' He clicked it open and then clicked it again to reveal a hidden inner casing with an inscription.

Lady Davencourt's voice faltered as she read. '"My beloved son, go forth and become the man you wish to be with my every blessing for the choices you make. But most importantly, find your one true love, as I have with your mother." Oh, Peregrine!'

She breathed. 'I always thought that... that I wasn't good enough for him!'

He pulled her into a hug. 'If only I'd known, I would have shown you this years ago! Is that why you thought no girl could be good enough for me?' At her nod, he hugged her again. 'But Constance—'

Lady Davencourt held up her hand and wiped her eyes. 'Constance will be every inch the best wife you could ever have chosen. She stood by you, Peregrine, through all the scandal. I wouldn't ask any more.'

Leaving them alone, Eleanor crept out of the vestry, down the aisle and back out into the afternoon sunshine, where she was stopped by a pair of impossibly shiny shoes.

'Clifford! You should be in the church by now. Constance and Beatrice both insisted you attend for all your help in clearing Peregrine's name and finding Bertie.'

'Hardly appropriate for a butler, my lady.' But just for once, his face failed to hide how delighted he was to have been asked.

'Go sit with Hugh. I bet he's as uncomfortable as you are at being invited, too.'

Waiting outside the church door, Constance held her father's arm, chattering excitely. She broke off and laughed as Eleanor joined them. 'We were wondering where you were. It's tradition for the bride to be late, not her bridesmaids.'

Inside, the majestic sound of the organ rose to the medieval rafters. At the end of the long, red-carpeted nave, in front of the enormous oval stained-glass window, Peregrine stood next to his best man, an old friend from college.

'Ready, my wonderful daughter?' Sir Grainger whispered.

Constance nodded and reached behind to gently squeeze Eleanor's hand. Beatrice and her other sister stroked Constance's hair, while the flower girls stopped spinning in circles and tried to keep their legs from jiggling.

Eleanor peered down at the young boy beside her in his white-and-blue sailor suit. 'Are you ready, Bertie?'

He blinked back slowly from under his matching hat and reached for her hand. 'Bravo, my lady!'

The wedding guests in the pews turned to watch the bride glide along the aisle. All except one. A pair of deep-brown eyes remained fixed on a certain bridesmaid. Her. Seldon's face flushed as Eleanor drew level.

'Beyond beautiful,' she heard him mutter.

The procession stopped at the altar as Eleanor glanced back and wondered if one day it might, just might, be her...

A LETTER FROM VERITY

Dear reader,

I want to say a huge thank you for choosing to read *Death Down the Aisle*. If you did enjoy it, and want to keep up to date with all my latest releases, just sign up at the following link. Your email address will never be shared and you can unsubscribe at any time.

www.bookouture.com/verity-bright

I hope you loved *Death Down the Aisle* and, if you did, I would be very grateful if you could write a review. I'd love to hear what you think, and it makes such a difference helping new readers to discover one of my books for the first time.

I love hearing from my readers – you can get in touch on my Facebook page, through Twitter, Goodreads or my website.

Thanks,

Verity

www.veritybright.com

facebook.com/veritybrightauthor
twitter.com/BrightVerity

HISTORICAL NOTES

BREACH OF PROMISE

It was around Charles II's time that the idea of being able to sue for breach of promise first started to take hold. Marriage was seen as a contract to benefit both parties and losing the benefits, especially for the woman, was a serious matter. Therefore, it made sense to have the right of redress in the courts. In a society run by, and for the benefit of, men, the breach of promise was something of an anomaly as the weight of legal – and public – opinion almost always favoured the woman. Indeed, some women, commoners among them, were awarded huge sums even by today's standards. The law was finally abolished in 1971, causing Clifford and Seldon to both turn in their graves no doubt!

WOMEN'S INSTITUTE

Since the Women's Institute in Britain held its first meeting in 1915 in a garden shed in Anglesey (and then Chipstone) it's been a force to be reckoned with. In 1921, the first British-born

woman to be elected to Parliament, Mrs Margaret Wintering-
ham, was an active member. And in 1979 in the Great Jam
Debate, the Women's Institute persuaded the government that
their members' kitchens should be exempt from local council
regulations so they could continue to sell their jam directly to
the public. There are now over 6,500 institutes and over
200,000 members.

WOMEN IN THE POLICE FORCE

At the beginning of WWI around four thousand women
became voluntary police officers, keeping order in a variety of
places from parks to munitions factories. However, none of
them had the same powers as their male colleagues. The first
woman to be appointed with full police powers was Edith
Smith in 1915, although her main duties consisted of
cautioning prostitutes and spying on the wives of servicemen
sent abroad to cut down on infidelity! The Chipstone Women's
Institute's Petition was sorely needed, as all but one hundred
women were dismissed from the police force at the end of the
war, and by 1936 there were still only one hundred and thirty-
six women police officers in the entire country.

WWI AIR RAIDS

Germany bombed Britain, mostly London, from 1914 to 1918
using a variety of methods. The earliest was Zeppelins, a type of
airship filled with hydrogen gas. Most of the attacks occurred on
London, but some fell off target (including Hartbridge) as the
Zeppelins were hard to steer in strong winds and had to stay
high to avoid getting shot down. Given that the Zeppelins were
highly combustible and very slow, they were soon replaced by
planes.

CONSCRIPTION IN WWI

Over a million people had enlisted by 1915, but even this huge figure wasn't enough to keep up with casualties. This forced the government to introduce conscription. At first it only included single men aged eighteen to forty-one, but it was extended to married men in 1916 (hence Aubrey being called up) and the age raised to fifty-one in 1918.

IDENTITY TAGS

From 1907 British identity tags were aluminium, but at the outbreak of WWI it was obvious the country would not be able to produce enough, so they were changed to vulcanised asbestos. However, existing supplies of the original aluminium discs were still issued for several years. The information on the disc included a soldier's number, rank, name, regiment and religious denomination. The rank was later dropped as it meant reissuing a tag every time a soldier changed rank.

GHOSTS AND WWI

Soldiers coming back from the dead are not that unusual, especially in large-scale conflicts like WWI. Laurence Marriott's name is on the Menin Gate Memorial to the Missing in Ypres, Belgium. He turned up later, however, injured but very much alive. And Fred Joslin's family were told he had died in battle at the age of nineteen, yet he survived to celebrate his ninety-fifth birthday. When their son wrote to them from a hospital bed in Malta where he was recovering, Fred Joslin's family's problems, however, weren't quite over. The War Office refused to believe that he was alive and it took the family – and Fred himself – some time to convince them otherwise.

HYPNOTISM

In the early 1900s most people's introduction to hypnotism was via vaudeville acts in theatres such as the one Eleanor's staff visit. Then, after WWI, hypnotism started to be used to treat conditions such as shellshock and became more credible. Eleanor going to a hypnotist to try to recall past events would still have been highly unusual in its day with most 'patients' being too scared of what might happen to countenance it.

ACKNOWLEDGEMENTS

Thanks to our ninja editor, Kelsie, and the rest of the team at Bookouture.

Printed in Great Britain
by Amazon